Protecting his Past

Guarding Royalty 1

Elouise East

Contents

Author Note

If you would like to see any potential triggers for this book and any other books I've written, please go to this link on my website: https://elouiseeast.com/triggers

1

Dominic

Dominic Ainsley studied his surroundings. The room he was in was far too big for his liking and had too many exits and too many people, but he could hardly deny the king his birthday celebration, especially when there were children involved. He doubted he would hold the Lead Protection Officer position for long if he put his foot down too harshly with the king. Though it hadn't stopped him from trying. The event differed from the Trooping the Colour that happened every year. That official birthday celebration happened on a different day and took place at Buckingham Palace. This event was the king's personal celebration, and he'd invited kids from all over the country to join him.

King Andrew was currently talking to his son, Prince Frederick, which made Dominic even more nervous. Having so many royal members under one roof was not something he ever thought they'd do again after the events of the past few years. When a member of their own family attempted to kill others, it made most people hesitant to group together.

But not the Sutcliffes.

The Sutcliffes rallied around, gathered their strength and pushed the assassination attempts behind them, showing the country and the commonwealth just what they were made of.

Pure steel.

"Check in," he ordered his team through his earpiece.

"Clear," said Colt, his second-in-command.

"Clear," added Nick.

After receiving five more all-clear answers, he relaxed marginally. "Brett, how're things on your end?"

Brett Cage was the Head of Security, which meant he was technically Dominic's boss, although Dominic was in charge of his own security team, which concentrated on the king's protection alone. Regardless, he still answered to Brett.

"All clear this end," Brett confirmed. "I'm not going to jinx it, though."

"Please don't," Dominic muttered. "I'd be ecstatic if we went an entire month without some security issue or another."

"You and me both."

Dominic snapped to attention when Andrew hugged Frederick and moved away, Colt slipping to his front and Dominic stepping to his back. They met up with Kean and Kendal, the king's partners.

"We just have the children's choir to listen to, and we can go," Andrew said over his shoulder.

"Yes, Your Majesty."

The choir consisted of forty-five children who had been practising for months for this event. Dominic could understand why Andrew didn't want to leave until they performed. And he enjoyed it, too, even as he wished they could leave before they tempted fate more than he was comfortable with.

His phone vibrated in his inside pocket, but he ignored it. He couldn't have any distractions, and if there was an emergency, it would come across his earpiece. When it vibrated again, he wished he'd silenced the thing completely instead of just muting it. The only reason he kept it with him was for the unusual times when the earpieces didn't work, and as Brett had just received some new ones that passed the tests their security teams had put them through, he doubted anything would go wrong with them.

"Time for home," Andrew said, kissing Kean and Kendal on their cheeks. "I'll see you back there." He turned to Dominic, who waved him towards the exit. "Thank you for indulging me, Dominic."

"London is moving," Dominic said into his earpiece. Then, he focused on Andrew's comment. "It's not my place to dictate your actions, Your Majesty, only to keep you safe. I may have…strong opinions about certain aspects, but in the end, it's your choice and my job to make it happen."

Andrew chuckled as they headed towards the exit Dominic had already decided on taking him out of, the other members of his team coalescing beside them.

"Your Majesty! Can I have a minute of your time, please?"

Dominic and Andrew groaned in unison as Malachi Sanders, the up-and-coming reporter who dogged their every step, jogged over to them. Colt held out a hand to stop him from moving any closer.

"Please, Your Majesty. Do you have a quote for the paper about the children's choir?" Malachi asked.

Andrew smiled, though Dominic could see he was tired. "The children's choir was absolutely beautiful. They did the songs justice, and I hope they have many more years of song ahead of them."

Dominic encouraged Andrew to continue moving, which he did.

"Thank you, Your Majesty!"

"He won't quit," Andrew muttered.

The black town car with tinted windows waited for them, and Dominic halted Andrew before he exited the palace while Colt and Viola checked out the driver and that there was no one else waiting inside the car or boot. When they gave him the all-clear, he guided Andrew to the now-open back door. Kean and Kendal would leave in a separate car. It was one thing Dominic had insisted upon. There was no way he was having three important members of the royal family in one car at the same time.

Andrew slid inside, followed by Colt, and Dominic stood in the doorway, waiting for his team to climb into the two cars, one in front, one behind, before climbing in beside the king.

"Go," he ordered as soon as he had closed the door.

As the cars sped towards Windsor, a journey that would take around an hour, Dominic didn't relax. He couldn't. The life of the monarch was in his hands, and after being given this position when the previous bodyguard, Simon, had been killed while protecting Andrew, he was always second-guessing himself. Was he doing enough? Was it a good idea? Could he do something different? Questions went around and around in his head that he doubted would ever be answered.

"Dominic?"

He blinked and focused on Andrew. "Yes, Your Majesty?"

"Is something wrong?"

"No, Your Majesty."

Andrew sighed. "One of these days, you're going to call me Andrew."

Dominic doubted that, but he let it go. "Are you heading straight to your suite when we get back?"

"Yes. I think I'll call it a night after this." Andrew rested his head back and closed his eyes. "I'm not getting any younger."

Dominic smiled at Colt, who rolled his eyes. They were both of the opinion that Andrew would outlive them all. And they weren't even taking their jobs into the equation.

After escorting Andrew to his suite and checking that it was safe, he left Landon outside and headed for the security briefing room with the rest of the team, finally able to relax a little easier knowing the king was under Windsor Castle's roof. He slumped into an uncomfortable chair—purposefully so he didn't fall asleep—and pulled out his phone. He froze when the missed caller's name showed up.

"Everything okay, Dominic?" Colt asked, standing over him.

Dominic nodded, putting his phone away again, though his heart pounded at what the caller could want. They were only supposed to call in an emergency, but he couldn't call them back now. He had to finish the debriefing before he could deal with that.

"Fine, thanks. Just tired."

"Ain't we all," Nick said, kicking his feet up onto the table and resting his head back. It didn't seem comfortable but to each their own. "If you ask me, His Majesty should take a year-long holiday in the Caribbean. We can all go with him and sun, sea and—"

"Okay, we get the picture, Nick," Brett said as he entered the room, followed by a troop of bodyguards. "I'll be sure to bring that up with him at our next meeting." He dropped into the chair behind his desk and sighed. "Let's get this done so we can go home. Dominic?"

"No issues that I saw. Everything ran smoothly. The earpieces seem to work great. No distortion or interference. Easy to get in, easy to get out. I feel like I missed something, but..." He shrugged.

Brett nodded. "Yeah. It was almost too smooth."

"Exactly."

"Anyone else have any input?"

It took twenty minutes to get through everyone's information and opinions, and Dominic wiped his palms on his trousers several times, wishing they'd hurry so he could find out what was going on. Something had obviously happened, and they needed him, but what?

"Dominic?"

His gaze snapped to Brett's, and he cursed himself for his inattention. "Hmm?"

Brett stared at him for a long second. "Anything to add?"

He had no clue. "Don't think so."

Brett clapped his hands. "In that case, go home, rest up and return refreshed."

The guards filtered out slowly, and Dominic followed as patiently as he could. If anyone noticed his haste and stopped him, there would be far too many questions he couldn't answer. Luckily, no one did, and he aimed straight for his car. Tapping his fingers against the steering wheel as he navigated the Windsor streets, he finally parked outside his house. It was a small two-bedroom place on the outskirts of the town, but it was big enough for him. He locked his car, darted up the path and let himself in the house. When the door closed behind him, he leaned back and yanked his phone from his pocket. Dialling the number he would know by heart even if it wasn't programmed into his phone, he waited as it rang. And rang.

Heart pounding, he paced the hallway.

"Hello?" a soft voice said, and Dominic closed his eyes at hearing the voice he hadn't heard for so long.

"May?"

A sigh sounded. "Dominic, thank god."

"What's wrong?"

"I think they've found me, Dom."

Dominic stopped, heat curdling inside him. "How?"

"I don't know. I noticed a car following me yesterday, but then it turned off, and I thought I was wrong. I went to work today, and the same car followed me again. I took the long way home and thought I'd lost them. There's a car outside now, Dom. I don't know what to do."

Dominic's heart raced. She needed to get out of there.

"Have you spoken to Yousef?"

"I can't get hold of him." May's voice sounded more and more stressed.

"Okay. May, listen to me." He paused. "Are you listening?"

She exhaled. "Yes."

"Can you get to the safe room in the house?" He wished he knew where she was and what her house looked like.

"No, there isn't one."

"Goddamn it. There was supposed to be one!" Dominic glared at the wall, his mind whirling through all the possibilities. He lowered and calmed his voice. "Describe your house and location, May."

"Um, two-bedroom. Semi-detached house. The front garden has a stone driveway, and the back is just concrete. Um, what else?"

"Further afield of the house. What is around you? Trees? Streets?"

"The street backs onto an enormous field surrounded by trees. There's an alleyway behind the house. To the front, there are just more houses."

How could she get out of there? "Go upstairs and peer out the back window." He heard thumping. "Can you see anyone either in the alley or in the field or trees? You might need to look for a few minutes to see if someone moves."

Those three minutes were the longest of his life. "I can't see anyone," she whispered.

"Grab your backpack. I assume you still have it?"

"I do." Rustling sounded. "I've got it."

"Comfortable shoes?"

"Yes. Trainers."

"Waterproof coat?"

"Already on."

"Earpiece?"

"In my hand."

Despite the circumstances, he smiled; he'd taught her well. "Good. Switch to the earpiece now."

It took a few seconds to switch over, but then her voice came through again. "Done."

"Remember that sneaky training, as you called it?" She chuckled in response. "You need to use that to get yourself to the first set of trees. Quiet as a mouse. When you reach the trees, pause. Listen. Look. And listen again. When you know it's clear, run like hell across that field to the other side."

"Okay."

"Do it. I'll stay on the line, but I won't say anything unless you talk first."

Dominic rested his forehead against the window of the door to his conservatory. He closed his eyes, listening for every inhale and exhale, every stumble, every click or squeak coming through the line. He glanced at the clock on the wall, measuring the time. It went against his instincts to let her do her thing, to do what he trained her to do, but he had to. He turned his back to the door and slid down, keeping the phone to his ear. May's harsh breathing belied her calm exterior, but he was so proud of her.

How had that fucker found her? She was in witness protection, for fuck's sake. They'd changed her name, her history, her routine, everything. No one should've been able to find her. When May was safe, he was going to have words with her handler. Yousef should've been available day or night. So why the fuck wasn't he?

"I'm in the first lot of trees."

"Okay, May. Well done. Stop here and breathe for a moment. Keep your eyes scanning, and keep your ears listening. Get to know the sounds around you."

He fell silent again, wishing he could be there to help her, but not even he knew where she was, and he refused to ask unless they had definitely found her. If she had been found, there was no reason for him not to know her location any longer. Raking his fingers through his hair, he listened.

"Nothing," she whispered.

"Then go."

May's panting filled his ear, and he imagined her racing across the field as fast as her five-foot-two legs could carry her. The wait was excruciating, but it didn't take her long. Two minutes after his words, she said, "I'm in the second lot of trees."

"Good. Now, wait again. Look around you and look back the way you came. See if anyone follows you."

He'd have done anything to have eyes on her at that moment. To see what she saw. To protect her.

"Holy shit!"

Dominic's heart took off again. "May? What's wrong?"

"Someone's in my house. It looks like gunshots. Flashes of light in the windows, just like in the movies."

Fuck. They'd found her. "It's okay, May. You're out. Let's get you somewhere safe. Is there one place you can think of where you have never visited, never shown an interest in, doesn't have any connections to your new friends or anything?"

"Um, fuck, um... I don't know!"

"Okay. May, breathe for me. We don't have much time, but we have enough for you to think."

She inhaled and exhaled twice and then said, "The theatre."

He chuckled despite the seriousness of the situation. "Still don't like plays, then?" He didn't wait for her answer. "Do you know how to get there from where you are without using the major streets, if possible?"

"Yes. I can get there."

"Then go. Where are you, May?"

"I thought you didn't want to know?"

"If they've found you, it's a moot point. Where are you?"

"Carlisle."

Dominic sighed. "You're fucking miles away."

May chuckled. "Wasn't that the point?"

"Yeah, but three hundred miles?" He sighed again. "I suppose I should be grateful it wasn't John O'Groats." He bit his lip. "I'm going to hang up and try to get hold of Yousef. You keep going and call me back when you're nearly there."

"Do you have to go?"

"I need to find out if Yousef can get someone to you quicker than I can. I don't know anyone close to you."

May was silent for a moment. "Okay."

"You'll be fine, May. You've done so well already. I'm so proud of you. Keep going a little longer."

"It should only take me half an hour at most to get there. If I've not called by then…"

Dominic swallowed hard, not wanting to consider that. "What's the theatre called?"

"It's Carlisle Community Theatre."

"Right. You can do this, May. I know you can."

"Speak to you soon," she whispered.

Dominic couldn't say any kind of goodbye. He refused to believe she wouldn't get out of this after everything she'd already been through. He scrambled to his feet and thumped up the stairs, aiming for his guest room, which held his desk and safe. Unlocking his safe, he riffled through the contents to find the business card for Yousef, a number he had promised not to use unless there was no other option.

He dialled. It rang and rang and went to voicemail. He tried again. Same thing. He flipped the business card, dialling the second number on it.

"Detective Addams," a deep voice said.

"Detective, this is Dominic Ainsley. Do you remember May?"

"Mr Ainsley. I would say it was nice to hear from you, but I suspect that's not the case. Especially since I have just attended a crime scene at Yousef Azizi's house."

"Crime scene?" Dominic knew what was coming, but he didn't want it to be true.

"Yousef Azizi was found tied to a chair in his dining room with his throat cut this afternoon. I'm assuming your call is related."

He dropped into his desk chair. "They've found May. She's on the run."

"Is anyone with her?"

"No. I have no one there who can help her. I don't know who to trust."

Addams was quiet but then said, "Where is she?"

And wasn't that the crux of the matter? Could he trust this detective he barely knew with May's life? He wasn't sure he had a choice.

"She's in Carlisle. I'm not saying where, but if you have someone you trust, get them to call me. I'm going to make my way there as soon as I can." He headed for the door.

"I know someone in Manchester. They might get there quicker than anyone else I know."

"Ask them, please. And get them to call me."

"Will do." Dominic was about to hang up when Addams said, "Do you think he gave her up?"

Dominic sighed. "Yes. I think he did."

"Me, too."

The call ended, and Dominic stared at his phone, willing May to call back. He wished he could call Vance, a pilot friend, and get his piloting skills up in the air, but it would most likely take longer for Vance to file the flight request and get the plane going than it would if Dominic drove. He grabbed his go bag and opened the front door, stopping with a start when he almost ran into Brett.

"Going somewhere? I thought you were resting."

Dominic hadn't told anyone about May for obvious reasons, but something must've shown on his face because Brett became all business.

"What do you need?"

Taking a leap of faith, he swallowed. "My sister has been in witness protection for five years. She called earlier to say she thought someone had found her. She's on the run, and I need to get to her, but I don't know if I'll make it in time."

Brett didn't bat an eyelid at the 'sister' part of his words, making Dominic wonder if he already knew. "Where?"

"Carlisle."

Brett pulled out his phone. "I'm sorry to bother you, Your Highness. I wonder if you can help me..." He explained what little Dominic had told him and then ended the call. "We need to get to Windsor Castle now."

"But I need—"

"No one will get you to Carlisle faster than Freddie. A helicopter will be waiting for us when we get there."

"What about security?"

"Felix and Nick are very capable. Besides, we won't be long." Brett headed for his car. "We'll have your sister settled in Windsor Castle before you know it."

Dominic stared at Brett's retreating figure for all of a few seconds before locking his house and following. He didn't know what to say. But if the royal family could help him, he wouldn't do anything to stop them, and he would repay them with his devoted service for the rest of his life.

2

Randall

Prince Freddie entered Randall Metcalfe's office quickly enough for the door to bang against the cupboard behind it and make Randall jump. "Damn, sorry," he said.

Randall placed a hand against his chest and inhaled. "It's fine, Your Highness. What can I do for you?"

"I need a helicopter here as fast as possible."

Randall picked up his tablet and scrolled through several screens to get what he needed, then he picked up the phone and dialled. "Good evening. A helicopter at Windsor Castle immediately, please."

"On its way in five," his contact said.

"Thank you." He ended the call and turned to Freddie. "It should be here in twenty minutes, Your Highness."

"Great." Freddie headed for the door.

"Do you need anything else?"

Freddie paused. "Actually, yes. Could you arrange for a guest room to be readied, please? We have a visitor coming to stay, though I'm not sure for how long."

"Of course. Do they need to be close to anyone in particular?"

"Maybe near the security rooms." Freddie paused again and then came closer. "Okay, I wasn't going to say anything yet as I'm not sure about who is supposed to know, but you might have more random requests, so... Dominic's sister is staying here. She's been in witness protection, but someone found her. I'm flying us to get her as soon as Dominic arrives."

The moment the bodyguard's name passed Freddie's lips, Randall perked up. He hadn't had much to do with Dominic before the atrocities of the past few months. But when Simon—and many others—had been killed and Dominic had taken over his position, they'd changed a few things. Now, instead of the guard staying outside of the offices completely, they sat in a chair outside Andrew's office—and in Randall's. He'd spent many hours with all the guards, but only Dominic made conversation. The others, while answering questions when asked, kept to themselves a little more, which Randall understood. Not everyone wanted to chat when they were supposed to be concentrating on their work. Randall had enough work for several people, but he managed it all with the help of Portia, his recently acquired assistant.

Portia had been the late queen's personal assistant but had distanced herself when Queen Louisa had been killed eighteen months ago. King Andrew had requested her for the position of Randall's assistant when Kendal, one of the king's partners, had insisted Randall have help with his endless to-do list.

But Dominic was an enigma Randall was trying to figure out, and maybe his sister was part of the puzzle. He hadn't even known Dominic *had* a sister.

"Of course. I'll see that she's comfortable and has everything she could need for when you return. I'll also set up a room for Dominic, as I'm sure he'll want to be close to her."

"Thank you, Randall."

Freddie left, and Randall started on his new task list despite the late hour. He called the household staff to get two rooms ready, near each other and the security room, during which he heard the helicopter arrive. He contacted the kitchen to arrange for some food and drinks to be available in each room as well, and then after the sounds of the helicopter disappeared, he arranged for clothes and toiletries to be sent to the room in case they both came back with nothing but the clothes on their backs. When he decided there was nothing else he could do, he settled back and waited.

It was way past the time he would usually finish working, but he wouldn't leave until he knew everyone was back safe and there wasn't anything else they needed. Only then would he go home to sleep. Or he would settle in the room the king had set aside for him.

He knew exactly how long it took for them to get back because he watched the clock. Two hours and forty-five minutes after they left, the helicopter landed back at Windsor. Randall wished he could be outside waiting with, undoubtedly, several of the royal family, but he didn't want to overwhelm them. So, he stayed in his office until he heard voices.

The rooms they'd allocated Dominic and his sister were down the corridor from where Randall's was, and they had to pass the office to get there. He stepped into the hallway as they drew closer. An entourage consisting of Brett, King Andrew, Princes Freddie and Christian—with Oreo, Christian's Labrador, trotting beside them—and then Dominic had who Randall assumed was his sister wrapped in his arms as they wandered past him.

Dominic met his gaze and nodded, mouthing, "Thank you."

Randall smiled, glad he could be of help. He entered his office again, made sure everything was turned off and then followed in the wake of the new residents. His room was small by Windsor standards, but he loved it. He could've easily stayed there instead of having a small house on the outskirts of the town, but he thought it would be better to get away from his work occasionally. That night, though, he needed sleep and to ensure he was available should anyone need anything.

But he wasn't needed, and even though he slept fitfully because he was concerned about Dominic and his sister, he was at his desk by six-thirty with a cup of strong tea in his hand. He had enough work to keep busy, even with it being a Sunday, but his mind wandered.

A knock and the click of a door opening caught his attention, and for a second, he froze, remembering the ordeal he had gone through five months prior.

Randall cursed himself as he entered his office. He'd almost been home when he remembered he'd left his wallet in his desk, and he needed it. So he returned. Sitting in his chair, he unlocked the drawers and pulled his wallet free. As he did, he heard the door open, and he glanced up with a ready smile, but no one entered. He frowned and shook his head. He must've imagined it. But then the bite of cold metal pressed against his temple. He froze and glanced to the side.

"Good evening, Randall," an icy voice said. "Please don't make any sudden movements. I would hate to lose you. At least while I need you."

Randall swallowed hard. He hadn't heard that tone coming from Prince Ernest before, but he had recently become aware of what he was capable of. He had no idea whether he would survive whatever the man had planned.

Ernest stepped around to the front of the desk, still pointing the gun at Randall, his mouth curling up and his nostrils flaring as he stared like Randall was a bug he wanted to squash. And he probably was. The man had killed so many people already. What was one more?

"Now, I'd like you to call Andrew and get him here right away. And no funny business. I know your secret codes and everything else. Just ask him something that wouldn't alert anyone and put it on speakerphone."

Randall couldn't see a way out of it, so although he didn't want to bring the king into this, he picked up the phone, dialled and pressed the speaker button.

"Hello?" King Andrew said.

"I'm sorry to interrupt your evening, Your Majesty," he said, holding Ernest's gaze, "but I've realised I've forgotten to complete one set of paperwork that needs your signature. Would you mind coming to the office to sign it, please? I wouldn't usually ask, but it's the papers for the Chancellor."

Andrew sighed. "Of course, Randall. I'll be there shortly. Although...why are you still working? I thought you'd gone home?"

Randall wished he had never returned. "I had, Your Majesty, but I'd forgotten something, and when I got back to my desk to collect it, I found the paperwork."

"All right. I'll be there in a few minutes."

"Thank you, Your Majesty. And I'm sorry again."

"It's fine, Randall."

Randall ended the call.

"Well done. Let's get prepared for his arrival, shall we?"

Ernest nudged the gun in the direction of Andrew's office, and Randall rose slowly. Walking around the desk, he headed for the door, his heart in his throat, his head pounding, and his body trembling. The gun pressed into his back, which didn't help. They entered the king's office, and Ernest pushed him towards the desk.

"Sit behind his desk and put your hands flat on the surface. I know about the security buttons underneath there, and if they accidentally get pressed, you accidentally get shot. Understood?"

Randall nodded. Andrew would never forgive him for his treachery. Helping a villain? It's enough to get him sent to jail. As he settled behind the king's desk, he tried to control his breathing, not wanting to freak out until he knew what was going to happen. Had he signed Andrew's death warrant?

He wasn't sure how long it had been until he heard a voice, then silence. The office door opened, and Andrew stepped through. His gaze immediately found Randall, and Randall watched the emotions flow across his face. The betrayal. The shock. But then the door slammed shut behind him, and Ernest pressed the gun against Andrew's neck.

"I'm sorry, Your Majesty," Randall whispered.

"I told you to stay quiet," Ernest said.

"What do you want, Ernest?" Andrew asked.

"What do I want? I want you gone. I want the entire Sutcliffe line to disappear. Is that too much to ask?"

"Why?"

Ernest snorted. "Why, he says. For god's sake, Andrew. I sometimes wonder why you're on the throne at all." Ernest walked around him. "Sit, brother-in-law, and let me tell you a story."

Ernest motioned to the sofa next to Andrew. Randall could see everything unfolding, but Ernest's words were distant because Randall was trying to figure out a way for them to get out of there. Could he reach for the button without Ernest knowing? He moved slightly, wanting to get his knee to the side, and the desk chair squeaked.

"One wrong move, Randall, and you know what will happen."

He froze.

"Would you like a drink, Ernest?" Andrew asked.

"Do you know? I think I will, actually. Randall, get me a whiskey. And get Andrew a bourbon, and then sit back down."

Randall did as Ernest asked, handing him a glass filled halfway with the golden liquid, then handing one to Andrew. Then he returned to the chair, trying but failing to hit the button as he sat.

A *while later—time had lost meaning—Andrew glanced at Randall and mouthed, "Shout at three," holding up three fingers.*

Shout what? Did it really matter? He needed to get the attention of the guards who waited outside as usual, and he trusted Andrew with his life. Andrew continued the conversation as if nothing was happening, but Randall tuned in, hearing the numbers as Andrew spoke.

"John was...three."

Randall screamed at the top of his lungs, and Andrew leapt over the back of the sofa. Ernest's gun went off, but Randall had already dropped to the floor. Doors slammed open, guns fired, and Randall crawled to the wall, out of the firing range, hugging his knees to his chest and burying his face. He didn't want to see whose death he had caused. He didn't think he could deal with it.

When Andrew knelt in front of him, Randall started babbling. "I'm so sorry, Your Majesty. He just came out of the wall. I didn't know there was a secret doorway. He startled me and then pulled the gun. I wasn't sure what to do, but he gave me no choice. I'm sorry." Randall's voice gave, and he sobbed into his hands.

Andrew grabbed Randall in his arms and held him as he cried. He didn't deserve it, though. He would've been responsible for Andrew's death had Ernest managed what he started. There was no way the king could trust him again. No way.

But Andrew had and still did. He'd ensured the secret doorway had been sealed up with no chance of it being opened again, which is what Randall reminded himself of as Dominic entered through the main door. Randall kept his smile in place as he inhaled and exhaled a couple of times, pushing down the fear that still caught him unawares at times. Even though his therapy sessions with Derek helped, it was a long process and one he would have to be patient with.

"Good morning. How can I help?" he asked.

Dominic stopped in front of his desk. Randall peered up at him, wanting to stand but knowing it wouldn't help with their height difference. The crease between his eyes was more pronounced than usual, and his stubble was longer than normal. The suit he wore every day was missing, and in its place were jeans and a polo shirt, things Randall didn't think he'd ever seen him in.

When Dominic's hazel eyes met his blue ones, his heart skipped a beat. "I wanted to thank you for what you did for me last night."

Randall shook his head. "I didn't do anything." Dominic lifted his eyebrow, and Randall's cheeks heated. "Okay, maybe I did a couple of small things, but that's it."

"Regardless of whether you think it's small or not, you helped get my sister out of there, and I appreciate it more than you know."

"How is she?"

Dominic sighed and sank into the chair on the other side of the desk. "She's okay. Scared, frustrated, pissed, and everything in between." He huffed a laugh.

"Can I ask what happened?" He wasn't sure he *should* ask, but he was nosey. Especially when it came to Dominic, not that he would ever tell him that.

"Her ex was abusive, and he eventually got caught up with the wrong people. He became a mule, amongst other things, and May testified against them all. She went into witness protection when she received death threats. That was five years ago. I haven't seen or heard from her in all that time. Until last night." He fidgeted, staring at his hands. "Someone found her through her handler. He was the only one who knew her old and new identity, as far as I'm aware."

"Was?"

Dominic's gaze met his. "The police found him dead. Tortured."

Randall's stomach churned. He was so sick of this shit. Why couldn't everyone just live happily and leave everyone else alone?

Dominic chuckled. "It would be nice, wouldn't it?"

Randall frowned, then closed his eyes. "I didn't mean to say that out loud."

"It's okay. You're completely right. Unfortunately, it comes with our territory, doesn't it?" He scratched his chin. "Well, mine, anyway."

"You have the royal family behind you now. That should make it easier to protect her."

Dominic shook his head. "I'm not bringing them into this more than I already have. It's my family; therefore, I need to deal with it."

Randall's mouth twitched as he tried to keep from smiling. "Good luck with that."

There was no way Dominic would be dealing with this alone if Randall knew the royal family at all. They were probably already working on trying to find whoever was after May, and he doubted it would take them long with how many contacts they had. Although saying that, they struggled when it had been Ernest, their own family member—even if he was family only through his marriage to Charlotte.

Randall shook away the thought and refocused on Dominic. "If you need help, ask. Don't go putting your life in danger because of your ego."

Dominic glared at him, but Randall didn't take offence. "I don't have an ego."

"Well, you do, but not much of one. But this is your family, Dominic. All bets are off when family is involved."

Dominic nodded slowly and then got to his feet. "Thank you, Randall. I appreciate your help, and I know everyone around here does, too."

Randall's face heated again, and he ducked his head. "No problem. I'm here if you need anything." *Absolutely anything.*

Dominic smiled and left the office, and Randall blew out a breath and leaned back, staring at the door. He had given up all hope of romance or relationships in his life, but it didn't stop him from dreaming about it. And he refused to admit how often Dominic played into those dreams. The man was ten years younger than him, and he had his whole life ahead of him. Randall was just waiting for retirement, and even then, he probably wouldn't retire until he was unable to do the job any longer. He loved working for the Sutcliffes, but it didn't leave much time for a social or romantic life. He was happy, though. He could deal with the loneliness if it meant he could do this job every day.

Brushing aside his dreams of love, he focused on his work. Portia wouldn't be in that day—as he shouldn't be—but he had a feeling it would be a busy one, anyway. Royal work didn't stop just because it was a weekend, and he was happiest when he was helping people.

Maybe he should check in with May and see if there was anything she needed.

But later.

He refused to ask her about her brother, though. That wasn't his business, as much as he might dream for it to be.

3

Dominic

As Dominic closed the door to Randall's office, his childhood best friend and the person who helped him get the job with the royal family in the first place called his name.

"I hear you've had an adventure, though no one knows specifics," Owen said, bumping shoulders with him as they headed towards the security room.

"You could say that." Owen had been his best friend since they'd started primary school together at five years old. He and Evan. Both men were as much a part of his family as his family was, and they considered May to be their sister, too. Evan had moved to Italy a few years ago, and they didn't see him as much as they used to. "They found May. I had to go and get her."

Owen stopped, grabbing Dominic's biceps. "What? Is she okay? Where is she?"

Dominic couldn't help his smile. "She's kick-ass is what she is. She got herself out of there, and Freddie flew us there to collect her. She's staying here for now." He gestured down the hallway.

"She needs a fucking medal for all the shit she's put up with." Owen put his hands on his hips. "I'll drop by and say hello later. I don't want to overwhelm her too much. I'll let Evan know, too."

"She'll be happy to see you. I think the strain of not seeing family was as much a burden as hiding from those who want to hurt her."

They resumed walking. "You would've thought after five years they would've given up," Owen said.

"Unfortunately, some people have long memories. Especially the ones still alive and in jail."

They fell into silence as they entered the security room for the daily briefing. Even when there weren't any events planned, they would always meet to ensure everyone was up to speed. Brett made it mandatory, unless a guard was on holiday, for everyone to attend, even if they weren't working that day. Usually, it would only last at most an hour, and they were always compensated for it. Some people wouldn't like that, but when the security of the royal family was at risk, they chose people who didn't mind attending the short briefing each morning.

"Good morning," Brett said to him when he approached. "How's May?"

"Tired. I think the stress has worn her out."

Brett nodded. "It's bound to. She'll be fine here, and we'll figure out what's going on."

"You don't need to. I can do it."

Brett raised his eyebrows. "I know you can, but you don't have to. See me after, and you can get me up to speed on the case. Oh, and I'm going to have to let everyone know who May is, or they'll challenge her if they see her roaming the hallways."

Dominic sighed but nodded and found a seat next to Owen. He crossed his arms over his chest and stared towards the front of the room while Brett called everyone's attention.

"Good morning, everyone. This should be a quick one." He ran through the events that were planned for the coming week, which were only two, thankfully, and confirmed everyone's assignments. "And one last thing before you go. We have a new resident staying at Windsor for the foreseeable future. Her name is May Ainsley." Several guards glanced at Dominic, but he stayed looking at Brett. "She has been in witness protection for five years, and the people who were after her found her last night. Therefore, she might be a little jumpy around new people. She is not a security risk to the royal family, and please keep her safe should the situation call for it. Any questions?"

Dominic tuned out as Brett answered the questions, and then he dismissed them. Dominic stayed seated, as did Owen. Brett raised his eyebrows at Owen's presence but didn't say anything.

"Okay, give it to me."

He spent around fifteen minutes explaining the case and answering Brett's questions while his boss wrote continually in his notebook. It was wearing having to go through it all again when he'd thought it was over and done with, but then, it was never over and done with, was it? Something always came back to bite them in the ass. Same with Ernest's betrayal. They were still dealing with the aftermath.

"Okay, we'll start looking into the people that were involved at the time and see where they are now. Can you get in contact with Detective Addams and see what information he now has and if he can get anything from the police in Carlisle?"

Dominic nodded. "I can, but you don't have to do this."

Owen punched his arm, and Dominic glared at him. "Wouldn't you want as much help as possible to keep May safe? No matter the cost?"

When he put it like that, how could Dominic say no? Which was exactly why he'd said it if the smirk Owen gave him was any indication.

"Fine." He glanced at Brett. "Thanks."

"You're welcome. Now go. You're not on duty until tomorrow, so chill the fuck out," Brett said.

"Yes, boss," he said, with only a hint of sarcasm.

They headed down the corridor towards May's room, and Owen hung back when they arrived.

"Ask her if she wants to see me first. I don't want to smother her if she needs a break."

Dominic clapped him on the shoulder and knocked on May's door. "May, it's Dominic."

"Come in!" she called, and still, the sound of her voice sent a wave of relief through him. When she was in hiding, there was no news from or about her, so he had no idea whether she was alive or dead. It pained him so much to know she was out there without his support. Which reminded him they needed to call their parents.

He opened the door and latched it again, leaning against it. "Hey, boo," he said, using his childhood nickname for her.

Tears glistened in her eyes as she stood in front of him, hands wringing together. "I never thought I'd see you again."

"There's someone who would like to see you if you're up for a visitor?"

May tilted her head but didn't seem unduly worried. "Who?"

Dominic smiled. "Are you up for a visitor or not?"

May backhanded his chest. "Fine. Yes. I'm okay."

Dominic opened the door and waved Owen forward. May squealed when she saw him and wrapped her arms around his neck. He lifted her, and she slid her legs around his waist like she used to as a child. Dominic closed the door, smiling at the antics of the pair. Before Owen had come out to him, Dominic had thought he had a thing for May, and he was gearing up to make peace with the relationship, but then Owen had floored him. He didn't have an issue with Owen being gay—Dominic was, after all—but it was because he'd had no inkling of it at the time. Thinking back now, he could see hints of it, and when Owen came out, Dominic thought his parents were expecting him and Owen to get together. They weren't each other's type, though.

"It's so good to see you," May said when she finally disentangled herself.

"You're a sight for sore eyes," Owen said, cupping her cheek. "I hear you've been busy."

May blew out a breath. "You could say that. Although, staying in a place like this is something a girl could get used to." She spread her arms and spun around.

They laughed, and Dominic grabbed drinks for them all while Owen and May caught up. Unfortunately, Dominic had to rain on their conversation because he needed information.

"May, I need you to go through exactly what you saw and heard last night and anything from before that, too. Every detail you can remember."

May sighed and slumped. "I know. I just wish it was over."

"It will be soon. Just stay strong for a little longer, okay?" Owen said, squeezing her hands.

"This is like when we were kids. We're just missing Evan." She sniffed. "I'd had the feeling I was being watched for a few days. Maybe since Wednesday. I went to the coffee shop, as usual, to get some breakfast before I went to work. As I ate at the table, I people-watched." She smiled. "You know how much I enjoy that." Dominic did. "I saw a man in a car across the road. I don't remember anything about the car except that it was dark blue and had really shiny wheels."

"Did you see what he looked like?"

May closed her eyes. "He wore black and didn't have much hair. He was quite big."

"How could you tell?"

"There wasn't much gap between him and the steering wheel."

"Okay. What happened?"

"Nothing. We caught each other's gaze once, but other than the cursory look I gave him, remembering details like you taught me, I put it out of my head."

"Did you see him again?"

May shook her head. "I didn't get any weird feelings the rest of that day."

"When after that?"

"On Thursday, I saw the same car. I remembered the shiny wheels. There was a different person behind the wheel. All in black again, lean, black hair, goatee, leather coat, polo neck jumper. I went to work, and the guy walked in about an hour later. I swear it was him, but he didn't wear a leather coat, so I could've been wrong."

"Did you serve him?"

"No. He went to another cashier. I couldn't be certain it was him, so I pushed it aside, thinking I was paranoid. On Friday, I didn't see anyone before work, but when I walked home, I kept hearing footsteps, as if someone was purposefully scaring me. Every time I looked around, there was no one there."

"What about yesterday?" Owen asked.

"I had a lie in like I always do on my days off. Didn't get out of bed until probably ten o'clock. Chilled around the house all day, doing housework, reading and stuff like that. There was a knock on the door around dinnertime that night. After checking the cameras, I opened the door to a pizza delivery guy." She stared at him. "I didn't order pizza. When I told him so, he apologised and left. But I saw the car a few doors down the street. This time, there were two guys in it, but I couldn't see if they were the same ones from before. That's when I called you."

Dominic didn't like any of it, but he was glad she had caught what details she had, though why they used such a distinctive car, he didn't know. Unless the point was to unnerve her purposefully before they killed her.

"All right. Well done, May. You did great," he said.

"I've had excellent teachers for my sneaky training."

Dominic grinned at her reference to him, Owen and Evan teaching her defensive and evasive skills. "We have one more hurdle to get over now." May tilted her head. "We need to talk to our parents."

May bit her lip, but there was no disguising her elation at the thought of seeing them. "Can we go to them?"

Dominic shook his head. "I will bring them here. I'll tell them it's a surprise tour or something."

He left May in Owen's capable presence and drove to their parents' house. They still lived in their childhood home, although the police hadn't believed it was safe. When May disappeared into witness protection, their parents stayed in Holyport. It was only a fifteen-minute drive, and when he pulled up, the door opened almost immediately. He truly believed his parents had a sixth sense about their kids.

"Dominic! I wasn't expecting to see you today," his father Chance said.

Dominic accepted the hug from him and chuckled. "But you always seem to know when I'm coming, anyway, Pops."

Chance laughed. "True. Though don't ask me how."

"A parent always knows," his dad said as he joined them in the driveway. Tom was a retired teacher, and with the glasses and clothing he wore, there was no disguising the fact.

"Hey, Dad." Dominic hugged him. "I see you're enjoying retired life, though still dress as if you're going to work."

Tom clipped his ear. "I happen to like these clothes, and they're comfortable. I don't care what I look like as long as I'm comfy."

Dominic shook his head, smiling. "I'm here because I thought you might like that tour around Windsor Castle you always asked for."

Chance gasped, his hands covering his mouth, his eyes wide. "Really?"

Dominic nodded, and though he hated lying to them, he knew they would forgive him when they saw May. "Grab what you need, and we'll go."

"Oh, Tom! Quick, let's get ready before he changes his mind." Chance disappeared into the house, muttering to himself.

Tom stayed behind, staring at Dominic. "A tour, huh?"

Dominic stayed strong. His training had taught him well, but he couldn't always pull it off when he faced down his parents. "Pops always wanted to see it. Things are quiet now, so it would be a good time."

Tom nodded slowly. "I better get ready then." He narrowed his eyes at Dominic for a long second and then turned back to the house.

Dominic let out a quiet breath and checked his phone while he waited. When his parents returned, Chance was wearing a T-shirt with a British flag on it, and he wore a small backpack, also with the flag. Talk about fitting in. Tom wore the same as he had before, though he'd added a jumper and a coat over his arm.

"Let's go!" Chance said, climbing into Dominic's back seat.

"Yeah, let's," Tom said, a little more unenthused.

Dominic's parents had been together for over forty years, even when it hadn't been the best time to be gay. They'd adopted Dominic when he was three years old—or rather, Chance had adopted him as a single parent because the laws back then hadn't allowed for same-sex couples to adopt. They'd done the same for May when she was a year old. Nothing fazed them, and now that they were both retired and their kids were not living at home, they could enjoy their time together.

They made small talk as Dominic drove them to Windsor, with Chance remarking on several things he knew about the place, obviously forgetting Dominic knew the place like the back of his hand. When the guards waved them through the gates, Chance almost squealed. Dominic shook his head. The man had been on the public Windsor tours several times through the years, but he was still excited.

Dominic parked the car. They headed through the doors Dominic usually used, which were not open to the public, and Tom grabbed Chance's arm so he didn't walk into something as he looked around them.

"I'm assuming you have something to show us, son, with how fast you're walking," Tom said.

Dominic chuckled and slowed. "Sorry. I do have something, yes. But you can still have the tour afterwards if you want."

"Lead the way."

He told them about the different things they passed and what they were used for if he could, and then led them down the hallway. He paused outside Randall's office, something urging him to check in, and he opened the door, popping his head in.

Randall's head popped up, eyes wide, until he saw Dominic, and then he smiled. "Hey, I wasn't expecting to see you again today. I thought you'd be with—"

Dominic quickly held up a finger to silence him, and Randall's eyes widened again. "I was just checking in with you. I've brought my parents for a *tour*." He hoped his slight inflexion got across his message.

Randall stood, smoothing down his clothes. "Oh, that's nice."

Dominic stepped inside, gesturing for his parents to follow. "Pops, Dad, this is Randall Metcalfe. He's the magic behind everything we do."

Randall's cheeks coloured as he rounded his desk with his hands outstretched. "It's lovely to meet you. I hope you have a wonderful tour. The place really is beautiful."

"Isn't it?" Chance said. "I can't believe I'm meeting you. You do such a brilliant job."

Randall stared at Chance, and Dominic laughed. "Pops is a huge royal family fan. He knows as much about them as we do. Probably more."

Randall smiled. "Well, we're glad to have you." He glanced at Dominic, including him in his words, and Dominic's heart skipped a beat.

It took his dad clearing his throat to shake him from his head, and they said goodbye before heading further down the corridor.

"Where are we going?" Chance asked.

"You'll see. We're almost there."

He stopped by May's door and knocked. Owen opened it and was thrown back with the force of Chance's hug.

"Owen! I've not seen you for far too long."

"I know. Life gets in the way, doesn't it?" Owen chuckled.

Dominic closed the door behind them. "I'm sorry for the subterfuge, but I didn't want to ruin the surprise."

"What surprise?" Tom asked.

May stepped out of the bedroom, tears already in her eyes.

Chance gasped. "My baby!" He reached for May at the same time May reached for him, and they hugged, tears streaming down their faces. Tom joined them, stoic but just as emotional.

Owen clapped him on the shoulder. "I'll leave you to it, but call me if you need anything at all."

"I will. Thanks, man."

Owen left, and Dominic watched the tearful reunion, barely keeping his emotions in check. There were so many things up in the air, and he hated it all. But he could give them this. He didn't know if May was going to have to go into hiding again or if they could give her life back, but he was going to do whatever it took to ensure she was safe. And if he could get help from the Sutcliffes, he wouldn't turn it down.

4

Randall

The unexpected visit from Dominic and his parents was a lovely surprise. Randall hadn't known Dominic had gay parents, but it added to his—and their—charm. He still wanted to visit May, but he would allow them to reconcile without his interruption. It was sure to be a tearful reunion. What he did do was call the kitchen and arrange for lunch and drinks to be taken to May's room for them all.

After he'd finished doing what work he could, he chose to take himself away from his work completely and head home. He had housework to get done and clothes to get washed—both his pet hates. But needs must.

He smiled at the guards he passed and pulled his coat tighter around him when he exited the building. Hurrying to his car, he unlocked it and slid inside, switching on the engine to get the heat flowing as quickly as he could. It was only mid-September, but the weather had turned colder the past few days. He checked his phone while he shivered, and it rang. He swore his mother had some sort of camera installed and knew when he'd finished work because she always called at the right time.

He sighed and answered. "Hey, Mum."

"Randall, are you coming for dinner tonight? We haven't seen you in over two weeks now." Despite his mother being almost seventy years old, she hadn't lost any of her personality or fight. Randall put it down to her having had him at eighteen. "I need an update."

This time, Randall kept his sigh to himself. "Not tonight, Mum. I've had a busy day already, and I have lots of housework to do. I need to catch up."

"They work you far too hard. You need to start saying no so you can go out and meet someone. How do you expect to find a boyfriend if you're never out of the house or always at work?"

"I don't need someone. I'm happy as I am." Total lie, but if he said it enough times, maybe it would become true. He clenched his hand on his lap.

"You're not happy, Randall. Not even a little. I can see it every time I look at you. Find yourself a nice man, and you'll feel much better."

There was no calming her down. This was her usual state when it came to the "woe is him" conversation about the state of his relationships.

"I'm doing fine, Mum. Anyway, I have to go. I need to get home."

"You're not home yet! Well, what do I expect? You're never home anymore." Rose sighed. "Fine. Get home and do your chores, but I expect to see you next week without fail. It's not like we live miles away from you."

They would if Randall hadn't got a job he loved more than he wanted to leave. He could deal with the fallout of not attending dinner, but he couldn't deal with another night of dissecting his love life. Especially not that day.

"Okay. See you next week."

He ended the call with a long exhale and started his car, diverting his attention from the previous conversation by thinking about home. The place where he sometimes rested his head was a small two-bedroom house on the outskirts of Windsor. He'd chosen the place because it had lots of character, but it was also modern enough to meet what little needs he had. He had painted it a dark green so it would merge with the trees and greenery of the forest during the summer that grew behind the house. Every time he saw it, he smiled because it was his little bit of heaven amongst the balancing act he kept up with his family and the upheaval and evil that continued to dog the royal family. He liked that owners appeared to be long-term instead of having new neighbours all the time. Except for the property opposite. Someone had recently moved in, but Randall hadn't seen who. It wasn't his business, really.

He put his keys in the dish in the hallway, slipped off his shoes and coat, and aimed for the kitchen. The kettle waited for him, and he flicked the switch before grabbing a cup and a teabag. Some people had a routine of what they did when they arrived home from work. Some people weren't him. He wasn't home enough to make a routine besides making a cup of tea. Sometimes, he read. Sometimes, he watched TV. Sometimes, he went straight to bed. It all depended on how he felt when he walked through the door.

But that day, he was unsettled. He couldn't decide what he wanted to do. So, he grabbed a blanket, tucked himself into the bucket chair by the back window and watched the trees blow in the gentle breeze as he drank his drink. By letting his mind wander, he could relax. No expectations from him—if he ignored the housework and washing.

His thoughts, as they often did, turned to Dominic. Randall didn't deny to himself that he liked Dominic as more than a friend, but he also knew that he was ten years older than him, and he didn't stand a chance with him. He was content just talking with him and being in his presence when he was looking after the king. In the dark of every night, his thoughts followed the path he wished he could take, but it made the harsh reality a lot harder to swallow.

His phone beeped, and he checked the screen, ignoring the new message from his mother and smiling when his friend's name came up. He swiped at it.

"Hey, you."

Geoff's deep voice came through loud and clear in the silence. "Hey, yourself. Are you relaxing right now or still at work?"

"Relaxing for a change, although household chores are calling."

"Don't you dare! They can wait a little longer. I can't believe you're at home at this time of the day. What happened?"

Randall sighed, wishing he could unload everything on his best friend. He'd met Geoff at pre-school, and though they lost touch during primary school because they'd attended different ones, they met up again at secondary school. And their friendship had continued as if those intervening missing years hadn't happened. "Nothing in particular. Another normal day."

"It doesn't sound like another day. You sound...fed up."

Randall focused out of the window, hoping the view would help him. "I'm not fed up. Maybe tired. I don't know."

"Are you sure nothing has happened?"

Randall chuckled. "Nothing relating to me that I can tell you."

"Ah. How are things with Dominic?"

Oh, how he wished he hadn't shared his dreams in a rare, weak moment. "He's fine. Busy, but fine."

"I still can't believe you're not going to try for him. He sounds perfect for you."

Randall had to be careful about what he shared with his friend, but he'd given the basics without going into details. Geoff knew who he worked for—most of the country did—but Randall couldn't share the internal goings-on of his job.

"I'm too old for him. He needs to find someone who's not worn out and jaded by life. Someone who *has* a life."

"If you were with him, I'm sure you'd have a life."

"Shut up, Geoff. You sound like my mother."

Geoff gasped, and Randall could just imagine him with his hand on his chest, mouth gaping. "How dare you!" he said in mock outrage. "I'm far more eloquent."

"I won't tell Mum you said that. She'd shit a brick."

"Nice visual. And yes, she would, so please don't."

Randall chuckled. "Your secret is safe with me." He sighed. "I don't know, Geoff. I'm just feeling a little melancholy today. Nothing some music won't cure, I'm sure."

"You should come swimming with me. It'll help relax you."

"Hmm, I think I'm more likely to drown. Anyway, don't you get sick of water?"

"I'm a lifeguard and a swimming teacher. What part of that makes you think I'm sick of water?"

Randall shook his head. "I'm sure you were a fish in a former life."

"It wouldn't surprise me." Geoff grew quiet, which is something he did when he had something to say. "As much as I don't like how your mother goes about the subject, she has a point. You don't do lonely, Randall. You like company. You need to find someone, or you'll wither away."

He hated that they were both right. He was lonely, but there wasn't much he could do about it. Going out to find someone at a bar or club didn't appeal to him at all. He needed it to be a natural progression, not something engineered, because he needed to find someone to take away the emptiness.

"I'll figure something out. Don't worry."

Geoff sighed. "Fine, but I won't stop bugging you."

"You never do."

They spent the next few minutes talking about Geoff and his family. His wife, Nadine, had just got a promotion at work, and their twins had just started university. Geoff was glad about the promotion because it helped Nadine with her empty nest syndrome.

When they finally hung up, Randall was feeling a little more like himself, and he set about his chores, putting his favourite eighties songs on to help his mood lighten further. Life wasn't always what people wanted when they wanted it, and he just had to deal with it.

It shouldn't be too hard. He'd been doing it for years already.

Randall made some time in his tasks the following day to visit with May. He knocked on her door with a gift he thought she might appreciate.

"Who is it?" a hesitant voice said.

"Hi, May. My name is Randall. I'm the king's personal—"

The door opened suddenly, and May's smiling face appeared. "Randall! Dominic has told me so much about you."

Randall's heart skipped a beat at that. "Oh, um..."

"Come on in."

He stepped inside and closed the door, holding out the gift to her.

"Oh, wow! It's beautiful."

It was a hamper filled with toiletries. Basically, a spa day in a box. He thought it might help her relax in an unfamiliar place.

"How are you settling in?"

May smiled at him, but he could see it didn't reach her eyes. "It's amazing. This place is just...wow."

"Feeling a trifle caged, by any chance?"

May snorted and stared at the floor, scuffing her foot back and forth. She met his gaze again. "Just a trifle."

"Would you like to go for a walk in the gardens?" His impromptu offer shouldn't inconvenience anyone, plus he had his phone with him if someone needed him.

Her eyes lit up. "Can I?

"Of course. We will need a guard with us, but it should be fine." He should ask Dominic, too, but he wanted to get the sadness from her eyes. He pulled out his phone, dialled and lifted it to his ear. "Hello, Brett. I'm going to accompany May to the gardens, but I thought it would be advisable to take a guard with us. Do you have someone you can spare for half an hour or so?"

"Of course. I'll send Nina over right away." He paused. "Have you mentioned this to Dominic?"

Randall cleared his throat. "No. I've not seen him."

Brett chuckled in his ear. "I'll let him know when he arrives, then."

"Thank you." He ended the call and faced May. "A guard will be with us shortly, and then we can get some fresh air."

May got herself ready, and a knock sounded a few minutes later. Randall checked who it was before opening the door.

"Hello, Nina. Thank you for this."

Nina smiled. "No problem at all. It makes a change from guarding Kieren."

Randall grinned. "He needs a guard, regardless of his opinions on the matter."

"Agreed." Nina waved down the hallway. "Shall we go?"

Randall turned to May. "Are you ready?"

"Yep."

Some of the weight had already lifted from her demeanour, and he could see her standing straighter as they walked further away from her room.

"What is it you do, May?"

"In Carlisle, I was a bank cashier, but I'm a photographer. I had to change my job as well as my life when I moved."

Randall's heart broke for her. She had been through so much for someone so young. "I can imagine that was difficult. A bit like cutting off your arm."

His words made her laugh, a loud bark of humour that lifted the darkness from her expression again. "Definitely. I had to leave all my cameras and equipment behind. I used to work freelance, sending my photos to travel companies, beauty magazines, anything like that, really."

"You must be really good."

She frowned at him as he gestured towards the door to the outside at the end of the hallway. "How can you tell? You haven't seen anything I've photographed."

"I can hear the passion for it in your voice. That kind of excitement about a job usually means you're good at it because you enjoy doing it and want to learn and get better."

She nodded. "Not to toot my own horn to use one of my father's phrases, but I was."

"You still are. If I put a camera in your hands now, you would get right back into it. I guarantee it."

She sighed. "I would love that. But everything is so up in the air. I don't know how long I'm going to be here. Whether I'm going to be sent back into witness protection again. Whether they're going to leave me hanging. I don't know."

They stepped out onto the stones in the East Terrace Lawn, and though it was chilly, it was a bright, sunny day. Randall inhaled deeply, staring across the expanse of greenery, stones, statues and water features that spread out before him. He rested his hands on the stone wall and smiled, grateful for being able to work in such an incredible place.

"It's beautiful. I've only ever seen it on TV before," May said from beside him.

"Shall we go for a wander?"

May nodded, and he led her down the stone steps to the garden. The crunch of the small stones beneath their feet was music to his ears—he loved all different sounds that some people might find annoying—and the scent of roses hung in the air. They walked down the straight path towards the fountain, completely at ease, no rushing, no stressing, with a cool breeze wafting off the water. It was wonderful. His phone vibrated in his pocket, but unless it rang, he was okay to ignore it for now.

"So, Randall. Tell me what my brother looks like when he's working."

Randall's mouth twitched. "I don't think it's much different from when he looks after you. Vigilant, focused, protective. He's fantastic at his job."

"He won't admit to having had injuries, but I'm assuming he has." Randall didn't answer, not wanting to cause upset. She sighed. "I heard all about what happened a few months back. Well, the past few years, really. It was a surprise—a good one, in some ways—to see him behind King Andrew. He'd never been in the main picture before, so I knew something must've happened. And then I heard about the loss of the guard."

Randall exhaled, glancing at Nina, who, though wearing a pained expression, was keeping an eye on their surroundings. "We've had far too many losses, but we're focusing on the future now. We have Princes George, Timothy and Eddie's joining coming up in a couple of months, and that's keeping us busy and upbeat."

"You've just had Prince Freddie and Prince Damon's wedding, too. You must be all wrapped up in a thousand to-do lists by now."

Randall laughed. "Don't I know it? I don't mind. I enjoy it."

"I wish you didn't enjoy it quite so much. You need a break."

Randall withheld a shiver when Dominic's voice rolled over him. He inhaled and faced him with a smile. "Good morning, Dominic."

"Dom!" May threw her arms around his neck and hugged him, and though Dominic hugged her back, his eyes were on Randall.

"Dom?" Randall couldn't help but ask.

Dominic ducked his head when he pulled back. "She won't quit."

May laughed. "You'll always be Dom to me, even though you don't like it. Or maybe *because* you don't like it. I'm not sure."

Dominic tickled her, and she squealed and squirmed away from him. "You would do better to remember who you're talking to, boo."

May rested her head against Dominic's arm. "It's my name for him," she explained to Randall. "He might not like it, but he's never stopped me from using it."

"After twenty-five-odd years, I can hardly stop you."

Randall could see in Dominic's expression that he didn't mind one bit. When he looked at his sister, his face softened, and the lines that were present during tense moments were gone. Randall had never seen the expression on him before, but what he wouldn't give for it to be aimed at him.

"Well, now you have Dominic, I will leave you to your visit. Enjoy the garden, May. It was lovely to meet you."

May let go of Dominic and hugged Randall. "Thank you for the basket. I can't wait to use them."

"You're most welcome."

He nodded and smiled at Dominic and headed back the way they came but stopped when Dominic called his name. "Do you need something?"

"Yes." Dominic grabbed his hand and squeezed. "I need to thank you for seeing what I didn't."

Randall's heart jumped at the contact, and he couldn't think of a response other than, "What?"

"You saw what she needed and gave it to her. A sense of freedom." He shook his head. "I thought by keeping her inside, she would be safer, but her wings are too long for a suite no matter how big it is."

Randall twisted his hand so he could return the squeeze. "You're doing great. Just remember, she's a person first and foremost. Let someone else be her guard while you're there as her brother."

Dominic huffed a laugh. "I can't believe I needed you to tell me that."

"You're welcome. Now, enjoy what little time you have together."

Dominic laughed heartily that time. "You've obviously seen my schedule for today," he said as he walked backwards, keeping his eyes on Randall.

"No, but I've seen the king's."

Randall waved and headed back inside, his stomach in knots. Dominic wasn't his and never would be. He was happy on his own.

Now, if he just reminded himself of that every hour, he might begin to believe it.

5

Dominic

"You like him," May said when Dominic returned to her side.

Dominic studied the floor as they continued on their walk through the garden. "I do. He's a good person."

"Don't pretend you don't know what I'm saying, Dom. You might be eight years older than me, but I still have years on you in accepting what my heart is telling me."

She had him there. She was light years ahead of him in that respect. He just couldn't let what his heart told him to be a factor in his life. He'd learnt many times that having his heart on his sleeve was something that sent more trouble his way, not less. Case in point was that he'd nearly killed her ex when he'd found out what he'd been doing. If Owen and Evan hadn't been there, he would have, and he would now be doing jail time instead of working for the most amazing family he'd ever known—besides his own, of course. Listening to his heart wasn't conducive to keeping him on an even keel.

He glanced behind him at Nina, who had dropped back a few more steps, and although he knew she could still hear them if they raised their voices, she would be less likely to if he kept his voice low.

"He's a friend, May. That's all."

"I can see the way you look at him, Dom." She followed his example and kept her voice down. "Like he's the sun, and you're the flower arching towards it. You've been alone so long. Why not accept what you already know in your heart and do something about it?"

"We're colleagues."

"He looks at you the same way, you know."

Dominic whipped his head around towards her, not missing the smirk on her face. "He does?"

May's mouth twitched as she stared ahead of them, running a hand along the wall they'd come to. "It doesn't matter. You're not interested."

Dominic huffed. "Bloody hell, May. I've not missed these 'know-it-all' conversations."

May laughed, and the joy in her voice warmed his soul, defrosting the ice that had grown since they had taken her in the witness protection, out of his reach, where he couldn't help her. Despite her meddling ways, he had missed the pure happiness she evoked in everyone around her.

She stopped and faced him. "From what I've seen, he cares about you as much as you care about him, despite how you pretend otherwise. Why not take the chance? He might just be your person." The light in her eyes dimmed a little, and she turned away, resuming their walk.

Why had she become sad? Had she found someone in Carlisle that she cared about? It was possible because she had been there for five years. If she opened up and told him, he could vet the guy. See if he was good enough for her.

As for Randall, well... Dominic had some thinking to do.

He glanced at his watch and sighed. "I'm sorry to love you and leave you, but I have to get back to work."

May smiled. "That's okay. I've had my fill of the outdoors now, so I can go inside, and you can relax that I'm safe while you do your job."

He couldn't help it. He pulled her into his arms and hugged the fuck out of her. Without having to say that he would be worried about her safety, she had given him peace of mind to enable him to focus solely on the king while he worked.

After kissing her cheek goodbye at her door, he hustled down the corridors to the security room, a place he'd renamed "Sec HQ" in his head. When he entered, everyone was already there. He nodded at Brett and took a seat next to Nick.

"Now that we're all here, let's get to it. Andrew has a meeting with the Prime Minister, as you are all aware. There will only be you six in attendance, but as the meeting is taking place here, those of us who have protectees on the grounds will be available should you require assistance."

They went through the protocols in place to keep Andrew safe, and then they dispersed. They had done this many times already, but they always went through the procedures again to ensure a coherent working relationship between them all.

Dominic dropped into step beside Nick as they headed for Andrew's suite, while the other four guards went to the King's Drawing Room to ensure everything was in place before the king himself arrived.

"How is your sister?" Nick asked.

Dominic snorted. "Bossy, as always. She's doing okay. We just need to find whoever is after her, and then she can relax. We can relax."

Nick nodded but said nothing more. A man of few words.

Dominic knocked on Andrew's suite and received permission to enter. When he did, Andrew was just finishing a drink in the company of his partners. Whenever Dominic saw them together, his heart thudded painfully against his ribs, reminding him he did want what the king had, what others had, but he had a job that made it nearly impossible to trust who he slept beside.

Except Randall.

With May's voice echoing in his head, he bowed his head to the royals. "Your Majesty. Nick and I are outside whenever you are ready to leave. The Prime Minister is on his way and should be here in twenty minutes."

Andrew stood, holding a cup. "Thank you, Dominic. I'll be ready in a couple of minutes."

"Yes, Your Majesty." Dominic bowed his head to them again and left the room, closing the door quietly behind him. "He's nearly ready," he said to Nick.

They settled in to wait, but it wasn't long before Andrew appeared. The man was always where he said he would be *when* he said he would be. Colt and Emmy were positioned outside when they arrived at the Drawing Room, which meant Viola and Landon should be inside, checking through the room. Nick entered the room first, giving the nod to Dominic when it was clear.

"After you, Your Majesty." He waved the king into the room.

"Thank you."

They said nothing more as Andrew settled onto a seat. If his actions followed his usual routine, he wouldn't get a drink for himself unless his guest had one when he arrived. True to form, when the Prime Minister entered, Andrew stood and held out his hand.

"Alan, nice to see you again."

Alan Grey was someone Dominic had never been able to read properly. He seemed to want to help the country prosper, especially when he was first elected, but recently, his views had changed, and not in a good way. The pressure of his colleagues to do what was best for *them* instead of the country was weighing down on him, and the country was suffering for it. Andrew, however, wasn't giving Alan an inch when it came to doing the right thing. Unfortunately, Andrew only had so much power despite being the king.

"Would you like a drink?" Andrew asked.

"Tea would be great, thanks."

Nick moved to fill their orders—something none of the guards minded doing if it meant the king was safe and there weren't more people in the room than necessary—and placed them by their sides as the men talked.

It was mostly menial stuff—not that Dominic would repeat anything he heard under any circumstances—until Andrew brought up the one topic they often butted heads about. Dominic braced for an argument, but Alan surprised him.

"I know, Your Majesty. I have taken a long, hard look at where I was when I was first given this job and my position now, and I've seen the discrepancy. I've finally remembered what I wanted to do for the country." Alan sighed. "I've removed the plans from our agenda. It won't help in the long run. We need to focus on what we can do now that will help our future, not risk it all on chance."

"I'm glad you can see my side of things, Alan. Can I ask what caused this change of heart?"

Alan laughed and shook his head. "My wife echoing your words. She made me see what you had been saying all along." He sighed. "And threatened to leave me if I continued along the route I was going."

"Ah," Andrew said. "Partners can be wonderfully succinct when they need to be."

"So true."

They continued discussing other agendas and plans within the government, Andrew giving his thoughts on the planned routes. It was over three hours later when they finished. After saying goodbye to the Prime Minister, Dominic and Nick followed Andrew back to his office. Nick stayed outside in the corridor, and Dominic checked Andrew's office before leaving him to his work and settling in the chair in Randall's office.

Dominic's eyes focused on Randall the moment he let himself look—which was why he always made sure to secure the king before he looked at him. May's words circled in his head as he watched the man go through what appeared to be several reams of paper. His gaze snapped to the door when it opened, but he relaxed when he saw Portia. She smiled and nodded at him and went straight over to Randall. Dominic watched their interaction, lifting his eyebrow when they started laughing. Randall glanced at him, his cheeks flushing a rosy pink. Dominic couldn't help his mouth curving into a smile, but he made himself look away and pick up the book he'd been reading whenever he was on duty.

He lost himself in the pages, though he was completely aware of everything going on around him, especially wherever Randall was, the sound of his laughter, the scent of his cologne, which he had still yet to identify.

"Dominic?"

Randall's voice brought his attention up. "Yes?"

"Would you like a drink?"

He smiled. "A coffee would be great, thanks."

Randall nodded and headed over to the coffee machine. "Nick will want coffee as well, won't he?"

"Yes, please."

Dominic watched Portia grab some paperwork and leave the room with another smile in his direction. He hadn't had much to do with Portia because he had been lower on the guarding lines before the queen had been killed. He knew her and that she had been the queen's personal assistant, but that was all. They had rarely crossed paths in his schedule.

When they were alone, Randall finished the drinks, taking one out of the room to Nick before returning and handing Dominic his coffee.

"Thank you."

"You're welcome." Randall carried his glass of water over to his desk. "How is May doing? Did she enjoy the garden?"

Dominic nodded. "She loved it. I think that will be a regular haunt for her from now on."

"I don't blame her. I find it peaceful, too."

"Your schedule is as full as the king's. Maybe more so."

Randall chuckled. "Definitely more so. His is more important and draining, but yes, I do have a lot to do most days. I'm glad Portia can help out."

"I'm glad you have someone to share the burden. All work and no play..." He left the phrase without finishing, knowing Randall would understand what he was saying.

Randall's mouth twitched. "I'm definitely a dull boy, then."

Dominic rubbed his chin, the stubble scratching his fingers. "I don't believe that for a moment."

Their gazes locked, and Dominic swore he could feel a link between them clicking into place. Randall's dark blond hair was combed back and to the side from his forehead, leaving his face—and expressions—available for him to see. He wore his stubble slightly shorter than Dominic did, giving him a slightly younger appearance than the age he knew Randall to be. His lips were pale pink, the lower one slightly plumper than the upper, and made Dominic want to bite them.

Crap. May was right.

As much as he wanted to walk over to Randall and drop a kiss on those delectable lips, Dominic couldn't. He was working, and if he got distracted, bad things could happen. But he couldn't help from wetting his own lips as if he was going to kiss him. Randall's eyes widened, and he lowered his head, breaking the lock they had on one another.

Randall busied himself with his work, and Dominic tried to read his book, but his attention was on the man across the room from him. At least, it was until his phone rang with a number he'd be waiting for.

"Detective Addams, do you have any news?"

"Good afternoon to you, too, Mr Ainsley."

Dominic rubbed his forehead. "Sorry. Good afternoon."

Addams chuckled in his ear. "It's okay. I'm used to it. To answer your question, yes, I have news, but it's not necessarily good."

"I would be surprised if we caught a break." Dominic sighed, leaning his elbows on his knees as he waited for the obviously bad news.

"The Carlisle police officers have finished with the scene, and there is no evidence of any shooting in May's house. No shell cases, no bullet holes, nothing."

"Gun powder residue?"

"Not that they could find." Addams sighed. "It's as if it never happened. Is May certain she saw and heard gunshots?"

Dominic nodded, even though the guy couldn't see him. "She said she saw the flashes."

"And it was definitely at her house? The police have interviewed most of her neighbours, but not all are available yet."

Dominic grimaced. "You think they hit a different house?"

"You said she was a distance away when she stopped and looked back. She could've got it wrong."

"I suppose." He paused, thinking it through. "It's possible, but she has a keen eye. It would surprise me if she got it wrong. I'm assuming they need to speak to her."

"They will, yes. They agreed I could give you this update, but everything else will need to go through the detective in charge,

Maloney. I'll send his number to you. I told him you would get May to call him so she can give her statement."

"Thanks. I'll get her to do that this afternoon." He sighed. "So there was nothing to show anyone had been in her house at all?"

"Nothing. Either May got it wrong, or someone has an extremely good gift for cleaning a scene."

Dominic frowned. "It seems unlikely if they're the crooks we believe them to be."

"You're not the only one who thought that." Addams cleared his throat. "I'm still going to be kept in the loop, so if you have any questions, call me. I will, however, be visiting soon. Detective Maloney wants someone to have eyes on May, and I offered, thinking it would be easier for her with someone she knew."

"I appreciate that. Just give me a call when you want to visit, and I'll clear it for you."

Addams chuckled. "You do realise I could just walk in without any problems, don't you?"

"You could, but there's no guarantee it would stay that way, even if you are a police officer. Remember what this family has been through lately." Dominic's heart skipped a beat, and he met Randall's gaze again. There was a sense of camaraderie between them from what they'd been through together.

"Duly noted."

They ended the call, and Dominic put his phone away.

"Everything okay?"

He glanced at Randall and smiled. "Yeah." He sighed again, running his hands through his hair. "There was no evidence of any wrongdoing at May's house in Carlisle."

Randall frowned. "How is that possible?"

"I don't know, but I intend to find out." He shook his head, transferring his gaze to the window. "Something doesn't add up," he murmured.

"If you want someone to bounce ideas off, I have a good listening ear," Randall offered.

Dominic chuckled. "Thank you. I might just take you up on that."

Randall's cheeks flushed again, and Dominic wanted to cup them and feel how hot they got. Instead, he stared across the distance between them, not making a move. Randall was the first to break eye contact again, and they dropped into a comfortable silence.

In his mind, Dominic played through the information he had about May, everything that had happened five years ago and everything that happened that weekend. He tried to see it from different angles. Were they even after May in the first place, or had it been someone else? A neighbour? A work colleague? If they had been after May, what was their end game? Did they still want revenge for what she did, or did they just want to scare her?

There were far too many unanswered questions for Dominic's liking, and he hated not having the information he needed to answer them.

But the scariest question of all… Had this all been a ruse to flush her out of the woodwork so they could get her now she had fled home?

Woe betide anyone who tried to get to her. Dominic would scorch the earth to keep her safe. The same for any of his family, the royal family, and a certain personal assistant, who he now realised meant a lot more to him than he had understood before his enlightening conversation with his sister.

Let anyone try to hurt them and see what he would do.

6

Randall

Sometimes, Randall's need to help made his mouth work before his brain engaged. Offering to listen to Dominic's problem was something he was happy to do, but Dominic would probably think he was being nosey. When Landon came to relieve Dominic at the end of his shift, Randall was almost pleased. He'd felt the man's eyes on him several times over the past few hours, and it had stopped Randall from working as much—and as efficiently—as usual. Landon, however, was the strong, silent type and barely spoke, except to answer when Randall asked if he wanted a drink or snack. It wasn't his job to feed and water them, but he enjoyed making them comfortable. They were doing an important job, after all.

By the end of Randall's working day, he was slightly behind on what he had planned, but he wasn't going to get any more work done. He locked everything up he needed to and headed for his car.

"Randall!"

He jumped at his name, his hand going to his chest as if to stop his heart from escaping. He closed his eyes when he saw Dominic.

"Sorry. I thought you'd heard me coming," Dominic said when he reached him.

"It's okay. I was lost in my thoughts." He inhaled. "Everything okay?"

Dominic ducked his head, but not before Randall saw his grimace. "Well, I wondered if you'd like to go out sometime? Maybe to get something to eat or just a drink if that's too much." Dominic lifted his head again and met his gaze.

Was he asking him on a date? Why? He's much too young for Randall. He had his whole life ahead of him. He didn't need Randall weighing him down with his insecurities and issues.

"I don't think so. It's not a good idea."

As soon as he said the words, he wanted to take them back. Despite knowing he didn't want to drag Dominic down, the expression that crossed Dominic's face was one he didn't want to see again.

"Oh, okay. I just thought... Never mind." He began walking backwards. "Have a good evening."

Randall watched him turn and jog back across the car park to the door. When he disappeared, Randall sighed and carried on to his car. Why had he done that? Had Dominic really wanted a date with him? Or was it something else he wanted to discuss?

Randall paused when he sat behind the steering wheel. Had Dominic wanted the listening ear Randall had offered? *Shit.* He rubbed his hands over his face, debating what to do, but he wasn't sure of the best course of action now he'd already declined.

Sighing, he drove home. It wasn't long before he settled into bed, but he tossed and turned for hours, dozing and waking repeatedly. It took a nightmare about what happened those few months ago for him to give up and drive back to Windsor Castle, despite it being three o'clock in the morning. The guards were used to him turning up at all hours, so his appearance wasn't anything unusual.

Entering his office, he made himself a cup of tea and settled at his desk. The work he hadn't completed earlier that day—well, the previous day—beckoned, and he pulled the first task towards him, rubbing his tired eyes.

He wasn't sure how long he worked before a noise startled him, and he rose and backed away from the sound even as he whipped his head towards it.

"For God's sake," Dominic muttered. "Sorry, I don't mean to keep scaring you. I'm used to moving quietly. I'll try to be louder next time."

Randall leaned back against the wall, closing his eyes and covering his face with his trembling hands. Breathing slowly was the only way to get himself under control, and as he did, he felt Dominic move closer. When arms came around him, as slowly as a tortoise making its way home, he melted into them, burying his head into the warmth Dominic provided. His arms tightened, holding Randall closer and making him feel safer than he had been in a long time.

"I'm sorry. So sorry," Dominic murmured over and over.

Randall let himself relax in those arms for as long as he dared, and then he pulled back, meeting Dominic's pained gaze. "It's not your fault. I'm still dealing with what happened. It's just closer to the surface because I had a nightmare tonight."

Dominic cupped Randall's cheeks, wiping away the tears that had escaped. "I wondered why you were here so late. Or early."

Randall's eyelids fluttered as Dominic cleared his cheeks, needing every touch he was given, and Dominic continued brushing his thumbs across his skin.

"Randall..." Dominic whispered.

Randall met his gaze, and the blistering heat he saw was unexpected. Was that for him? How? Why? "I..." He had no idea what to say.

"Yes or no?"

Randall's heart pounded, and he inhaled. Taking the chance of his lifetime, he nodded. Dominic licked his lips, lowering his head inch by inch until Randall was ready to scream from impatience. If this was the only kiss he was ever going to have with Dominic, he was going to make it worthwhile.

When their lips finally touched, Randall's eyes drifted shut, his hands clasping onto Dominic's biceps. Dominic brushed his mouth back and forth across Randall's lips and then pressed harder. He nipped, and Randall gasped, automatically opening his mouth and giving Dominic the invitation Randall so wanted him to accept. And accept he did. As Dominic's tongue swooped into his mouth, Randall's knees buckled, but Dominic's hand left his face and wrapped around his waist to keep him from falling.

The kiss. The taste. The scent. It was everything Randall could've ever wanted from a first kiss, and he would remember it forever.

As Dominic explored Randall's mouth, Randall's hands slipped around Dominic's back, gripping the fabric of his shirt and feeling the heat of him seep through into his body. He wanted more. He needed more. But just as he tightened his hold, Dominic softened the kiss until he dropped gentle kisses onto Randall's lips, cheeks and nose. He rested their foreheads together, and Randall breathed, his heart still pumping erratically.

"That was..." Dominic didn't finish the sentence, but Randall could think of several ways to do so. He didn't say any of them, though. Instead, he lifted his head, allowing Dominic to come into focus properly.

"Thank you."

Dominic chuckled. "You don't need to thank me for that. I've been wanting to do that all day."

Randall's cheeks heated, and he wanted to hide his face, but Dominic cupped his cheek again. He smiled and closed his eyes, hiding the only way he could unless he pulled away. Something he didn't want to do but knew he had to. For his own sanity.

"I should get on…" he said.

"It's four in the morning. Why do you need to work now? You should rest."

Randall sighed and lowered his head, dislodging Dominic's hand. "I don't think I'll sleep."

"I could help."

Randall couldn't help it. He laughed. "Could you, indeed?"

Dominic frowned and then covered his face with his free hand. "I didn't quite mean that the way it sounded. I just meant I could walk you to your room and help you to bed—while I stayed out of it—and then close your door and walk away. I'll even sing you a lullaby if you want to cringe your way through it."

Randall's mouth twitched, but he withheld his laugh. "I'm sure you're not as bad as you think."

"A cat would sing better."

Randall pulled out of Dominic's arms and took a step back, needing to breathe without inhaling his scent, but found his back against the wall he'd forgotten about. Dominic must've realised what he needed because he moved a few steps away from him, giving him the space to get his head back on straight.

"I think I'll get some more work done instead, but thank you for the offer," Randall said.

Dominic nodded, scratching his chin; a tell Randall was realising meant he had a question, but he wasn't sure if he should ask. Randall waited for it.

"Are you okay? Did I overstep?"

Randall held out his hands. "I'm just a little…taken aback."

"Taken aback? About what?"

Randall touched his lips, reliving the kiss as he stared at Dominic. "You wanting to kiss me," he whispered. "I'm ten years older than you, Dominic. You have better options out there." He waved his hand towards the invisible millions of people that Dominic could choose from, but the moment he spoke, Dominic froze. The blank expression that he usually wore when he was working and pushing everything else aside other than the important job he had to carry out flitted across his face, and he stepped further back.

"I'm sorry. I thought... Never mind. Have a good night, Randall."

Before Randall could take back what he said and explain, Dominic left his office. He slumped back against the wall, exhaling and banging his head back against it gently. What had he done? He'd hurt him unintentionally, but his words were true. Dominic could have anyone he wanted, so why had he kissed Randall? He was far too old and came with far too much baggage. Rubbing his hands over his face, he sighed and then headed back to his desk. As tired as he now was, there was no way he would be able to sleep.

Five hours later, he was refilling his tea when Andrew entered, with Nick following.

"Good morning, Your Majesty. Can I bring you a drink?"

"Tea would be great, thanks, Randall, and then I'll need you to come in with your notebook, or whatever it is you use now, and go through a list as long as my arm as to what the heck is going on."

Randall raised his eyebrows at his fed-up tone. "Yes, Your Majesty. I will be in momentarily." Andrew disappeared into his office, and Nick took the seat outside the door. "Would you like a drink, Nick?"

"I'm good, thanks."

Randall busied himself making drinks while trying not to ask the question that was on the tip of his tongue. He didn't hold back for long. "How come Dominic isn't here this morning? It was supposed to be his shift, wasn't it?"

"Yeah, he asked to swap, said he had something he needed to do with his sister."

Randall nodded and said nothing more. Nick, while full of humour and sarcasm, was never talkative when he was working. Besides, he was sure Dominic was avoiding him rather than having to see his sister.

Carrying the king's tea, he tucked his tablet under his arm and picked up his own cup. He realised his mistake when he got to the door, and Nick chuckled despite his usual stoic demeanour. Nick knocked on the door, and when Andrew called for Randall to enter, he held the door open for him.

"Thank you, Nick."

He placed the tea in front of Andrew and settled into the visitor's chair, crossing his legs to rest the tablet on and putting his cup on the edge of the king's desk. "I'm ready when you are, Your Majesty."

Andrew sighed and cupped his mug in his hands. "Freddie has reported back that the visit to Australia isn't going as well as they'd hoped."

Randall frowned. "Oh, did he say why he thought that?"

"More and more of the citizens want to separate from the Commonwealth. They want to be an individual entity in themselves. I can see their point, but it brings a lot of problems that need solving before it can happen. I had hoped Freddie could pave the way for helping to settle them and keep things as they are." He sighed again. "It doesn't seem to have worked. Freddie and Damon are getting pushback from the government, and protests are riling others up from what I can gather."

Randall glanced at his tablet. This wasn't his domain. He had nothing to offer in the way of advice, but he could listen, as he always had.

"This wasn't quite the gentle and easy honeymoon I had told them they would have." Andrew huffed a laugh. "I'll have to send them on a better one when they return."

"I'm sure a visit to the Caribbean would be a pleasant idea for them."

"Hmm, maybe."

"What do you need me to do to help with Australia, Your Majesty?"

Andrew didn't answer for a moment, but then he said, "Can you find out exactly what we need if this goes ahead, please? I've never had to deal with it myself, but I know my father did some research on it. I have no idea what to expect."

"Of course, Your Majesty. Is there a time constraint on this?" He made a few notes on his tablet and set a reminder in his calendar for the following day.

"No. I don't think it's going to happen anytime soon, but they will undoubtedly want to get the ball rolling."

Randall finished his notes and picked up his drink, sipping while he waited for Andrew to get to the next issue on his list.

"May Ainsley," Andrew said, meeting Randall's gaze. Randall's heart pounded. "I need you to liaise with Brett and find out exactly what is happening with the situation. I'm not convinced there aren't problems coming our way. I have no issues with her staying here, but I want everyone prepared for the possibilities. Talk to Dominic as well and get his opinion on what might be coming."

Randall swallowed hard. "Yes, Your Majesty." He added to his task list, though he wished he hadn't been tasked with speaking with Dominic. After what had happened earlier that morning,

Randall was probably the last person Dominic wanted to see and speak to.

"I received a phone call this morning," Andrew said. He transferred his gaze to the window, swinging his chair around. "I have no idea who it was or how they got my number, but their message was both clear and unclear." He met Randall's gaze. "'Get ready for number one,' was all they said. I can't decide if it's a credible threat or a prank, but I've passed it to Brett. I need you to collate emails and messages that the royal family receives or has already received that are anything similar to it. Brett said he would send you anything he finds."

Randall's stomach churned. He was used to threats to the safety of the royal family, but when it was so clouded by uncertainty, it made his stomach churn.

They spoke for another half an hour, going through the other issues that had cropped up overnight, including the half a dozen email requests from Malachi Sanders, asking for an exclusive interview, and Randall left Andrew with another cup of tea and a closed door so he could do what he needed to prepare for the meeting he had that afternoon.

Randall settled behind his desk and got to work on what he could. He checked the email accounts he was in charge of, and nothing showed up as a threat or otherwise about "number one," so he breathed easy for the moment. He set to work on researching what was needed if Australia decided to remove itself from British rule. There was no way he was putting speaking to Dominic on the back burner because he was worried about seeing him again. Of course, he wasn't.

He sighed and slumped in his chair. Maybe he should get it over and done with. "Nick, do you know if Dominic is still with his sister?"

Nick shook his head. "I've no idea. I can contact Brett and find out if you want?"

Randall waved him away. "No, don't worry. I'll go and find him." He emailed the king to let him know he was going out of the office and could be reached on his phone if he needed anything and then locked his computer and headed out. The security room would be the first visit, so he could ask Brett. He could've used the phone to locate Dominic, but Randall wanted to use the time to steady his nerves.

Would Dominic still talk to him? Would he be a frozen mask of civility, or would he forgive Randall for his poorly chosen words?

As he wandered the hallways, he heard Dominic's voice and smiled despite his uncertainty. But at the harsh tone, he paused before rounding the corner.

"You have no right," Dominic hissed. "Stay away from her and our family." There was silence while—he assumed—Dominic listened. "No! You leave everyone else out of this. If you have a problem, you come to me. Touch anyone else, and I will see to it that you are found at the bottom of the Thames." Silence again. "You think I'm fucking around? Just try me, Fletcher."

Randall heard a smash and several curses falling from Dominic's mouth, and he peered around the corner to see the man picking up the shards of his phone.

"That's one way to end a call," Randall murmured as he stepped towards him, picking up a piece of plastic on his way.

Dominic glanced up at him, and his eyes gave voice to the anger and pain he felt. Dominic stood and sighed, his shoulders lowering. "Did you need something?"

"For two things, actually." Randall inhaled, gathering his courage. "First, I want to apologise for what I said earlier." He wrung his hands together, scraping his palm on the plastic he'd forgotten he held. "I couldn't understand why you wanted to kiss me, and I voiced that in the wrong way. I'm sorry."

Dominic huffed a laugh and stepped closer, taking the piece of broken phone Randall held. "It's okay. It smarted a little, to begin with, but I realised you weren't aiming your words at me. You were aiming them at yourself. Once I understood that, I planned to visit you and explain exactly how much you've come to mean to me."

Randall's heart skipped a beat, and his breathing turned erratic. "Oh," was all he could manage.

Dominic chuckled. "A man of few words." He cleared his throat and ducked his head. "I'd like to start again. I can tell you exactly what you could give me that others couldn't. Will you let me take you out to dinner?"

Randall licked his lips. "Okay."

"Good. What's the second thing?"

"What?" Randall's brain had scrambled.

"The second thing you wanted to talk to me about?"

"Oh, Andrew would like us to talk about the situation with May. He wants a report on everything that could be heading our way, so he needs background information. Are you okay with that?"

Dominic stared at the broken phone in his hands. "I suppose I'll have to be."

Randall could understand his reluctance. Dominic didn't like relying on other people unless there was no option, which was surprising considering he was the king's protector, who needed to work as a team all the time.

"Are you on shift this afternoon?" Dominic nodded. "We'll talk then."

"Yes, sir," Dominic teased.

Randall swallowed hard and backed away. "Oh, is everything okay with that call?"

Dominic didn't answer for a moment, but then he nodded as if he was debating with himself. "Not really, but I'll fill you in this afternoon."

Randall wanted to press, but he didn't. "See you later."

He escaped while he still could instead of throwing himself in Dominic's arms like his entire body wanted to do. He didn't want to be the needy little submissive he was when Dominic was going through something. He wanted to be strong. For Dominic.

7

Dominic

Dominic watched Randall leave, and then he stared down at the ruined remains of his phone. He exhaled and headed back towards Sec HQ. When he entered, Brett raised his eyebrows.

"Back so soon. What's up?"

Dominic sighed. "Do you know, whenever you say that, I expect to see you holding a carrot while saying it in Bugs Bunny's voice?" He dropped the remains on the table, and Brett frowned.

"Need I ask?"

"Let's just say I had a phone call that riled me up a little too much."

Brett stood and disappeared into the adjoining room, returning a few seconds later. He threw a packet at him. "Don't break this one. I'm running low on stock."

Dominic chuckled. "I can imagine. Do you have shares in the company?"

"I wish. I'd be a bloody millionaire."

Dominic unpacked the new phone. "I'll get this set up as quickly as possible."

"Let Felix know when you're done, and he'll get your old number transferred over." Brett slurped his coffee.

"Does he have to?" Dominic whined.

Brett stared at him. "What's going on, Dominic?"

"You know what's going on. Everything with May. Balancing her and my job. And now..." He trailed off.

"Now?"

Dominic glanced at him and winced. "And now, Randall."

Brett's mouth curved, though he tried to hide it behind his mug. "Randall, eh?"

"Fuck off."

Brett laughed. "You mentioned him, not me."

Dominic dropped into a chair and kicked his feet up onto the corner of the desk. He stared at the ceiling and gave up the pretence. "I asked him for dinner yesterday, and he said no. So, I left it. Then, when I heard he'd arrived back at three o'clock this morning, I went to check on him. I kissed him. Then, when I asked him for dinner again, he said I shouldn't have anything to do with him. It threw me off balance. If he didn't want me, why did he kiss me back?"

"Oh, for fuck's sake, Dominic. He wants you. I've seen it for weeks. Months even. And I know you want him, too. There's just been a misunderstanding. Fix it, and we can all live happily ever after."

Dominic put up his middle finger. "I want to. I'll be speaking with him this afternoon about the May stuff. He said yes to dinner this time." He exhaled. "I really don't want to mess things up and him pull away again."

"So don't give him a choice. You're doing the afternoon shift. Take dinner with you or arrange for it to be delivered to the office."

Dominic lifted his head and stared at Brett. "You know, you can be romantic when you want to be."

Brett threw a piece of the broken phone at him, and Dominic laughed as he stood. Despite the anger that had coursed through him after the phone call, his interactions with Randall and Brett had helped calm him. It was a shame his phone was the unlucky recipient of his temper.

"Who caused this?" Brett asked, nudging the remains.

Dominic put his hands on his hips and lowered his head. "Fletcher Pinton. He was one of Gavin's right-hand men before Gavin was incarcerated. Seems like he's gone up in the world. He called to tell me that May needed to pay for what she did. And if he couldn't have her, he would find someone else who would be just as beneficial to him." Dominic glanced at Brett. "I might have threatened to let him visit the bottom of the river."

Brett rolled his eyes and sighed. "Your words will get you into trouble one of these days."

"It wouldn't be the first time."

He left Brett to his work and headed to his room. He took a quick shower and dressed in his work clothes. As he went for the door so he could visit his sister for a couple of hours before his shift started, he paused, staring at his new phone. He strode across the room to where the landline phones were and dialled the kitchen.

"Kitchen."

"Good afternoon. Could I please arrange for lunch for two people to be sent to May Ainsley's room?"

"Of course. Is there anything, in particular, you would like?" the staff member asked.

"No. We're not fussy."

"Okay. We'll get something over to you within the hour."

"Thank you. Could I also ask for dinner to be sent to Randall's office at five o'clock, please?"

"No problem, sir. Would that be for one person or more?"

"Two, please." He was being presumptive, but they both had to eat.

"All sorted. Can I help you with anything else?"

Dominic thought he'd already asked for too much. "No, that's great, thank you."

"You're welcome, sir. Have a good day."

He had never felt good about getting other people to do the work he could easily do himself, but the only way he could get food that wasn't prepared by the Windsor staff was if he headed out to get it himself. No one would let him near the kitchen. And not because he couldn't cook. Because he could.

When May let him into her room, all he could scent was roses. There was an enormous bouquet of pink roses displayed on the side table.

"Have you been picking the king's flowers?" he joked.

May backhanded his chest. "No, they were a gift from Randall."

Dominic blinked. "That's kind of him."

"It is. Do you want a drink?" She headed for the small fridge. "Coffee?"

"I should stop asking," she said with an eye roll.

"You shouldn't need to. It's all I ever drink. Well, almost." He waited until she had brought the drinks over before he said, "Have you heard anything from anyone who should know better?"

She chuckled. "That's a good way of putting it." She sipped her tea and crossed her legs underneath her. "Actually, yes. Fletcher."

Dominic tensed. "When?"

"Around three hours ago. I told him, none too politely, to leave me alone."

"So that's why he called me. He's not used to you standing up for yourself."

May snorted. "I've certainly grown a backbone since all this happened."

"You've always had a backbone; otherwise, this would never have happened in the first place. You've got more strength in one hand than some people have in their entire bodies." He studied her expression. "What else did he say?"

She put her cup down on the coffee table and wrapped her arms around herself. "Paul's out."

Dominic stopped himself from gripping his mug so tightly it broke. "Out?"

"He got out a few weeks ago, apparently."

"Why weren't we notified?"

"No idea."

Dominic put his mug down and pulled out his phone, dialling.

"Detective Addams."

"Addams, it's Dominic. Why weren't we told that Paul Leary was out of prison?"

"I didn't know he was." Dominic heard the rustling of paper and then some clicking of a keyboard. "Shit. We were supposed to have been told, but somehow, they never sent it through."

"I can imagine why." Dominic sighed. "Do you know when he got out, exactly?"

"July twenty-eighth. Why?"

"Doesn't it seem convenient that they found May not long after he was released? He's not the only one after her, but he would have more of a vested interest as they had been together. He's the type of guy who would be pissed off that a *woman* got the better of him. I know that for a fact."

Addams exhaled. "I'll look into where he is and see if we can get any more information from him. I can't make promises, but we'll try."

"Thanks."

He ended the call and barely refrained from throwing it again.

"Even if they find me, there's no way they can get to me here," May said.

He shook his head. "Nowhere is impenetrable. Even here. It's difficult but not impossible. We need to find the sons of bitches and finish this once and for all." He stood and paced, flicking his phone end over end as he walked. "Why now? No one bothered with you for five years. The only difference is that Paul is now out of prison. He has to be the one orchestrating this."

A knock sounded, and May jumped. Dominic went to the door and opened it an inch, relaxing when a staff member rolled in a trolley with their delicious-smelling lunch on it. He doubted either of them would be hungry, but they needed to keep their strength up. Especially May.

"Thank you," he said to the staff member as they exited. "Come on, eat up. Even if it's only a little."

They settled at the small dining table that was placed near a window, and Dominic flipped his gaze between the window and May, trying to see where her emotions lay.

"This will never be over, will it?"

Dominic put down his sandwich, brushing his hands. "Yes, it will. One way or another, it will end. I promise you. You will not be running for your life forever."

He could see May didn't believe him, but he couldn't reassure her any other way. They finished lunch, talking about everything and nothing. As he readied to leave for the start of his shift, he pulled her into a hug.

"You are not a prisoner here. I know it seems that way, but you're not. Maybe tomorrow I can take you over to Book Drunk. We have an in with the owner."

May laughed, lifting Dominic's mood. "So I've heard. Have Prince Christian and Oscar announced their wedding yet? I bet it won't be long."

"Not heard anything yet, but everyone else is slowly tying the knot. I'm sure you're right, and it won't be long until they announce it."

He kissed her cheek before he left, hating to go when she was feeling down, but he couldn't ignore his job. That afternoon would be fairly easy, as Andrew only had one meeting in his office and the rest of the time would be spent alone. It meant Dominic had an afternoon of watching and talking to Randall. His soon-to-be favourite activity.

When he entered Randall's office to take over from Nick, he found Randall and Portia talking rapidly, leaning over the desk and pointing to things on the papers resting there. He glanced at Nick.

"Everything okay?" he murmured, not wanting to interrupt.

Nick nodded and stood. "He's been given a job to do that requires a lot of work, it seems. He's been like this for several hours already. He's barely stopped. I even had to make him a drink because he'd not touched one for over two hours. I've no idea what it's all about."

"If it's important for us to know, they'll tell us, I'm sure." His eyes found their way back to Randall again. "Anyway, get off with you."

"I'll be getting off all right." He winked and left, leaving his laughter in his wake.

Dominic knocked on Andrew's office door and entered when called. "Good afternoon, Your Majesty. I'm just checking in with you. Nick has gone off shift now, and I'll be here if you need anything."

"Thank you, Dominic." Andrew's tired voice barely reached him. "I must admit to wishing it was the end of the day already."

"It sounds like you've had a busy morning."

"You could say that." Andrew sighed and waved him in. "I suppose I better let you know what's going on. Have a seat."

Dominic settled in the visitor's chair, his stomach churning. He waited patiently, knowing Andrew would get to the point when he was ready.

Andrew sighed. "I received a phone call earlier. It came up as an unknown number, but I often get that when it's people who call me. I answered, and the person only said, 'Get ready for number one.' I have no idea what they mean, but it's not sitting well with me. I've asked Randall to collate all the emails, calls, texts and any other means from anyone who has received something similar. It's not a simple job, which is why he's probably running around like a hare on drugs out there, but it's necessary."

"Have you notified Brett?"

Andrew nodded his head. "I didn't feel like there was much point, but I did. The more I think about it, the more I'm concerned about the words. 'Get ready for number one.' It could mean anything, but something is tickling the back of my mind, and I don't like it."

"Neither do I, Your Majesty. Brett will get to the bottom of it."

Andrew nodded. "Thank you, Dominic. And if I haven't said it enough, I appreciate everything you're doing for us."

"You don't have to thank me, Your Majesty."

Andrew chuckled. "Yes, I do. I made a promise to Louisa that I would never take my staff for granted, and I'm keeping to it."

Dominic smiled and bowed his head. "It's a pleasure."

"How is your sister?"

He exhaled. "Worried. Annoyed. Anxious. Wishing it was all over. There are so many words to describe it. We just want it finished so she can live her life without looking over her shoulder."

"I know how that feels." Andrew sighed. "We'll figure it out, and she'll be free from it before she knows it."

"You don't have to—" He stopped when Andrew glared at him. "Thank you."

Randall knocked and poked his head in the door. "Sorry to interrupt, but your guest is here."

Andrew stood. "Thank you, Randall. Just give us a moment." Randall smiled and closed the door, and Andrew focused on Dominic again. "Use whatever resources you need to help with figuring out what's going on, and if you need anything we don't have, please ask. You're as close as family, Dominic, and I mean that."

Dominic could barely talk through the lump in his throat. "Thank you, Your Majesty."

"Andrew, please."

Dominic chuckled. "No, Your Majesty."

Andrew sighed and shook his head. "One of these days..."

"Don't hold your breath."

He exited the office, and Randall showed the chancellor in while Dominic called Brett and double-checked what Andrew had told him. When Randall came back out, he busied himself making drinks and carried them back into the room before returning and closing the door firmly. His shoulders slumped as he turned to Dominic.

"Hey," he said with a small smile. "Would you like a drink?"

Dominic stood and slid an arm around Randall's waist. "How about you sit down, and I'll make us both a drink?"

Randall exhaled. "Yes, please."

It proved how tired Randall was with his simple acceptance of a job he always said was his to do—which it wasn't. Dominic made them both drinks and settled on the seat in front of Randall's desk instead of in his usual seat in front of Andrew's office. He was still within easy reach if he was needed, but he wanted to be closer to Randall.

"So, Andrew filled me in on the phone call."

Randall sipped his tea despite it being so hot he must've burnt his lips and nodded. "I don't really know what I'm doing, but I've contacted the rest of the family to find out if they've received anything strange, and so far, no one has."

"Brett will get Felix and Sam on it."

"Good, thanks." He closed his eyes briefly.

"You're tired."

Randall smiled, small though it was. "I am, but I'll push through as I always do." He put his cup down and pulled a notepad towards him. "So, Mr Ainsley, tell me your woes."

Dominic chuckled and settled in, going right back to the beginning of May's relationship with Paul and how they got together—according to May—and what happened up to the point when she said goodbye and left for witness protection. It was a long story, and Randall only interrupted when he had questions. And when prompted, Dominic continued to the phone call he received from May three days earlier up to the present time and the phone calls they had both received that day.

Randall stared at his notepad for a long time and then said, "Do you think this has anything to do with the phone call Andrew received?"

Dominic frowned. "What made you think that?"

"Well, you've both received calls today, and so did Andrew. It could just be coincidence, but I'm not a fan of that way of thinking. It seems too convenient."

"If it is linked, I have no idea about the reference for 'number one.'"

Randall waved his hand. "I'm probably trying to link it when it's not. Ignore me."

The door opened, and the king and the chancellor exited. Randall stood and showed the chancellor out. Andrew sighed and nodded at Dominic. "I'll be in here working if anyone needs me."

"Yes, Your Majesty."

When Andrew closed himself back in his office, Dominic pulled out his phone and called the kitchen. "Can I request dinner for the king to be brought to his office at five o'clock, please?" He was beginning to sound like a broken record.

"Of course, sir."

Randall sat in his chair and smiled at him as he ended the call. "You must've been reading my mind."

"I'd love to be able to." Dominic winked, and Randall flushed.

"You really wouldn't."

8

Randall

T he idea that Dominic could read Randall's mind when all the things he wanted to do with the man were front and centre was not good. Dominic had mentioned going to dinner, but was it a good idea? They were close in their working relationship. Would having a romantic relationship ruin it?

Before he could answer that question, the kitchen staff brought in two trolleys. Randall frowned. Dominic had only ordered for Andrew, so what was the other for?

Dominic stood and knocked on Andrew's door and held it open for the staff to wheel the trolley in.

"Ah, thank you, Emily. I was just wondering why my stomach was growling at me," Randall heard the king say.

Randall opened his mouth to ask about the second trolley when Dominic closed Andrew's door, and the staff left. Dominic smiled as he strode for the trolley.

"I thought we could have one dinner here—because I know you've barely eaten today—and if this goes well, we can arrange another one when neither of us is working. What do you think?" Dominic said.

Randall was speechless. Kendal was the only other person who had been worried about his eating habits. And they were also the person who insisted he have an assistant.

"Um, sure. Thanks."

He cleared the space directly in front of him, and Dominic placed a plate full of potatoes, vegetables and chicken pie if he wasn't mistaken. The smell was divine and made his stomach grumble. Dominic laughed and handed him some cutlery.

"I'm backing away slowly. Don't eat me." He grabbed his own plate and settled opposite Randall but balancing the plate on his knees.

That wouldn't do. Randall stood and cleared the front of the desk. Then he indicated for Dominic to use it. "If this is dinner, we need to eat at the same table."

Dominic smiled at him and lifted his plate, scooting his chair closer. "So, how is your family?"

Randall swallowed his mouthful. "They're okay. Mum keeps bugging me about visiting for dinner." He caught Dominic's frown. "I've missed the last three weeks of Sunday dinners."

"Why?"

Randall put a forkful of potato in his mouth so he could think about what answer he could give. One that didn't make it sound like he was a loser whose mother was trying to set him up any way she could.

"She wants me to be happy, but for her, that means to have someone in my life. She's very vocal about it, but that means she's constantly on me for working too much, for not socialising enough, and so on. It gets...wearing after a while."

"I know the feeling." Dominic sipped his drink. "My fathers are similar but maybe less vocal about it. I can see it in their eyes whenever we're on the subject, though."

"I know she means well, but I can't face it most weeks." Wasn't that the understatement of the year?

"How are your—you have siblings, right?" Randall nodded. "How are they with it all?"

Randall chuckled. "Ryan is happily married to his wife and has been for fifteen years. Rae has a fiancé and is hoping to get married next year. They're not at all bothered about my relationship status." He sighed. "I don't see them very often."

"How come?"

"Ryan is a nurse, so he's got crappy shifts. Rae is a nursery assistant, which makes things easier, but she's always out with her fiancé or friends." He snorted. "I sound like I'm moaning about it, but I'm not. It's just…" He shook his head. "Sorry, you don't want to hear this."

Dominic put down his cutlery. "I wouldn't have asked if I didn't."

Randall stared at him, wanting to make sure he was serious and then continued. "Because they have their own lives, they don't receive the constant hounding from Mum. I feel like… I don't know. Like I'm letting them down, I suppose."

"You're not letting them down. You're finding your own way."

"That's not done me so well, has it?"

Dominic chuckled. "You've found me, haven't you?"

Randall's cheeks heated, and he focused on his food. If only he could believe that Dominic wanted him for longer than a few dates. They were so different, and Randall didn't trust that "opposites attract" sentiment. Dominic ran headfirst into danger while Randall hid from it. Dominic had a close relationship with his family, while Randall…not so much. Dominic spent time with his family, while Randall worked every hour he could get away with.

"I didn't mean to make you uncomfortable," Dominic said.

Randall glanced up. "You didn't." He sighed. "I'm not good at interpreting conversations. I like things spelt out for me. When someone says something but means something else, I struggle. I've learnt with Andrew. I know his tells and how he talks now, but it took me a long time to get there. With anyone else, I'm stuck."

Dominic pushed his plate aside and leaned his arms on the desk, putting them closer. "How about if I make myself completely clear?" Randall nodded, wondering where he was going with it. "I like you a lot, Randall. I know you see our age gap as an issue, but I don't. Ten years is nothing. There's nothing wrong with you. Everything I see is something that intrigues me and urges me to find out more. I want to spend time learning about you, about your family. I promise to always say what I mean, even if it might hurt one or both of us." He licked his lips. "Does that help?"

Randall tried to answer, but the lump of emotion in his throat stopped him. He nodded, blinking away the tears that threatened to overflow, and hid his hands in his lap to stop the trembling.

Andrew's door opened, and the king stepped out, pushing the trolley. "Ah, Randall. Why are you still here? It's nearly six o'clock. Go home and get some rest. We have a lot of work to do tomorrow." He left the trolley by the door and glanced at Dominic. "I hope you're not distracting my assistant, Dominic."

"Not at all. I'm making sure he eats, Your Majesty."

Andrew smiled. "Even better. Finish your food, Randall, and go home. I'll see you in the morning." He returned to his office and closed the door.

Randall chuckled. "I have my orders. I think I'll sleep here, though. I can't be bothered to drive tonight."

Dominic cleared both their plates and set them on the trolley. "I'll arrange for these to be collected, so don't worry about that." He returned to the desk but rounded it to stop beside him and pull him up. Sliding his arms around Randall's waist, he just held him, staring down at him, and Randall's cheeks flushed again. His curse. "Can I kiss you?"

"We shouldn't. You're working," Randall protested.

Dominic smiled and shook his head. "Can I kiss you?"

Randall's mouth twitched. He wanted to say yes. So he did. "Yes, please."

Dominic lowered his head and brushed his mouth across Randall's lips. Then he pressed a little harder. His hand reached up to cup Randall's head, and he teased his lips with his tongue. Randall inhaled at the sensations bombarding him from such a simple, innocent kiss, and Dominic took advantage, sliding his tongue inside, taking it into a not-so-innocent kiss, after all. Randall slid his arms around Dominic's neck and held on as Dominic deepened the kiss further. After far too short a time, as far as Randall was concerned, Dominic pulled back. His thumb brushed across Randall's cheek.

"Thank you."

Randall's mind was blown. He hadn't been kissed like that in...ever. "Thank *you*."

Dominic smiled and dropped a chaste kiss on his mouth and then let go. "I'd walk you to your room, but I can't."

Randall waved him away. "It's fine. Maybe next time." He gathered his belongings, locked everything away that needed to be and headed for the door. Dominic was back in his usual seat by the office door, and Randall paused. "I look forward to our next dinner."

Dominic beamed at him. There was no other word for it, and Randall felt like he'd given the man the world. How could he be so happy about such a simple gesture?

"I can't wait."

Randall smiled and aimed for his room, his mind lost in the kiss and the dinner and the conversation. It was all so easy with Dominic. Much easier than he thought it would be. Apart from feeling like he was out of his depth, everything else fell into place.

Tiredness washed over him when he entered his room. The freshly made bed welcomed him, and he stripped and headed for the en suite first. He didn't linger in the shower; instead, he climbed into bed wearing clean boxers and pulled the covers over him. It was far too early for him to sleep, but he didn't have the energy to stay up any longer. He'd happily stare at the ceiling and revisit the kiss again and again.

Hours later, a knock on his door pulled him from the doze he'd fallen into. Not fully asleep, but not fully awake either.

"One minute!" he called as he stumbled towards the sound.

He braced one hand on the doorframe and opened the door, brightening when he saw Dominic.

"Did I wake you?"

Dominic looked all kinds of apologetic, but Randall shook his head. "Not really. I was only dozing. I haven't been able to sleep well lately. A light doze is about all I can manage."

"I won't be long. I just wanted to say goodnight after I finished my shift." Dominic stepped closer, eyes travelling down his body. "And maybe have a goodnight kiss to tide me over until I can steal the next one."

Randall chuckled and opened the door further. "I'm sure I can oblige. Just not out in the hallway."

Dominic crossed the threshold, and Randall closed the door, suddenly realising how intimate it would seem when this was basically Randall's bedroom.

"Sorry. I don't have a living area like others do." He wrung his hands, trying to ignore the fact he wore just his boxers.

"It's fine by me." Dominic moved closer, and Randall instinctively stepped back until the wall supported him. Dominic's arm caged him in, but there was no worry, no fear, just heat blooming inside him. A heat that would show in his groin if he didn't concentrate enough.

Dominic nuzzled Randall's cheek with his nose, his lips taking a teasing path along his jaw to his mouth but never quite reaching it. Randall gripped Dominic's hips, hooking his fingers through the belt loops of his trousers. Whether that was to tether Dominic to him or the other way around, he wasn't sure.

"You always smell delicious," Dominic murmured, his lips tracing down Randall's neck and along his collarbone. "Whenever you walk past me, I always inhale, teasing myself with your scent."

Dominic's hands moved to cradle Randall's head as he stared into his eyes, the pupils wide and heavy with lust. Randall had never felt more desired than in that moment, and it caused him to do something he'd never tried before. He stepped into Dominic's embrace and joined their mouths, sliding his arms around him and anchoring them together. Dominic groaned and deepened the kiss immediately. They fell against the wall, Dominic's arms protecting Randall from getting hurt. Their groins met, thrusting against each other as their arousal climbed.

Randall needed more. He needed everything Dominic was willing to give him, and he wanted it now. But the thing he wanted more than anything...?

He pulled away from the kiss and stared into Dominic's eyes. When Dominic paused and waited, Randall smiled and dropped to his knees.

Dominic's eyes widened. "You don't have to—"

"I want to. I *really* want to." He nuzzled his face into Dominic's groin, closing his eyes as his scent seeped through the fabric. Dominic's hand brushed through Randall's hair. "I've thought about this. What it would be like. If I would have the courage to ask for it." He peered up at Dominic. "But I'm not asking this time." He licked his lips. "I'm taking."

He unfastened the belt, leaving it in the loops, unzipped the trousers and pushed them down Dominic's thighs. He nestled his nose against the rapidly hardening cock again, staring up at

Dominic as he did so. Dominic's nostrils flared, and his free hand fisted against his side.

Randall slipped his thumbs into the briefs and worked them over Dominic's cock and down his legs, freeing his erection from its confines. Randall wrapped a hand around the shaft, the heat warming his palm, and stroked. Dominic hissed, and Randall smiled but had a momentary pause. It had been years since he had done this, and as much as the phrase didn't fit this scenario, he hoped it was like riding a bike and he never forgot.

Dominic's hand cupped Randall's jaw. "Whatever you want or don't want is fine."

With those words, the tension released, and Randall parted his lips, letting Dominic's cock rest on his tongue and slide into his mouth. The musky taste had always been something he'd enjoyed, even when it turned others off. To him, it was a sign of strength, though he wasn't sure why.

He swiped his tongue all around the shaft, wetting it, then focused on taking him as deep as he could. It had been a while, so he could only manage around half of it, but he used his hand on the other half. Up and down, he bobbed, swiping his tongue around the head on every up move. His free hand gripped Dominic's hip, and he could feel the trembling of his body, how he held himself back. But now, Randall didn't want that. He wanted to feel Dominic's strength, his need, his dominance.

Randall let go with his hands and put them behind his back. Keeping his cock resting on his tongue, he stopped moving and looked up at Dominic. He waited. Dominic frowned and moved to pull out, but Randall grabbed at his hips again. This time, he pulled Dominic's hips forward as he stayed still, and then he returned his hands behind him again, hoping Dominic would get the idea without Randall having to explain. That would embarrass the hell out of him.

"Are you sure?"

Randall nodded a little, flicking his tongue across the underside of his cock. Dominic exhaled.

"Okay."

Dominic thrust forward, gently at first, as if gauging how much Randall could take, but Randall wanted more. He needed him to take what Randall was freely giving him.

His submission.

Dominic's hand speared through Randall's hair, keeping him in place as he increased his movements. "Fuck, Randall. Your mouth is hot. Jeez." He panted, and sweat dotted his brow.

Randall watched everything with keen eyes, wanting to remember everything in case this never happened again. The sounds Dominic made, the scent of him, the taste of him, the sight as he came closer and closer to orgasm. He catalogued every minute expression, even as his own climax barrelled forward, readying to escape.

"Fuck. I'm almost there. I can't believe you want this with me."

Randall filed those words away to analyse later, but he used his tongue whenever Dominic withdrew, hoping to send him higher.

"That's it. Fuck, yeah. Oh, fuck, fuck, fuck. I'm coming!"

Dominic tensed, and Randall watched the contractions rip through his abdomen as his mouth flooded with his release. Everything together sent Randall following over the edge, his entire body shuddering as his cock released into his boxers. He concentrated enough to swallow everything Dominic gave him, and when Dominic pulled free, Randall licked his lips to ensure he got it all.

Dominic dropped to his knees in front of him and palmed his cheeks. He opened his mouth to say something, but nothing came out. Instead, he shook his head and kissed Randall as if his life depended on it.

When they pulled back, breathing heavily, Dominic whispered, "Thank you."

Randall leant his head against Dominic's shoulder. "I think I could sleep now," he murmured.

Dominic chuckled, and before Randall could complain, he stood and swept Randall into his arms. Carrying him over to the bed, he laid him down. "Let me get a cloth." He disappeared before Randall could say anything and returned a moment later.

Randall threw an arm over his burning face as Dominic removed his boxers and cleaned his groin. But then he covered him with the duvet and sat on the edge of the bed.

"I'll leave you to get some sleep."

"Do you want to stay?"

Dominic smiled. "I would love to, but not tonight. I don't want to overwhelm you when you wake up tomorrow. I know you like to think things through. My only request is that if you start to worry about anything, please talk to me first."

Randall nodded. "Okay."

Dominic leaned down and kissed him and then headed for the door. He paused before he left, glancing over his shoulder. "That was one heck of a goodnight kiss. I wonder how we'll top that next time." He winked and disappeared, closing the door behind him.

Randall froze for a second before chuckling.

How indeed.

9

Dominic

The "goodnight kiss" stayed with Dominic for hours. By the time he was home—for the first time since May arrived—his body cried out for more of Randall. He barely slept, tossing and turning as memories and dreams collided to create a whirlwind of images sent to drive him from his bed and into Randall's arms.

When he finally got up after realising no more sleep was on his agenda, he had the whole day ahead of him with nothing planned. Well, he did have plans, but nothing work-related except for the morning briefing. He did his morning routine, the workout helping to centre him, and then showered and dressed. Making breakfast, he brought his computer to the kitchen table and ate while starting his research. He wasn't sure what he could access himself and what he would have to ask Brett or Felix to help with, but he could try.

Fletcher Pinton had been a low-time crook when Dominic had been younger. They were around the same age and had grown up in similar circles, but what worried Dominic the most was that Fletcher knew of Dominic's past. A past he had told no one except those that were there. Fletcher could easily use that to his advantage, and although it wouldn't stop Dominic from doing whatever he could to save May, it might mean the end of his job if it got out.

From what he could find on the internet, Fletcher had been involved in several crimes, but nothing had ever been pinned on him. He went free of any charges every single time. Did he have an excellent lawyer, or was he just that good at hiding things?

Other than that basic information, he wasn't able to find much; therefore, another visit to Sec HQ was in his future. He closed his computer and headed for the kitchen. He needed more coffee. He'd indulged and bought himself a coffee machine, even though he drank normal coffee with milk, nothing fancy, but he couldn't resist. May loved the fancy drinks, and despite her not being with him at the time, he'd bought it with her in mind.

As he inhaled the aroma and took his first sip, the doorbell rang. His mind immediately went to Randall, but then dismissed it because he would be working, not taking time off to visit Dominic on the sly.

He peered through the peephole and paused. Why was May's ex on his doorstep? Opening the door, he crossed his arms over his chest.

"What do you want?"

"Long time no see to you, too, Dom," Paul said, grinning. It was that grin that had mesmerised May in the first place, and if Dominic didn't know him, he could've admitted he was handsome in a rugged way.

"As I said, what do you want?"

Paul slid his hands into his jacket pocket, and Dominic braced for him to remove a gun or something, but Paul just shrugged. "I just came to say hi."

"Bullshit. You've been in prison for five years, Paul. You made no contact then, so why now?"

Paul leaned against the wall to the side of the door, but Dominic didn't trust his easy posture. The man was slimy; there was no other word for it. Despite his good looks, his personality was on par with an enraged elephant.

"I want to apologise to May."

"Really." It wasn't a question. "You could have done that at the time."

"I did, but I need to do it again now I've done my stint. I'm a changed man, Dom."

Dominic hated that the man had taken on May's use of his name, but he could hardly stop it after so long.

"I don't believe a word of it."

A dark expression briefly crossed Paul's face, belying his words and confirming Dominic's thoughts, but he suppressed it quicker than Dominic remembered him being able to.

"You could always see behind my bullshit." Paul smirked, the glint in his eyes proving the lie of his earlier words.

"So, I ask again. What do you want?"

Paul straightened. "May. Plain and simple."

Dominic laughed. He couldn't help it. "I have no idea where she is."

Paul shook his head, his mouth quirking. "Bullshit, to quote you from earlier. You picked her up in a fancy helicopter a few days ago. You know exactly where she is. And it's in your best interests to tell me."

Dominic stepped forward. "Are you threatening me?"

"No. I'm not allowed to touch you. May, however..."

"Leave her alone. It's in *your* best interests to stay away."

Paul chuckled. "Oh, yeah. I forgot. You have the royal family on your side now. I wonder what they'd think of your past indiscretions."

Dominic's palms sweated at his words. How did he know about that? He ignored the threat. He'd deal with it if he had to. He gave no quarter to Paul, though. "Leave and stay away. I'm warning you."

Paul clicked his tongue. "Don't say I didn't give you the chance." He stepped back. "Have a good day, Dom."

Dominic watched him leave and only closed the door when he knew he was no longer nearby. He rested back against it, staring across his space. Despite knowing she was safe, he dialled May.

"Hey. Everything okay?" he said when she answered.

"Yep. Just going for a walk with Felix before the rain starts. How are you doing?"

"Good. Just trying to decide—" *how to destroy anyone who ever hurt you,* "what to do with the rest of my day."

"Sleep," she said. "You hardly ever sleep. Or has that changed?"

Dominic chuckled, accepting her words as a way to lighten his mood. "Nope. Not changed at all." And for reasons he wouldn't explain to her. Randall was his business only, for now.

"Then sleep, my dear brother."

"You never know; I might just do it."

May laughed. "Yeah, and the sky is purple today."

Dominic smiled. "Have a good day, boo. I'll see you later."

"I'll be here."

Slightly mollified that she was doing all right, he paced and went over what Paul said. He was looking for May, but was that because he wanted revenge, or was there another reason? He truly didn't seem to know where she was, although his nod towards the royal family might show where he thought she might be.

He frowned. What did he mean when he said he wasn't allowed to touch Dominic? Why? It wouldn't surprise him if someone had put a hit out on him, but wouldn't that have given Paul even more reason? He needed to talk this through with someone.

"Owen, are you free?" he said when his best friend answered.

"I've got just over an hour. Why?"

Dominic sighed and settled into an armchair by the window. "I've just had a visit from Paul."

"Paul?"

"May's ex."

Owen's curses were long and loud. "What the fuck did he want?"

"May's location."

Owen laughed. "Yeah, as if you'd give that up."

"He knew I wouldn't, so why did he ask?"

"Hmm. He didn't leave anything behind, did he?"

"I didn't invite him in."

Owen tutted. "You know better than that. He doesn't need to come in to leave something behind."

Dominic rose and opened the front door. He stood there and checked the area was clear of people before he went through the interaction with Paul—where he stood, what he did. He'd leant against the wall, and Dominic inspected it. Nothing.

"Check the door itself. Did he knock or use the doorbell?" Owen said.

Dominic checked it. "Little shit," he said when he found the tiny bug attached to the side of it.

"What did you find?"

"Hold on." He removed it, trying not to knock it too much to show he'd found it, took it inside and put it on the kitchen counter. Did he destroy it or turn it around and use it to find Paul? "Can I call you back in a minute?"

"Make sure you do." Owen hung up.

Dominic turned on the radio in the kitchen and headed up the stairs to the bathroom. He switched on the shower and called Brett.

"Everything okay?" Brett said.

"Not really. I had a visit from May's ex, and he left me a parting gift. A bug."

"Ah, is that why there's so much background noise?"

"I wasn't taking any chances about what he could hear. I'd already called May before I found it, but hopefully, that's not an issue. My question is, do I destroy it, or do I bring it in to trace it back?"

Brett was silent for a moment. "Bring it in. Put it in a metal-lined box so it stifles the signal. When you get here, I'll make sure we have a scrambler ready to interfere with it until we can figure out where he is. Then we'll destroy it."

"Is it a good idea to bring it to Windsor?"

"As long as it's in the metal box, it should be fine."

Dominic didn't like "shoulds," but he'd do what Brett asked.

He entered his bedroom and grabbed the metal cash box he had. After emptying the contents into his safe, he grabbed his gun, tucked it into his holster and headed back downstairs again. He cushioned the box with a scarf, carefully slid the bug into the box and closed the lid. It wasn't a perfect solution, but it was the best he could do.

After messaging an update to Owen, he drove to Windsor. Luckily, he was able to make it look like any other day when he was on his way to work. After all, he had the briefing to attend, anyway. He greeted the guards as he entered through the gates. Brett must've warned them because they said nothing to him other than the usual hello. It was only as he parked that he wondered whether his car had been bugged, too. It had been sitting in the driveway when Paul had been there, so anything was possible.

Grabbing the box, he headed straight to Sec HQ. When he passed Randall's office, he wanted to go in, but he needed them all to be safe first. Brett was the first person he saw when he entered the security room, and he pointed to the table near the back of the room, where a scrambler sat waiting. Felix took the box from him, and Dominic left him to it. He wasn't bad at technology, but retracing it was far out of his league.

Dominic wanted to talk, but they couldn't until the signal was disabled. If Paul had learnt more about technology in prison, then he might already know it had been found and the new location, but the man had never been one for doing the required reading. It wouldn't surprise him if Paul had got someone else to do the heavy lifting, and he just planted the thing.

Or maybe it was Paul planting it, but someone else was the one behind it all? That sounded more like something Paul would get behind.

So many questions and no discernible answers.

Felix pumped a fist in the air silently and then dropped the bug into a glass of water. "All done. The receiver is on Queens Road."

"That's a little closer than comfort," Brett said.

"It doesn't have a large range. It could have probably reached around half of Windsor, but any further than that, and it would've lost the signal," Felix said.

"Do we visit them to see who they are?" Dominic asked.

Brett shook his head. "You stay close to home. I'll send someone to investigate." He moved off and took out his phone, disappearing into the back room.

Dominic rubbed his face. "This whole thing is a bloody mess."

"We did find some more information about Yousef Azizi. He'd been receiving phone calls from the same number for the past five weeks. They lasted a couple of minutes, sometimes a few seconds, but nothing longer."

"Who?"

"Don't know yet."

"Threats?" Dominic asked.

Felix shrugged. "Maybe. He'd also put in for a holiday at work. He'd just started that time off when he was killed."

"Did anyone know where he was going?"

Felix shook his head. "From the police reports, his colleagues were surprised about him taking time off because he was a workaholic. They didn't bother to ask if he was going away or anything." Felix frowned. "It's strange to me."

"What is?"

"If someone's behaviour changes, you ask questions. They didn't."

It was true. The first sign of discontent was usually a change in behaviour. They looked for similar clues when trying to figure out if a person was plotting against the crown. People loved being in a routine mostly, and when things in their life changed, so did their patterns.

Brett returned. "I've got someone going to check out the house. They'll report back soon." He glanced at Dominic. "Go and see your sister. There's nothing else we can do now. And don't glare at me. You know we'll let you know anything we find out."

Dominic huffed but thanked them and exited the room. All the way down the hall to May's room, he second-guessed his actions, but it was too late to change them now. He knocked on May's door and waited.

"Who is it?"

"Dominic."

She opened the door, smiling until she saw his face, and then she frowned. "What's happened?"

Dominic slipped into the room. "I received a visit from Paul today."

May gasped and covered her mouth with her hand. "What did he want?"

"You. He left behind a present, which I'm assuming was to help find you, but we've got it under control."

"I should leave. Find another safe house."

Dominic gripped her shoulders. "You're fine here. Even if they find you, it would be difficult for them to get to you. Not impossible, as I've said before, but difficult."

She closed her eyes and shook her head. "I shouldn't impose."

"You're not imposing."

She sighed and then smiled. "Well, someone likes me being here." She freed herself from his embrace and wandered over to the small side table, which held a vase and a single red rose.

Dominic frowned. "Who is that from?"

May shrugged. "I don't know. It was on the floor outside my room when I got back from my walk. Felix didn't seem concerned."

Dominic moved closer. "Was there a note or anything?"

May held out a small white card. On the front was the logo for the florist, which wasn't Robert's shop—Robert was Prince Henry's fiancé—and on the reverse was the letter A.

"I can't think of anyone with that initial, apart from the king, but it's unlikely to be him."

"If it was, he would be more likely to deliver it himself," Dominic murmured, though he was distracted by the note. "There was nothing else with it?"

May shook her head. "Should I not have accepted it?" Her voice shook.

Dominic put the card down and pulled May into his arms again, holding her tightly. "It's fine, May. Sorry. I'm suspicious of everything at the moment. It looks fine, so don't worry."

"I'll pretend it's from an admirer." She chuckled, though it was tight and forced.

Why couldn't they just leave her alone? He had no clue if this flower was linked to anything, but his instincts were flaring. Hopefully, as May said, it was from an admirer within the grounds and not someone who had found out where she was. What else could he do to keep her safe? She was surrounded by guards.

People were vetted before they were allowed on the premises. He wasn't sure what more he could do.

Other than take the fuckers out. And he planned to do that as soon as he could. But he needed to figure out what Paul wanted, which meant he needed to hear what Brett had found out from that address he'd sent those men to. Maybe there was someone there who could give them an insight into whatever was happening.

All he knew was they couldn't keep going the way they were. May couldn't be kept like a zoo animal indefinitely. She needed freedom to thrive. So, he needed to figure it out and give her wings back.

No matter what it took.

He sighed, said goodbye to May and headed for Sec HQ. He had to explain his past to Brett and hope he wasn't fired. What would he do if the royals turned their back on him when he needed their help more than ever?

10

Randall

Randall wasn't sure what alerted him to the fact that something was amiss with the guards, but they seemed even more alert and suspicious than usual, and that was saying something. He'd not seen Dominic at all, which wasn't surprising as it was his second day off, but he'd inwardly thought he might drop by to see him, which was a silly reaction as they'd only spent a small amount of time together, and it had only been a blow job. Maybe it hadn't been a good one, though Dominic had seemed to enjoy it.

He brushed thoughts of the handsome bodyguard from his mind for the twentieth time that day and refocused on the draft he was compiling. It needed to be completed quickly so he could get Andrew's signature on it before he left for the day.

When Andrew dismissed him for the day, Randall packed his things and headed home. He didn't want to stay at Windsor, where the memories of what he'd shared with Dominic were still fresh. He showered and changed into his fluffiest pyjamas before making a hot chocolate with cream and marshmallows, along with some butterscotch, his favourite treat in the world. Switching on the TV, he settled on a new film he had yet to see and tucked himself into a corner of the sofa and snuggled under a blanket.

He was stifling tears at the lovely marriage proposal when the doorbell rang. He frowned and paused the film. Who would be visiting him at ten o'clock at night? In fact, who would be visiting him at all? His parents never came, and his siblings rarely did either.

He shuffled to the door, hesitating to open it when the doorbell rang again.

"Randall, it's Dominic. I promise it's no one untoward."

Randall's heart picked up to a gallop, and his mouth twitched. Who said "untoward" in this day and age? He opened the door with raised eyebrows, leaning on the doorframe. "Are you sure about that? I might be worried about my virtue."

Dominic's smile was slow in coming, but Randall was rewarded with the full lips stretching across his face, a peek of his dimples showing. "I wouldn't worry about your virtue. It's safe with me."

Randall chuckled. "I don't believe that for a moment."

Dominic's smile fell, and Randall was about to apologise when Dominic stepped forward and claimed his mouth in a kiss that made him grasp at Dominic's shirt to keep him on his feet. His mind went blank, and all he could do was feel. And taste. And smell. And all of it sent his arousal skyrocketing.

When Dominic softened the kiss, little by little, Randall had the chance to calm enough to realise they were still on the doorstep. With a strength he didn't know he had, he dragged Dominic across the threshold and into the house, shoving the door shut behind him. Dominic slid his arms around Randall and held him close.

"Sorry about that. I know I haven't been to see you for a couple of days, but something happened, and I needed to deal with it. It ended with a difficult conversation with Brett, and I'm exhausted, but I couldn't think of anywhere—or anyone—I would prefer to be with right now."

Randall's heart skipped a beat, and he smiled, resting his cheek against Dominic's chest. "I'm sorry you've been through whatever it is, but I'm glad I could be of help."

Dominic hooked his finger under Randall's chin and lifted his head until they were staring at each other, and then he cupped the sides of his face. He traced Randall's face with his gaze for a long moment before saying, "I know we need to talk, but can I make love to you tonight?"

Tears brimmed in Randall's eyes, and he nodded. "Yes, please."

Dominic licked his lips and rested their foreheads together. "I do have a couple of questions before we go any further." Randall nodded as best he could with the hold he had on him. "I thought I felt something happening the other night, but I need to ask explicitly. Do you like BDSM of any kind?"

Randall felt his whole body flush. He swallowed hard, chewed on his lip and nodded. It was the best he could do at that moment. He hadn't expected that conversation so soon. "Yes, Sir."

Dominic's eyes darkened. "What do you like?"

Randall inhaled shakily and blew it out, taking another risk. "Almost anything," he whispered.

"You're submissive." It wasn't a question, but Randall nodded anyway. "What do you have experience with?"

Randall closed his eyes, knowing he needed to answer if they were to go any further. "Not a lot. I've watched lots of videos, been to Club Royal and seen things, but I've only personally experienced bondage."

Dominic traced his lips with his fingers. "Thank you for being honest, sweetheart. I know that was difficult for you. What is your safe word?"

"Guacamole."

Dominic's lips quirked, and Randall's cheeks heated. "Duly noted. Hard limits?"

Randall shrugged. "I'm not sure entirely, but from what I've seen, I don't like the idea of pet play or medical play. I'm not sure about anything else."

Dominic smiled, sending Randall's heart rate through the roof again. "I look forward to finding out everything you like and dislike." He lowered his head and kissed him. "I'm feeling a little dominant tonight. Would you like to play?"

"Yes, please." He hadn't meant for his words to come out as breathy as they did, but he couldn't help the need that flooded him.

"You can address me as sir or Master, whichever you prefer. We will use the traffic light system for ease, and you will immediately say your safe word if you are not happy with how things are. Do you understand?"

"Yes, Sir."

"Will you share your bedroom with me?"

Randall nodded. "This way, Sir."

He led the way down the hallway to the stairs and started up, halting when Dominic took his hand and threaded their fingers together. He received a smile, and that eased him more than anything else could have. He didn't hesitate at his door, nor when he stopped beside his bed, and not when he faced the man he wanted to share everything with.

"I like giving orders usually," Dominic said distractedly, "but I find I want to ask your permission this time."

Randall didn't need it, but if that was what Dominic needed, he would oblige. "Whatever you wish, Sir."

"Can I undress you?" Randall nodded. "I'll need your words, sweetheart."

"I'll try," he whispered. "I sometimes go quiet when I'm overwhelmed," he admitted. What was it about Dominic that made him want to bare every secret he had?

"Then it's now my aim to make you vocal instead." Dominic stepped closer. "Can I undress you?"

"Yes, Sir." Randall's entire body trembled as if he was standing in a walk-in freezer.

Dominic's hands smoothed over his fluffy pyjama top, and Randall closed his eyes, his cheeks heating when he realised Dominic had seen him in his pyjamas.

"This fabric is as soft as your skin, I'm sure," Dominic murmured, catching the hem and sliding his hands underneath. His fingers traced Randall's stomach. "Mmm, definitely just as soft."

Randall wanted to touch him, taste him, but he couldn't. He hadn't been told he could, so he fisted his hands beside him, letting Dominic do whatever he wanted to do to him. Goosebumps covered his skin despite still being covered by his pyjamas. Dominic nudged him backwards, and the back of his knees hit the bed.

"Lay down with your head on the pillow."

Randall sat down and scooted back until he rested against his feather-filled pillows. He stared up at Dominic, wondering what he had planned. Dominic didn't make him wait long and straddled Randall's thighs. His hands went to the hem of his top, and he nudged it up and up, further and further, until Randall had to lift his arms, ready for it to be removed. The fabric slid over his face and then stopped while it still covered his eyes.

"Do you know what? I like the idea of you not being able to see what I'm doing to you. Is this okay?" Dominic asked.

Randall's arms were still in the pyjama top just above his elbows, and the soft material covered his eyes but left his nose and mouth free. It wasn't dark, either, because he could see a little light from where his nose lifted it a bit.

"Yes, Sir." His voice was breathy, and his heart rate climbed. What would it feel like to not be able to see anything? Would his other senses be heightened like he'd read about?

"Keep your arms above your head unless you need to safe word, and it's even more important now that you use your words because I can't see your face."

"Yes, Sir. I will do my best." That was the most he could promise.

"Good."

Dominic's mouth covered his own, and Randall sank into the kiss, letting his master take what he wanted and receiving so much in return. Dominic nipped at his lips, and Randall gasped, opening for the invasion that muddled his brain. His master left no space unexplored, and Randall arched towards him, needing everything he gave him. His cock was rock hard and leaking in his pyjamas, and still, he needed more. He wanted more. He wanted Dominic inside him, taking him, claiming him.

"Damn, sweetheart," Dominic said when they parted, his voice as raw and hoarse as he believed his own would have been if he tried to formulate words.

Dominic kissed along Randall's jaw, down his neck and along his collarbone, nipping and licking as he went. Prickles of heat and sensation rose where he touched, and Randall squirmed. Dominic's fingers flicked at Randall's nipples, and Randall went stock still, trying not to move because his nipples were his most sensitive area, and it wouldn't take much to blow while they were being touched—it was often how he got himself off quickly when he didn't have much time or strength to make himself wait.

Dominic's hands paused. "Talk to me, sweetheart. You've frozen. Do you not like this?"

Randall's heart pounded, and he licked his lips, interlocking his fingers above his head. "They're really sensitive, Sir."

"That wasn't quite what I asked. Do you not like it?"

"I do like it, but…" He swallowed and exhaled. "It will set me off quickly, and I don't have a big refractory period. I don't want to let you down."

Dominic's lips met his, and Randall groaned into the mind-blowing kiss. When they came up for air again, Dominic said, "You will never let me down. Ever. I will leave these alone for now, but that doesn't mean I won't come back to them time and again. I'd love to make you come just from sucking on them."

"Oh, god." Just the idea sent fire down Randall's spine.

Dominic tongued down the centre of Randall's chest, lower and lower, until he reached the waistband of his pyjama bottoms. His fingers slid inside and tugged at them, taking them down, inch by slow inch. Randall's cock was lodged beneath the band, being inadvertently stroked until it broke free and rose back to his stomach with a slap. He wasn't bragging, but he didn't have a small dick, and the fact that he could only feel what was happening and couldn't see anything was heightening *everything*.

His pyjama bottoms were yanked from his legs, and Dominic pushed Randall's legs apart, baring him to his master. His cheeks heated again as he thought about what he must look like, spread out and restrained for Dominic's perusal.

"You're divine, sweetheart. Absolutely perfect as you lay there, waiting for me to do whatever I want to do. Do you realise how precious you are?" Dominic snorted. "Of course you don't. Well, it'll be my pleasure to make sure you understand."

His hands skimmed across his skin, starting at Randall's ankles and rising until he paused at Randall's hips. "This is mine." Dominic blew a waft of heated air across his shaft, and it pulsed at the extra sensation.

Randall opened his mouth to reply, but Dominic swallowed his cock, and only a hiss came out. Fire licked at his groin, his balls tightening from the stimulation. He bit his lip, trying anything he could think of to ensure this didn't end as soon as he thought it might. If he came now, there would be no way he could come again for at least a few hours. He was no spring chicken, after all.

"Oh, fuck, ah!"

Dominic slid his cock free and licked it like he would an ice cream, his tongue rough along the nerve on the underside.

"Sir!"

Dominic's mouth left him, but his hand stroked in a lazy rhythm, keeping Randall's arousal heightened. "Tell me, what do you need, sweetheart?"

"Please! I need you, please!"

The bed dipped and bounced, and then it was still as if Dominic had climbed off. All Randall could hear was some rustling, and he waited, his cock leaking onto his stomach. When things went quiet, he strained to hear anything.

"Sir?"

A hand on his ankle startled him, and he jumped. "Sorry." Hands soothed him, rising up his legs as they had previously. The bed dipped at the bottom, and Dominic's body heat warmed him as he crawled between his legs. His tongue lapped at each of his nipples in turn but didn't linger. Dominic laid his body over Randall's, and Randall sighed, loving the feel of it. He wrapped his legs around him despite not being told he was allowed, but he couldn't resist.

"How are your arms feeling?"

The words didn't register initially, but then he said, "They're fine, Sir."

"How close are you?"

Randall checked in with his body, even as more heat invaded his cheeks. "I won't blow yet."

"Good. I still have more I want to do."

"Oh, god," Randall murmured.

Dominic chuckled and kissed him. "Can I make love to you, Randall?"

"Yes, please, Sir." He wanted that more than anything he'd ever wanted in his life.

Dominic pulled back a little, and Randall wanted to stop him, but his bound arms stopped him. There was a click, which Randall associated with a lube bottle, and he clenched in anticipation. Cool air rushed in against his groin as Dominic moved away, and Randall's legs dropped to the bed. Warm fingers massaged cold lube into his pucker, and despite the embarrassment of Dominic seeing his most private area, Randall groaned and widened his legs, needing more. He'd never been this desperate before. Even with other partners. What was it about Dominic that made Randall's need shoot through the ceiling?

"That's it. Relax for me, sweetheart."

Dominic's finger pressed inside him, and Randall's body curled. He lost track of everything as Dominic's finger became two and three, each time stimulating his prostate but not enough to send him over the edge.

"You're ready for me now."

"Yes, Sir. Please," Randall panted. He doubted he'd last long when Dominic got inside him, but at least he'd get to feel it.

Dominic's cock rested against Randall's hole, and he wished he could see him. To take in everything about their first time. As if reading his mind, Dominic pulled the fabric from over his eyes and tucked it behind Randall's head, keeping his arms bound. Randall blinked against the brightness, and Dominic's hand cupped his cheek.

"I need to see you," Dominic said. "I want to watch you fall apart for me. Only me."

"Only you, Sir," Randall agreed, meeting his gaze and meaning every word.

Dominic pressed forward, and Randall bore down, allowing his master to slide deep inside him. The burn was present, but more in the background as Randall concentrated on Dominic's expression—his mouth opened, his eyelids became heavy, and his pupils dilated, and Randall wanted to remember every second of it.

The moment Dominic passed over Randall's prostate, it was all over for him. His orgasm barrelled over him, and he arched and exploded, automatically closing his eyes as the pleasure overwhelmed him. When his brain came back online, he was cocooned in warmth, and he opened his eyes, meeting Dominic's gaze.

"That was exquisite," Dominic said. "My turn."

It was then Randall realised Dominic was still inside him and hard. Very hard. Randall licked his lips. "Take me, Sir."

Dominic growled, braced on his hands and withdrew before slamming back in. Randall's sensitivity made small contractions ripple out from his groin as Dominic started a fierce rhythm. He wished he could have his hands so he could dig his nails into Dominic's back and wrap himself around him. Instead, he lifted his legs, resting his heels on Dominic's lower back, giving him easier access to him.

"Oh, fuck, Randall." Dominic's growl reverberated through him, and his speed increased. Randall saw the moment his orgasm reached its peak because the tightness of his features eased before pleasure effused across every inch of his face. He watched as Dominic trembled and jerked, taking his release in Randall, and Randall had never known a happier moment.

Dominic's body relaxed, and he rested his head on Randall's chest, hot air heaving across his nipples, tightening them even though he wouldn't be able to come again yet. He pulled at his pyjama top, wanting to be free, and eventually managed it. Pins and needles attacked his limbs, but he wrapped his arms around Dominic, needing to surround him and be surrounded after experiencing something as big as what they'd just done.

It might not have been anything mind-blowing for Dominic, but for him, it was. He could honestly say he'd never experienced that before. And he would never be able to forget it.

Would Dominic think the same? Did they have a chance of a relationship, or was this just physical for him? Randall hated the doubt that always crept in, and he tried to push it aside and enjoy the moment. Even if this was all he could have, it was better than a cold bed.

Wasn't it?

11

Dominic

Dominic listened to Randall's heartbeat, closing his eyes and counting them as if it was all he needed to do in his life. He didn't want to move, even when his cock slid free of Randall's body. He was right where he wanted—no, needed to be. It was also the perfect place to let his fears free.

"I'm scared," he confided, breathing the words across Randall's skin.

Randall's heartbeat skipped and then restarted a little faster. "Of what?"

"Of losing May, of not doing my job and something happening to Andrew, of not being enough, of… God, everything." He huffed a laugh, but there was no humour in it.

Randall tightened his hold on him, and Dominic sighed. He was usually the strong one. The one who had his shit together. But at that moment, he wanted to crumble, to lean on someone else. But that wasn't fair to Randall. No one deserved to be fucked and then have an emotional mess unloaded on them. He hadn't even completed aftercare for him.

He pushed to his hands, although Randall tried to stop him. "Sorry. Can I use the bathroom?"

Randall nodded. "Of course. It's the door opposite this one."

He dropped a kiss on Randall's lips, wanting to leave him with what he could while he got his head on right. Cleaning up in the bathroom, he wet a flannel with warm water and, with a deep inhale, took it back to Randall, along with a glass of water. As he'd expected, the man had hidden himself beneath the bedcovers, and Dominic wondered if he should disturb him. But he wasn't asleep, and the dominant in Dominic needed to tend to Randall's needs.

"Let me clean you."

Randall shook his head. "You don't have to. It's okay."

Dominic met his gaze. "I want to. I *need* to."

Randall wrung his hands and then nodded. Dominic lifted the covers from his still naked body and wiped at the crusty remains of his release. He gently pushed against Randall's legs and cleaned between his ass cheeks. He could feel the embarrassment washing over Randall, but the pride rising in Dominic was overwhelming. When he finished, he slid into bed next to his lover and took him into his arms.

"Thank you for letting me do that." He reached for the glass. "It's not the drink I would prefer you to have after a scene, but it's better than nothing." He held it to Randall's lips, and although he hesitated initially, he drank it all.

"Thank you," he said when he finished.

"You're welcome. I feel like I didn't talk to you enough about the scene and what would come after, and I'm sorry for that. I will do better from now on."

Randall turned his face into Dominic's neck and chuckled. "You can't do much better than what you've done. It's already one hundred times more than anyone else has done for me."

Dominic wanted to find and punch whoever had treated Randall so badly in the past, but he couldn't, so he made himself feel better by holding Randall closer.

"I'm here now. And this isn't a one-time thing. To make me sound like a teenager, I really like you, Randall, and I'd like to do this again soon."

There was silence, to begin with, and Dominic allowed it, letting Randall get used to the idea of them being together.

"You're not invincible, Dominic. Everyone gets things wrong occasionally, but I can say with complete confidence that you will do everything in your power to keep everyone safe. And if it's not within *your* power, you won't hesitate to ask for help. There is no weakness in asking for help. But you're also allowed to be scared. The fear is what keeps you fighting." Randall's voice was strong and fierce, and Dominic could imagine him standing up for what he believed was right. At least until he continued. "Unlike me. Fear paralyses me. It makes me easy prey because I would happily do whatever anyone asked of me if they pointed a gun in my direction." His voice broke on the word "gun."

Dominic cupped Randall's cheeks, bringing his head up so he could stare into his mesmerisingly blue eyes. "That's called self-preservation, and it's what I would expect ninety-five per cent of the population to do. You did good, Randall." Randall snorted and closed his eyes, a tear trickling from the corner of each. "You did what you needed to do to survive. Andrew did the same when he got you to shout out. It could've gone wrong, but you do whatever you need to. You did nothing wrong."

"Apart from bringing the king into something dangerous."

Dominic wiped at the tears. "Andrew can walk out of the front door of Windsor Castle and be in danger. It's something that comes with his role."

Randall sniffed and opened his eyes, peering up at him. "You're wonderful, Dominic. You're doing an amazing job, and I've heard nothing but good things about you."

Dominic inhaled and leaned his head back against the headboard. "I had a visit from May's ex yesterday. He left a bug behind, and I had to bring it in and get Felix to track it back. We found who it belonged to, and although Brett gave the men permission to arrest them when they found out who it was, they didn't."

"Who was it?"

"The same group who May put behind bars five years ago. It seems they've grown their numbers again." He sighed. "Brett told the men to stay and observe for a couple of days to see what they have going on. It seems to be more than drugs and blackmail this time."

"And they've settled here? In Windsor?"

"They were always here. But their operations look a lot bigger from the photographs I've seen. A lot of people coming and going that have bigger connotations than before."

"You're worried they've got more power behind them this time," Randall said.

Dominic nodded. "How can May be safe when so many people could be after her? Including many we don't know about?"

"We will find them all. She'll be safe. It might just take a little time."

"Time is not our friend."

"It never is," Randall agreed.

They fell into silence, and Dominic's mind went over the evidence they had again. Trying to see something he'd missed before. There had to be something he'd not seen. A little, tiny clue somewhere in the words or actions of those trying to hurt May. Their parents would not survive if something happened to either of them. Which brought him to another thought.

"Will you come with me to see my parents tomorrow night?" Randall jerked, and Dominic hid his smile. "Sorry, that was a little random. But it holds true. I'd love for you to see the house I grew up in."

Randall blinked at him and then said, "They still live in the same house?"

Dominic nodded. "It's a nice house, and they're waiting to fill it with grandchildren. At least, that's what I've been told several times."

Randall chuckled. "Every parent's dream. My parents aren't much different." He cleared his throat. "You should spend time with them by yourself. You don't need me to accompany you."

Dominic laughed. "They've had me and May with them for years. They would be glad of the new conversation." He squeezed Randall to him gently. "Please come?"

Randall was quiet for a moment. "If you think it won't be an imposition, I'd love to."

His tone made it sound like he wasn't certain he wanted to come, but Dominic would take anything he could get. And if it meant spending more time with him outside of work, then he was all for it.

He picked Randall up from Windsor the following afternoon. After having left him in the early hours of the previous night, he had nothing but Randall in his mind, even when he'd been working. Or rather, especially as he'd been working. Andrew had nothing but meetings that day, and he'd spent long hours in Randall's office, watching the man work his magic as he seamlessly ran Andrew's calendar like he'd been born for the role.

Maybe he had. But he could see the nerves in him now. A man who managed the king's workload as if it were nothing more than a fly buzzing around him.

"You've already met them, so it'll be fine," he said, trying to calm him.

"I know. It's more that... They're going to assume... It's a big thing..." He exhaled. "I know."

When Dominic pulled into the driveway, he switched the engine off, but he didn't climb out. Instead, he turned to Randall and took his hand.

"I know meeting parents is a big deal. If you really don't want to do this, you don't have to. I would never force you to." He took the leap he'd been wanting to for a while. "I want to share you with them and them with you because you mean a lot to me, Randall. I know we've not discussed it, but I'd like for us to consider calling this a relationship. It's only been a few days, but my feelings have been there for a while, sweetheart. And if I've learnt nothing else in the last few years, it's that life is short, and I intend to eke out every inch of happiness I can from it."

Randall had been staring at him while he spoke, and a tremulous smile crept across his face when he finished. "I wholeheartedly agree." He palmed Dominic's cheek. "I'm scared this is a dream, but no matter what, my answer will always be the same. Yes. I can't guarantee I'll be any good as a boyfriend, but let's give it a try."

Dominic wanted to yell his joy and deny Randall's claim, but he grabbed the back of Randall's head and fused their mouths, taking all the breath from both their lungs and exploring every inch of him. Pulling back when the need for air was more than his body could take, he rested their foreheads together.

"Thank you, sweetheart."

They exited the car, and Dominic threaded their fingers together as they walked up to the door. It opened before they got there, and his dad smiled at them, making an obvious nod towards their joined hands.

"Hey, Dad."

"Glad you could both make it," Tom said, pulling Dominic in for a hug. He paused before Randall but then did the same to him. "I'm happy you're here. Come on in. Chance is just setting the table."

"Hey, Pops," Dominic said when they entered the dining room.

"Dominic!" Chance put the last plate in its place and hugged him. "Tom mentioned we were having a guest tonight. I'm glad to see you again, Randall." He held out his hand and shook Randall's.

"Thank you for having me. You have a lovely home. Dominic tells me this was his childhood home, too."

Chance nodded. "It was." He gestured to a chair, and Randall sat, folding his arms and leaning on the table towards Chance as if to glean any information he could. "We found this place in quite a state when we first started looking for a home. We weren't sure we could fix it up, but with some patience and a lot of love, we managed. And then we filled it with the joy and laughter of two children."

"That's the short story, anyway," Tom added as he entered carrying two serving bowls. "Nothing fancy, I'm afraid. Just spaghetti and meatballs."

"It smells delicious," Randall said.

Chance leaned closer. "Tom won a trophy for this meal years ago, though he would deny it."

Tom waved his hand and sat. "Don't believe him. It was nothing exciting. There was a cooking competition at a nearby college, and Chance entered me—without my permission, I might add—and I won." He frowned. "I can't even remember what the prize was now."

Dominic chuckled. "Wasn't it that two-night stay in Wales?"

Tom clicked his fingers and pointed at him. "That was it." He shook his head. "Anyway, Chance uses any excuse possible to hype it up." He smiled at his husband. "Dig in. There's plenty more if we run out."

They spent an enjoyable evening chatting about anything and everything, but eventually, Dominic called time on their fun. Chance pulled him aside. "We've received a phone call from Malachi Sanders asking about May. We said no comment, but I wanted you to know."

"Thanks." Dominic turned back to face Randall. "I promise to bring him back another day." It was the only way they could get out of the door.

As they put their coats back on, Dominic laughed and pointed at the vase. "One rose, Pops? Is that all you could afford?"

Chance snorted and held up his hands. "It's not from me. I think Tom's got an admirer myself."

Dominic froze. "Why do you say that?"

Tom went over to the vase and fingered the red rose. "It was waiting on the doorstep when I got home today. It's beautiful in its simplicity but still a little strange."

Dominic stepped closer. "Was there no note or anything?" His heart rate increased, and he hoped, with everything inside him, that his father's answer wouldn't be what he knew it would be.

"Yes, but there was nothing but a B on it and the florist's logo." Tom stared at him. "What's wrong, Dominic?"

He shook his head and made himself smile. "Just wondering if it's you or Pops who are the recipient."

"We'll probably never know," Chance said. "I might buy a bunch tomorrow to fill the vase. It looks lonely."

Tom smiled at him and slid his arm around Chance's waist, kissing his cheek. "You big softie."

Dominic couldn't help the genuine smile that graced his face, and he turned to Randall. "They're both big softies." He winked, and Randall grinned. "Are you ready?"

Randall nodded and stepped towards Dominic's parents. "Thank you so much for having me. I really enjoyed the evening, and the food was delicious."

"You're welcome. Anytime. And I mean that," Tom said, wagging his finger at him. "You don't have to wait for this one to bring you. Anytime you need a breather or a chat, knock on the door. I almost guarantee one of us will be home with us both being retired now."

"Thank you. I appreciate that."

Dominic hugged his parents, maybe a little tighter than usual. "Keep safe."

"We will," Chance said.

Tom studied him a little more closely and palmed his cheek. "Something's bothering you," he murmured.

"I'm okay. Tired. That's all."

He could tell his father didn't believe him, but there were no more reassurances he could give. Ideally, he'd like to get his hands on that rose, but he couldn't do that without causing them to worry. He glanced at the rose one last time and led Randall to the car. Before he even got there, Tom called Randall's name. They stopped while Tom strode over to him, carrying that damn rose.

"Chance is right. I think this rose will be lonely here. How about you keep it? I'm sure there are flowers around Windsor that will keep it company."

Randall shook his head. "Oh, I couldn't."

"Yes, you can." Tom smiled and held it out to him. Randall took it and thanked him, and Tom came over to him, squeezing his hand and sliding something into it. "Something's bothering you about this rose, so do with it what you need to. This is the card."

Dominic huffed a laugh and shook his head. "I can get nothing past you."

Tom hugged him. "Please tell me whenever you're able to."

"All I can tell you is that I need you both to be careful and watchful. Something's coming, and I don't know what it is yet."

Tom pulled back and cupped his face. "We will. Take care of yourself and Randall." He glanced at the man in question. "I like him."

Dominic chuckled. "I knew you would."

Tom smiled, kissed his cheek and headed back to where Chance waited for him. Dominic climbed into the car and waved as they drove off.

He sighed. "I'm really sorry, Randall, but I'm going to have to take that rose when we get back."

"Oh? That's okay. I know it's from your parents, so it's only fair that you have it—"

"It's not that." He explained about the rose May had received the previous day. Same card, same handwriting, same MO. "I don't know what it means yet, but it's something, I'm sure."

Randall stared at the rose as if it had teeth. "Do you think..."

Dominic could understand where his brain might have gone, but he had no answers. "I don't know. Will there be others, and they're spelling something out?" Dominic shook his head. "It seems like a long-winded way to send a message. I'm going to take it to Brett and get his forensic contacts to look at it. As well as May's one." Dominic sighed again. "I'm sorry for bringing this mess to your door. I'd understand if you don't want anything to do with me now."

Randall snorted. "I don't have any problems with what's happening. Am I worried? Yes, but not about me. I'm worried about you, about May, about your parents. I'm worried about what this could mean. But us? No. Once I set my mind to something, I usually stick with my decision."

"I'm glad to hear it. I would hate to have to chain you to the bed so you didn't leave me," Dominic joked.

"Hmm, kinky."

Dominic laughed, and the mood lightened. When he parked in Windsor's car park, he walked Randall to his car and kissed him chastely.

"I want more than that, but not here. I'll see you again tomorrow."

Randall unlocked his car and opened the driver's door. "Not as much, though. Andrew's out and about, remember?"

Dominic grimaced. "Oh, yeah."

Randall chuckled. "You can't keep him locked up, either."

Dominic scrunched his face, not liking where his thoughts went, and he discarded them immediately. He pointed his finger at Randall. "Not nice."

Randall bit his lip, trying to contain his smile. "Sorry. Couldn't resist." He held out the rose. "I hope it helps."

Dominic took it and closed Randall's door. He waited until he exited the car park before turning to the building. He had a feeling he would be having a late night, and so would Brett.

12

Brett

When Dominic entered the briefing room holding a rose, Brett frowned over at him. "Did you forget to give that to Randall or something?"

Dominic shook his head and placed it on the table in front of him. "This was a rose my fathers received today. It was left outside their front door, and the note only said 'B'."

"Okay...?"

"At any other time, I wouldn't have been concerned about it, but...May received one yesterday. It was on the floor outside her suite when she and Felix got back from their walk. Her note said 'A'. Something's going on."

Brett closed his eyes and dropped his head into his hands. "I'm sick and tired of all these bloody games. If someone has a problem, talk it out. Stop throwing knives or bullets or...bloody roses!"

He breathed deeply and exhaled before lifting his head again. Dominic stared at him with raised eyebrows.

"Feel better now?"

Brett glared. "No." He stared at the rose. "Get both roses to forensics. See if we can't get some fingerprints or something from either the rose itself or the note. It's a long shot, but we can try. Felix?" His right-hand man came closer. "Can you check out the florist from the note and see what they have to say about it?"

"Sure thing."

Felix bent over the rose and snapped a picture of the florist's details. "It's not Floresco, that's for sure."

"Robert's shop would have nothing to do with this. If anyone knew anything about us, they'd know that. That's why they used someone else," Brett said.

"What do you think the letters are for?" Dominic said. "As I said to Randall earlier, it seems a long-winded way of spelling out a message if that's what they're trying to do."

Brett had his ideas, but until he had more information, he wasn't sharing. What he did need to do was keep an eye on his team and his protectees. All of them. It was far too easy to think about the smaller picture and miss out on the big one, and the fact that several different things were happening at once made him wonder if they weren't connected in some way. It also made him queasy.

"I'm not sure," Brett said, and Felix stared at him. Damn the man. He always saw through his words and actions, especially when he didn't want him to. "We'll figure it out."

There was nothing else he could do that he wasn't already, but that had never sat well with him. After sending Dominic off to retrieve May's rose and sort the forensics, he settled in for a long night.

"What do you really think it is?" Felix asked from his desk in the corner, surrounded by computers.

"It's the same thing as always." Felix raised his eyebrows. "People trying to take what isn't theirs or people trying to be something they shouldn't be or people wanting others to suffer for imagined errors. It's always the same. The only difference is how they go about it."

Without conscious thought, his mind conjured an image of his father, but Brett brushed it away immediately as he did every time it happened. He had no business interrupting Brett's work with his woe-is-me expression. It had never worked on Brett, and it would never work on him.

"That's rather...pessimistic, isn't it? Even for you."

Brett sighed and stared at the paperwork in front of him. "Guess I'm feeling like the glass is half empty today instead of half full."

Felix jumped from his seat, the legs scraping across the floor, and disappeared out of the door. Brett stared after him and chuckled, shaking his head. He was used to Felix's flights. He no longer took it to mean he'd said something wrong. The man would be back eventually.

When he did, however, he brought with him the scent of freshly brewed, *decent* coffee. Brett could've kissed him.

"You are my new favourite person," Brett said as he drank.

13

Randall

Randall palmed his forehead. "Are you able to manage those? And I'll take care of the changes to the menu."

"Of course. Let me take the table designs, too. You have enough to do."

"Thanks, Portia. I honestly don't know how I fit all this in before you arrived."

Portia chuckled and handed a cup of tea to him. "I don't know either, but at least you've got me now. You can spend some extra time with Dominic." She winked.

Randall's cheeks heated, and he flicked his gaze to Viola, who was sitting in the chair by the king's door. Her mouth twitched, but she pretended not to hear as she read her book.

He ignored Portia, even when she nudged his shoulder. "Shush, Portia."

She laughed and gathered up what she needed. They could've easily fit another desk into the space there, but Portia didn't want to be part of the "centre hub", as she called it. She much preferred her quieter office down the hall.

"Claim him quickly, Randall, or someone else might."

"I don't need to claim him, Portia. He's already mine." Randall smirked at his computer as she gasped.

"Yeah! I knew it."

Randall chuckled and rubbed his face. "You're so juvenile."

"Maybe, but... Randall and Dominic in a tree, K-I-S-S-I-N-G."

"God, you sound like George," Randall said, and he was sure he heard a snicker from Viola.

"I don't care." Portia leaned down, lowering her voice. "I'm so happy for you, Randall." She kissed his cheek and left the office, and Randall leaned back in his chair, taking a minute to stare at the ceiling and breathe before he had to handle the phone calls that needed to be completed that day.

"I'm happy for you, too," Viola said, and Randall lifted his head to look at her. "And him. He's been alone for too long."

"Thanks."

Randall settled in to work when Andrew's door opened.

"Right, Randall. I'm off. According to the calendar, I have three meetings now. Is that right?"

Randall stood. "Yes, Your Majesty." He rounded the table and handed Andrew the folders he needed. "They said lunch would be included, but I've arranged for something to be available in the car in case they don't provide anything."

"Thank you, Randall. Wish me luck."

"You don't need it, Your Majesty."

Andrew rubbed a hand over his face. "I'm not so sure."

He left, Viola following in his wake, and Randall headed back to his desk. He had a session with his therapist that evening, but he had so many things going around in his head that he wasn't sure it was a good time. Although, maybe that was the best time to go. Hopefully, Derek could help him clear things up.

The day ran as smoothly as it could when it involved the royal family. George made his presence known around lunchtime, wanting information about their ceremony, and Randall had to point him towards Portia. His exuberance, while enchanting, was overwhelming at that moment.

He hadn't seen Dominic all day—he would've gone with Andrew when he left—and Randall missed him. As he packed his belongings at the end of the day, the door opened, making him jump.

"Sorry!" Dominic said, wincing. "I really need to learn to open that door more quietly."

Randall chuckled, his heart rate calming. "It's okay. I should be used to it by now."

Dominic pulled Randall into his arms. "How has your day been?"

"Busy."

"When isn't it?"

"Never."

Dominic raised his eyebrow. "Exactly my point."

"Did everything go okay with Brett? I didn't hear anything, so I'm assuming you don't have any more information."

"We have a little." Dominic dropped a kiss on his lips and then pulled back. "We're waiting on DNA results from the card and rose petals and stem, but we're not holding out much hope. Brett got in touch with Commissioner Thomas, who put someone on the case. They visited the florist and got a statement from the owner. Apparently, she received the order via phone call and wrote the initials herself, but the caller wasn't clear on the meaning behind it. It wasn't her business, so she didn't pry. She took the payment via card, and Felix is tracking it now, but I doubt there'll be anything to it. They gave her an address to send them to and asked to leave them at the door and not hand them directly to the person."

Randall frowned. "Is that standard procedure? I thought flowers were supposed to be signed for?"

"Not all companies ask for signatures. Usually only for larger bouquets." Dominic sighed. "I doubt it'll lead to anything. It might not even have anything to do with May's case."

The door opened, and Nick came in. "There's a guy at the guard's station saying he's the detective in charge of May's case. Detective Addams. Do you know him?"

Dominic nodded and stood. "I've been expecting him. Thanks, Nick. I'll fetch him."

Nick left, and Dominic turned to him. "I'm sorry. I thought I'd have more time tonight."

Randall smiled, and though he was disappointed, he understood. "It's okay. We can catch up another night. We have time."

They shared another sweet kiss, and then Dominic disappeared. Randall finished packing his things and headed for his car. As it was Friday, he wasn't officially supposed to work weekends, except if there were events planned, but he always did some work. He didn't have much of a social life, after all.

But he was in for a surprise when he arrived home. A car he didn't recognise waited at the curb as he pulled into his driveway. With everything that had been happening at Windsor, he was unsure what to do about his unknown visitor. He climbed out of the car and waited for the person to get out of theirs.

He sighed and shook his head, his heart rate decreasing when Geoff climbed out. "What the hell! You scared the life out of me! Whose car did you pinch?"

Geoff rolled his eyes. "It's mine, you cretin. Bought and paid for."

Randall loved winding him up, though it was more often the other way around. "Come on in. I don't have alcohol, but I can order pizza."

"Sounds good to me."

Randall deposited his bag by the door and closed them inside. By the time he reached the kitchen, Geoff was already looking through the takeaway leaflets he'd found in the kitchen drawer.

"Just make yourself at home," Randall teased.

"Don't I always?" Geoff pointed to a leaflet. "How about Indian instead of pizza?"

Randall groaned. "Do I have to?"

"No." Geoff raised his eyebrows.

Randall snorted. "Yes, I do. Okay, you're ordering and accepting the delivery at the door, though."

"Deal."

There was a particular guy from the Indian takeaway place who seemed to have taken a liking to Randall. After grimacing through several interactions and sidestepping many dinner requests, Randall had stopped using the place, but it was Geoff's favourite.

While Geoff placed the order, Randall went upstairs to get changed. He checked his phone and sent a message to Derek, his therapist, to cancel his appointment as he headed back down again, but there was nothing from Dominic. Not that he expected there to be when he was busy with the detective. He wished he could be there to support Dominic, but it wasn't his business, even if he was on the edge of the situation. He'd only recently started a relationship with Dominic, so it wasn't like he was part of the family, as much as he wished he was.

"Food should be here in half an hour."

"Great." Randall made them a tea each, and then he settled opposite his best friend on the sofa. "So, spill. What's wrong?"

"What do you mean?"

"It's rare you turn up on my doorstep without prior notice because you've always said you never know what time I'll get in. And the only times you ever do it are when something is wrong. What's happened?" When Geoff still didn't say anything, Randall prompted, "Is Nadine okay? The twins?"

Geoff sighed. "I told you Nadine got the promotion?" Randall nodded. "Well, it appears like the only reason she got it was because her boss wanted more from her than what was in the job description."

Randall gaped at him. "She's having an affair?"

Geoff held up his hands. "God, no! Shit, sorry. No, she's not. But the boss propositioned her and basically said that he had promoted her solely on her looks and the fact that he wanted her."

"Fucker. What did she do?"

"She walked out of the meeting and continued her job until it was time to come home, and then she told me everything."

"Is she going back?"

Geoff shrugged. "I don't know. I left the decision up to her. Personally, I wouldn't want to work for someone like that, even in a different department, because if that is what he is like with her, then what is he like with others?"

"He could get arrested for sexual harassment."

"I don't know if she will press charges." Geoff exhaled. "I just feel so bad for her. She's worked damn hard to get that promotion, and he's wrecked it all in five minutes. I doubt she feels worthy of it anymore."

"I've always told her she was worth more than that company, anyway. Tell her to call me if she wants to find something else. I'm sure there are positions I can find that would suit her well."

"Thanks." The doorbell rang. "My job awaits." Geoff rose and headed for the front door, and within three minutes, he was back. "Your admirer wasn't happy it wasn't you." Geoff laughed.

Randall shoved him. "Shut up and give me my food."

Three hours later, Randall threw Geoff out of his house and told him to go home to his wife.

"Treat her like the princess she should be, and she'll be able to weather anything."

"How do you know what to say?"

Randall chuckled. "It's in my job description."

Before he went to bed, he sent a message to Dominic.

RANDALL: *I hope everything is going okay. I'll be back at work around eight o'clock in the morning. If you need anything, either let me know or leave a note on my desk, and I'll get it done as soon as I get in. Please get some rest.*

He didn't see the response until he woke up the next morning.

DOMINIC: *There's nothing I need except you beside me every night. I hope you sleep well. I'll see you tomorrow.*

Waking up to a message from Dominic was Randall's favourite new thing. It put a smile on his face that didn't disappear throughout his morning routine. Not even when he got re-routed through a diversion that had cropped up overnight and added ten minutes to his journey. And when he arrived at his desk, there was a note for him and a plastic fish.

"A fish?" he murmured as he opened the envelope.

Randall,

I hope you slept well. In case you're wondering, the fish is a clue to where our next date will be. I checked the calendar and have pencilled in the 27th. It seems like that is our best option, but I know you work on Wednesdays. We can rearrange if necessary. Don't work too hard. I'll see you later today.

D. x

The note had the same effect on him that the message had done, and Randall found himself smiling again. He picked up the fish. Were they going fishing? He'd never done it before, but he'd give anything a try once.

He tucked the note and fish into his desk drawer and switched on his computer. He had plenty of work to keep him busy until he could hopefully see Dominic that day. Going through the next batch of emails and calls was something he didn't enjoy, but Andrew needed it to be done. Some emails were worthy of newspaper headlines, but he would never do that, though others might. In some ways, checking emails was a way of helping to keep abreast of situations that might eventually blow up in their faces. Randall had curated a list of possible problems that he was going to bring up with Andrew as soon as he had some spare time, including that reporter, Malachi, who had contacted nearly every member of the royal family. For some reason, the king was extremely busy lately and had so many more appointments than he'd had for a long time. Did it have something to do with the upheaval they'd faced? Possibly, but it didn't stop it from being draining for the king.

A knock sounded, and Randall frowned. No one ever knocked. "Come in!"

The door opened, and a man who looked to be in his mid- to late-forties entered. He wore a black suit without a tie and a black jacket. It took a second for Randall to realise Dominic was behind him. Randall stood, smiling.

"Good morning."

"Morning, Randall. Can I introduce Detective Addams?" Dominic said though he didn't move his gaze away from Randall. "He's here to do some investigating."

Detective Addams chuckled. "You make it sound sinister."

Dominic wiped a hand over his face. "Sorry. I need more sleep."

Addams stepped forward and reached out a hand. "Nice to meet you, Randall."

"You, too, Detective. If there is anything I can do to assist you, please let me know."

Addams smiled. "Thank you, but I think I'm covered with Dominic and Brett. They've helped me plenty so far."

Randall grinned at Dominic. "I'm sure they have."

"Addams, I just need to speak with Randall, and then I'll take you to May."

"No problem at all. I'll wait outside with Colt." Addams turned to Randall. "It was nice to meet you."

Randall nodded once, and Addams left the room. Once the door closed behind him, Dominic took Randall in his arms and sighed as if the weight had been lifted from his shoulders. Randall rubbed his back and murmured nonsense.

"I wish I could stay like this forever," Dominic murmured against his shoulder.

"That would be nice."

Dominic lifted his head and slid his hands all the way up Randall's body to cup his cheeks. "I've missed you."

"I've missed you," Randall agreed.

Dominic lowered his head and kissed him, and Randall completely forgot where they were. His hands gripped Dominic's back, taking everything he gave and giving everything he could. When he needed air, as much as he wished he didn't, he dragged himself away and gasped.

"You really...shouldn't kiss...me like that."

Dominic licked his lips, humming slightly. "Why not?"

"Because I forget everything."

"Isn't that a good thing?"

"Not when I have work to do."

Dominic chuckled. "I can always try to kiss you again, and then you might remember?"

Randall's mouth twitched. "I'm not sure that'll work. We can try that test another day, though. Right now, you're needed."

Dominic sighed. "That I am."

"I'm assuming he's here to help."

Dominic nodded. "He was the original detective in charge of the case when May testified five years ago. He's been mostly kept up to date with the case, except for certain aspects that have been missed. He's catching up fast, though. I persuaded him not to see May yesterday, but I have no choice today."

"I'm glad you have someone else helping you. I hated that this was mostly on your shoulders, even if you do have some help from Brett and the team."

"It'll be over soon. One way or the other. It has to be."

Randall hugged him, and they shared one more air-stealing kiss before Dominic left. There wasn't much he could do to help the man apart from being there when he needed to let it all go. He could also help May by giving her the garden walks, the spa baskets, the flowers, and anything else he thought of. Maybe he could get permission to take her to Book Drunk one day. That might be pushing the boundaries of keeping her safe, but he could ask even if nothing came from it.

He sat down at his desk and stared at the screen, wishing he didn't have to work and that he could be with Dominic while he was going through it all. The best he could do was send him a message and ask him to come home with him that night. If Dominic could get away, Randall had an idea of how he could help him relax, but he needed to grab a few items first.

Plans decided, he sent the message, wrote a list and then set an alarm to remind him to fetch the items.

RANDALL: *If you can, meet me at my house at nine o'clock tonight. Bring your pyjamas. x*

Then he set to work so he could leave as early as his conscience would let him. It would only be a minor fix for a larger problem, but many small fixes can help something bigger, as far as he was concerned. It worked for him. He didn't have particularly big problems, but filling in the hole little by little was helping him become complete again. And Dominic was also a big part of that, and something he needed to discuss with his therapist.

As his timer went off, he tidied up and went searching for the perfect—in his opinion—items to help soothe a battered soul.

14

Dominic

Dominic knocked on his sister's door and told her who it was. He'd warned her that Addams was there and that they would be visiting. When she opened the door, Dominic could see the reservations on her face. She had never liked Addams, but she had never been able to vocalise why. Dominic couldn't find anything wrong with the guy apart from him being a little of a "know-it-all."

"Nice to see you again, May. Though I wish it was under better circumstances," Addams said.

"You, too, Detective. Would you like a drink?"

"Coffee, if it's not too much trouble, please?" Addams removed his jacket and sat on the sofa, crossing his legs and flipping open his notebook.

Dominic moved over to help May. "Are you okay?" he asked quietly.

She nodded. "I just wish this was over. Even if I have to go back into hiding. I want my life back. Any kind of life except one lived in fear."

He rubbed his hand over her back and pressed his lips to her temple. "I know. We're getting closer. I can feel it," he whispered.

May gave him a small smile and finished the drinks, carrying her and Addams' drinks to the table.

"Ah, thank you, May."

Dominic sat beside May, opposite Addams, and leaned back, giving a relaxed appearance when he was anything but. He had no idea what the detective wanted to talk to May about because he wouldn't say when Dominic had broached the subject. Well, he did have an idea, and if it went the way he thought it might—accusing May of contacting people from her old life—he wasn't going to be happy. He'd gone far too long without talking to her to keep her safe, and he knew she wouldn't have risked *anything* just to speak to someone.

Addams sipped his coffee, the slurp almost echoing in the otherwise silent room. "Lovely brew, May. Thank you." He placed the mug on the table and sat back, the epitome of ease. "I know you have been through this with several people, but I want you to go through everything that happened from the moment you believed something was wrong."

May exhaled and began her tale. It was the same as what she had told him and Owen. Addams didn't ask any questions until she finished her retelling, one thing he admired about the detective.

"Thank you. Can you describe the car for me?" May closed her eyes and recounted the information. "And the men you saw in the car?" She did the same again. "Did you see anyone as you made your way to the theatre?" She shook her head. "Was it unusual not to see anyone at that time of night? It wasn't particularly late."

"I was using alleys and back streets where I could. The theatre isn't a popular place."

"Even so. Was there a theatre performance that night?"

May frowned. "I'm not sure. I hate theatre."

Dominic couldn't help his chuckle. "You always have."

Addams stared at his notebook, the crease between his eyebrows deeper than usual. "Did you see anyone around when you were picked up by the helicopter?"

Dominic opened his mouth to answer, but Addams glanced at him and shook his head.

"I wasn't looking around," she said.

"You weren't worried someone might have come after you, even with Dominic being there?"

May glared at Addams. "I was hugging my brother for the first time in five years. The rest of the world fell away."

"Literally," Addams murmured. "Okay, tell me about the phone calls."

May stared at Addams for a long moment, and as Dominic was about to ask what was wrong, she licked her lips and answered the question. "I received a call from Fletcher. He threatened to make me pay for everything I'd put them through. I told him to get lost and ended the call."

"How did he get your number?"

Dominic froze. "How the hell did I miss that?" He glanced at May. "It never occurred to me that he shouldn't have your number. What kind of guard am I?" he muttered, cursing himself to hell.

May put a hand on his arm. "You're doing everything you can, Dom. And you're working, too. You're not a miracle worker."

Dominic shook his head and sent a text to Brett while still listening to Addams' line of questioning.

"I don't know. I assume he has his ways of finding information, the same others do."

Addams rested his notebook on his leg and linked his fingers, staring at May. "And what about the other phone calls?"

Dominic frowned. "What other phone calls?" Addams didn't answer, so he looked at his sister. "May?"

She sighed. "I received two calls prior to everything happening."

"Why didn't you tell me?"

"I didn't think they were relevant."

Dominic glared at her. "Bullshit. You knew they were, and you were protecting someone. Who?"

May's chin trembled as if she was about to cry, but she breathed through it. "You."

"May, come on! I get death threats every week because of my job. What did they say?"

May stared down at her cup. "They called me by my real name and said that if I didn't come out of hiding, they would make you pay for my sins."

Dominic clenched his jaw. "You should've told me, May."

"Sorry."

He stood and paced, grimacing with every step.

"How did you know about them?" May asked Addams, and Dominic paused, wanting to know that answer, too.

"I looked into your phone records for the past few weeks. I needed to make sure you weren't *forgetting* to tell me anything."

May glared at him again but said nothing.

Dominic wasn't so restrained when it came to family. "Are you accusing her of something?"

Addams transferred his gaze from May to Dominic. "Not at all. But sometimes, victims receive calls or emails that they forget about, thinking it's irrelevant, when in fact, they're important to the case."

Dominic could understand that. He'd received many calls over the years, which he'd ignored. Any of those could've related to past events, and he wouldn't know about it.

"Anything else you need to tell me, May?" Addams said, and Dominic wasn't sure he liked his tone.

"Not that I can think of, Detective," May replied with a bite.

They stared at each other for a few minutes, and then Addams stood. "I'm done, then. Thank you for the coffee." He gathered his jacket and headed for the door. "I'll leave you to visit, Dominic. I know my way back to the security room."

Despite the answers he wanted from May, he couldn't stay. "You know better than that, Addams. You can't go wandering around Windsor unaccompanied."

"I could if I insisted."

Dominic held up his hands. "If you want to be arrested by a guard who doesn't know who you are and held until someone comes to acknowledge that, go ahead."

Addams sighed. "You really do take security seriously here."

Dominic lifted his eyebrow. "We have the royal family living here. What do you expect?"

He hugged May and whispered, "He'll be leaving soon. And don't think you're free from my interrogation, boo."

She groaned. "I know."

They left May to her day and headed back towards Sec HQ. At least now Dominic had an idea why May didn't like Addams—he saw too much. They didn't say anything, to begin with, but then Addams said, "I wasn't going to keep it from you. I wanted to see her genuine reaction to me knowing about the calls."

"And?" Despite hating how it had happened, Dominic understood the reasoning behind it.

"You're not going to like my answer."

Dominic's stomach churned. "Tell me."

"She's hiding something." Dominic was about to deny that when Addams said, "You're too close, Dominic. You love her. But even our loved ones do things they shouldn't to save their family."

"What do you think she's done?" The words were torn from his throat like shards of glass.

"I honestly don't know. But she's not being fully truthful. With either of us."

They reached Sec HQ, and Dominic paused with his hand on the door handle. "You have an idea what it is, though, don't you?" Addams said nothing but didn't break his gaze away. "If this is a threat that could hurt the royal family, we need to know," Dominic pressed.

"I don't believe it is."

"Let us be the judge of that."

Dominic parked outside of Randall's house and grabbed his overnight bag. He didn't own pyjamas as such, but he had some threadbare joggers and a T-shirt he could use—if he needed them at all.

He knocked and waited, glancing around at the patches the streetlights didn't reach. Randall needed some security lights to brighten the area a bit more. He made a mental note to fix that as soon as possible.

"Good evening," Randall said.

Dominic stepped inside, dropping his bag to the floor and sliding his hands down the silky pyjamas Randall wore. "Wow. You look gorgeous."

Randall's cheeks flushed, and Dominic smiled, loving that he could make his lover feel desirable. He lowered his head and traced Randall's lips with his tongue before claiming his mouth completely. A hint of something minty that didn't seem to be toothpaste warmed his lips, and he couldn't get enough of it.

When he pulled back, they were both breathing heavily, and Dominic licked his lips. "Have you had something minty?"

Randall smiled. "Mint tea."

"Ah, that explains it." He brushed his thumb across the warmed cheeks, tracing the colouring. "Thank you for inviting me over."

"I wasn't sure if you would be able to make it. Did everything go well with the detective?"

"He's gone back home now. We didn't think it was wise for him to stay too long despite him being a police officer. It could point to May staying there."

"If I'm honest, Dominic, I'm sure most people have guessed already."

Dominic sighed. "Yeah, you're right. I can keep hoping, can't I?"

Randall slid his arms around Dominic's neck. "I'll help you keep hope." He kissed him. "In fact... I have something for you." He stepped back and grabbed Dominic's hands, pulling him further into the house.

"Do I need my pyjamas?"

Randall's smile lit up the room. "I don't know. Do you?"

Dominic didn't stop to pick up his bag. Randall turned around, still holding his hands, and they went through the kitchen to a small room at the back of the house. When they entered, Dominic was speechless. There were candles lit all around the edge of the room, and a long padded table—or was it a chair?—stood in the centre. The flickering embers cast an orange glow, soft music played, and Dominic relaxed instantly.

"What's all this?" he asked.

"I was trying to think of something to help you relax properly, and I thought you might like a massage." Randall wrung his hands. "I'm trained. I did it on a whim one month when I was at a loose end."

Dominic raised his eyebrow. "You were at a loose end?"

Randall chuckled. "I know. It doesn't seem possible, does it?" He waved at the table. "If you want, you can undress and lay on your stomach. I'll come back in a few min—"

Dominic grabbed him and held him close. "Can you help me? I find I'm struggling with my fine motor skills today," he murmured.

Randall ducked his head, but not before Dominic saw his smile. "Of course, Sir." His fingers went to the buttons of Dominic's shirt, slowly pushing each plastic circle through the buttonhole and exposing inch after inch of skin. Randall leaned forward, pressing kisses to each area freed from the confines of clothing.

Dominic's cock responded as Randall's lips closed around his nipple and sucked. His groan tore out of him, and he tightened his hold on Randall's hips to keep himself tethered. When he regained control, he found his shirt on the floor and his trousers unfastened. He allowed Randall to push his clothes off, leaving him naked and then dragged him up for a punishing kiss.

"Wait, Sir," Randall panted, pulling away. He rested his hands on Dominic's chest. "Your massage..."

Dominic inhaled, closed his eyes and exhaled. "Where do you want me?"

Randall's eyes darkened, and Dominic could guess what he was thinking, but he rallied and said, "On your stomach on the table, please."

Dominic almost declined, but Randall had gone to so much trouble for him. He climbed onto the sturdy table and laid down, placing his face into the hole so he could breathe.

"Are you comfortable, Sir?"

"Perfectly."

"I'm going to place some oil on your back and rub it into your skin."

"Mmhmm." Dominic was already feeling relaxed, and Randall hadn't even started with the massage yet.

When Randall's hands smoothed across his skin, Dominic groaned. With each passing moment, as Randall worked at his muscles with his magic hands, he fell deeper in love with the guy.

"Oh, you tensed. What's wrong? Did I hurt you?" Randall asked, continuing to soothe him with long strokes.

What's wrong? He'd just realised he was in love with Randall; that was what was wrong. Or rather, right. There was nothing wrong with it, but he hadn't understood until that moment. Not fully, anyway.

Randall hit a particularly tender bit, and he moaned, which encouraged Randall to work on it. He had magic hands, for sure. He needed them on another part of his body. With a groan of effort, he pushed himself up and over onto his back, his cock jutting painfully from his body.

"Ride me," he said, his voice deeper and hoarser than ever.

Randall climbed up, throwing his leg over Dominic's hips. "I'm already ready, Sir," he mumbled, staring down at Dominic's chest.

Dominic lifted his chin until they gazed at each other. "I'm glad because this won't be an easy ride."

Randall reached behind him and grimaced, throwing a plug to the floor, which Dominic assumed he'd removed from the ass he was about to claim. Randall slicked Dominic with the oil he'd been using and then rose to his knees and scooted forward enough for Dominic's cock to press against his hole.

Dominic gripped his hips, holding him steady. "Hands behind your back, grip each wrist. Do *not* let go at any point."

"Yes, Sir."

Dominic pulled Randall down on him as he thrust up, and he slid fully inside him in one go.

"Fuck, Randall."

Dominic lifted him again, slamming him back down over and over, making his head spin. Randall's dick bobbed in front of him, but he was going to make him come handsfree.

"Oh, fuck. Sir, please!"

Dominic gripped him tighter. The table, no matter how sturdy, wobbled as they moved, but he couldn't stop them now. His orgasm was barrelling down his spine quicker than ever. It had to be something to do with Randall because no one had ever made him come this quickly before.

"Come for me, Randall."

"I can't!" Randall cried.

Dominic's stomach muscles clenched as he rose to a sitting position, holding Randall to him. He lowered his head to Randall's nipples, fastened his lips around them and sucked at the same time that he slammed him down again.

Randall screamed, and his release covered Dominic's chest and stomach as Dominic fell over, too. Synchronised climaxes weren't impossible, but Dominic had never experienced it before. It was sexy as hell.

Dominic breathed into Randall's neck, coming down slowly. Randall had collapsed into Dominic's arms, and it was only his waning strength that kept them from tumbling to the floor. Surprisingly, the table had survived.

"Let's get you cleaned up."

With effort, Dominic lifted Randall from his cock, wrapped the man's legs around his waist and swung his own legs over the edge of the table. He carried Randall—who had snuggled into his chest—down the hall, up the stairs and into the bathroom. Sitting on the edge of the bath, he reached around his tired submissive and started a warm bath.

He held on to Randall the entire time the water rose, and when he finally switched it off, steam surrounded them. He stood, manoeuvring Randall's legs to one side, and lowered him into the water. Randall moaned as he sank to his shoulders. But it was then Dominic noticed his arms were behind his back.

"Oh, Randall," Dominic murmured. "You can let go of your arms now." He hadn't even realised. He wasn't doing a very good job of being perceptive lately.

With a wince, Randall did, and Dominic massaged both limbs to get the feeling back into them. Randall's dopey smile made Dominic's heart skip a beat. He refused to say anything after such a quick but intense encounter, but he would say something soon.

By the time the water had cooled, their stomachs were growling, so Randall went downstairs to make them a sandwich while Dominic made sure the candles were safely out in the back room, and everything was secure.

"Dominic?"

He headed towards Randall. "Yeah?"

"Did you put this here?" Randall pointed to the kitchen table, and Dominic froze.

"No." He stared at the offending item. "No, I did not."

There, in a perfect glass vase, sat a red rose with a note resting against it. Dominic grabbed Randall and dragged him into the room they'd used for the massage. It had only one window and no doors, except the one they came in. Dominic shut them in and dialled his phone.

"Brett, we need some help at Randall's house. Someone left a rose on the kitchen table while we were...busy. I don't know if anyone is still here, and my gun is not where I am." *Stupid, stupid thing to do, Dominic.*

"I'm sending people there now. Hold tight."

Dominic told him where they were and hung up. He dragged a shaking Randall into his arms and tucked him under his chin. "You're all right, Randall. I'm here."

But what use was he when he had nothing to use as a weapon to defend them if someone came at them?

15

Randall

As Randall clung to Dominic, the idea of someone being in his house when he didn't know about it was unsettling. Would he ever feel safe again after this? Maybe he should stay at Windsor from now on. He loved his house, but if it was so easily accessed, what was the point? Who had left the rose? And not just his, but May and Dominic's fathers', too? Had they been watching them all?

And thinking about that, why had *he* received one? His relationship with Dominic had only just started. Whoever was sending them obviously thought Randall was more important to that family than he was. Either that, or they were missing something, and it wasn't about May at all.

He considered Andrew's phone call. Was this some elaborate ruse to get to the king? If it was, what was the endgame? Why go after May, Dominic's parents and him?

Nothing added up, and Randall didn't like it.

His trembling didn't subside, even when anger took its place, and he stayed tucked beneath Dominic's chin, clinging to him as if he were someone who couldn't take the stress. Which was exactly what he was. Give him the stressful job of organising a royal family's schedule, planning a royal wedding or finding some way of not offending a foreign official, and he was their man. But threaten his life, his home, and he was a scared little lamb.

Dominic's phone vibrated.

"Brett?" He went silent as he listened, and Randall lifted his head to watch the expressions crossing Dominic's face, and a frisson of delight flowed through him at what they might have in store for whoever might still be around. "Okay." He closed his phone. "They've arrived. They're going to go around the property first and then come inside to check it through before they come to us. It might be a few minutes." He cupped Randall's jaw. "How are you holding up?"

Randall sighed. "Scared. Pissed. Terrified. Pissed."

Dominic chuckled. "That's my Randall." He brushed his thumb across Randall's lips. "We'll find whoever did this. I promise. And if you agree, we'll arrange for someone to check over your security features and see if we can upgrade them to make you feel safer. I know it's worrying you now."

"It is. I might stay at Windsor for a little while. At least there, I have lots of people around."

"It might be a good idea until we can secure your house. I don't ever want you to feel you can't come back here, though. We will fix it. I promise."

Randall smiled. "I know you will." He inhaled. "I need to contact Derek and get another appointment. As soon as he can fit me in."

"Good idea. Just remember, I'm here for anything you need. Just ask."

"I will." Randall lifted his head and kissed Dominic. "Thank you."

Dominic dropped his hand and chuckled, but there was no humour in it. "You shouldn't be thanking me for bringing this to your door."

Randall traced his fingers across Dominic's face, the prickle of his stubble scratching his hand. "It's not your fault. It's not anyone's fault but the person who's doing this."

Dominic's phone vibrated again, and he checked it. Then, a knock sounded. Dominic let go of Randall and stood in front of the door as he opened it a crack to peer through. Randall's heart was in his throat as he waited for the verdict, but then Dominic opened the door further. Brett stood in the doorway.

"All clear. There's no one in or around the house." He glanced at Randall. "Are you okay?"

Randall nodded. "I will be."

Brett focused on Dominic. "Where's your gun?"

Dominic ducked his head, sighed and moved to leave the room. "In my bag in the hallway. I got...distracted when I got here." He glanced at Randall, who flushed, and Brett chuckled.

"I'm sure."

They exited the room, and Randall made a wide berth around the kitchen table that was being dusted for fingerprints. Dominic's curse had him rushing to where they were waiting.

"What is it?" Brett asked.

"It's gone," Dominic said from his crouch by his bag, cursing up a blue storm afterwards. "The fucker took my gun."

"Fuck," Brett said. He pulled out his phone. "Felix, can you register Dominic's gun as missing with the relevant people? If it crops up in any crimes, it won't point to him that way."

Dominic paced the small area, and Randall wished he could soothe him, but he didn't want to overstep when he was with his colleagues and friends. Dominic must've sensed his need or needed Randall in return because he reached for him and pulled him into his arms.

"Sorry about all this."

"Stop apologising." Randall rested his cheek against Dominic's chest, hiding the heat emanating from them as Brett smiled when he studied them.

"Let's get you both back to Windsor. After you get some sleep, we can go through everything we know," Brett said as other guards filed past them to the door.

Dominic took Randall's hand. "I'll come with you to pack a bag."

By the time they were fully dressed—Randall having forgotten they had only been in their dressing gowns while everyone was there—and he had enough clothes to last him a few days, everyone else had disappeared, and only Brett remained. Brett drove Randall's car, and Dominic drove his own, taking Randall with him. When he asked why he couldn't drive his car, Dominic told him he wanted Randall with him. The heat that had gone through him that time had nothing to do with embarrassment and everything to do with arousal, but he was too tired and stressed to do anything about it.

Dominic didn't leave Randall's side, even when they entered Randall's room at Windsor. He'd expected him to disappear to his own room but was extremely glad when he stayed. They settled into bed, with Dominic on his back and Randall resting his cheek on his chest, and fell into silence.

"I'm sorry," Dominic said.

Randall smacked his stomach and received laughter in return. "It's not your fault."

"Maybe not, but I'm still sorry."

"Let's try to sleep. We can continue this argument tomorrow."

Dominic pressed his lips to Randall's head. "Sleep well."

Randall smiled, but he didn't sleep. He listened to Dominic's breathing, noticing when it lengthened and deepened as he slept, but Randall stayed awake. Even when his arm was numb, and he had pins and needles in his side from staying in the same position, he stayed still, not wanting to disturb Dominic when he needed the rest. When Dominic moved position, Randall moulded himself around him when he settled again. He didn't want to be away from him because it was only when he was with him that he felt safe. And wasn't that something he needed to talk to Derek about?

Bleary-eyed and exhausted, he still smiled when Dominic roused and checked on him in the early hours of the next day.

"You didn't sleep?"

Randall shook his head. "Too many thoughts."

"You should've woke me." Dominic shuffled down the bed until they were eye-to-eye, and then he slid his arm around Randall's waist. "Are you okay?"

Randall exhaled. "Yes, and no. I'm...uneasy about what happened, but I'm glad you were there. If you hadn't been, I don't know what I would've done."

"You would've done what we did. Hid and called for help. I know you, Randall."

"It wasn't what I did when Ernest got to me."

Dominic tightened his hold. "That was a different scenario. It wasn't possible to run and hide in that situation. You adapt and move with the punches. That's all anyone can do."

Randall knew that, but it was hard to believe it. "I'm going to see if Derek can see me today."

"That's a good idea. I've been told it's good to talk things out."

Randall chuckled. "It is." He rubbed his nose against Dominic's. "I need to tell my family to stay away from the house for now and to watch out for anything unusual. Just in case this expands to them as well."

Dominic nodded. "I doubt they'll be involved, but it's good to keep them aware of their surroundings."

"What are you going to be doing today?"

"As you know, I have the day off." He winked. "Looking into what happened. Continuing to investigate May's situation. Oh, I forgot to tell you, we didn't get any DNA off the previous two roses, but we might get lucky with this one. You never know."

"I doubt that florist would have agreed to send another rose. I bet whoever sent it used someone else."

Dominic nodded. "Probably. I didn't look at the card." He slid closer. "Do you want to shower with me?"

Randall smiled, heat blooming. "I would love to."

An hour and a half later, Randall was as relaxed and loose as he had ever been. Dominic had gone to see Brett, and Randall held his phone, staring at Derek's number. He hated having to ask on a Monday morning, but he needed to talk to him.

"Randall? Is everything okay?" Derek asked when he answered.

"Yes and no," he repeated his words from earlier. "I'm sorry to bother you so early, but I wondered if you had time to see me?"

"Of course! When would you like to come?"

The idea of leaving the safety of Windsor sent shivers through him. "Actually, would you be able to come to Windsor Castle?" He'd already cleared it with Dominic and Brett.

"Sure. What time?"

"Whenever you can."

Derek hummed a little, something Randall had noticed he did when he was concentrating. "I can be there around ten o'clock if that's okay?"

"Perfect. Thank you. And sorry again for intruding on your Monday."

"It's absolutely fine, Randall. I'll see you in a couple of hours."

He messaged Portia, asking her to cover for him for a while.

What could he do for two hours? Derek often told him to try journalling, but he'd never liked the idea of writing down his feelings or thoughts. He'd seen and heard too many incidents of having those used against someone, and so he never had, but it might help organise his mind. He could always burn them later.

He grabbed a pad of paper and a pen and sat cross-legged on the bed. As he sat there, he felt stupid, but then he took a breath and started writing. At first, he detailed what had happened the day before. As he continued, the words poured out of him. Pages upon pages of words. When he finally stopped because his hand cramped, he hardly remembered a word of what he'd written. But one thing he did know...he felt lighter. Maybe there was something to this journalling after all.

A knock jolted him from his revelation, and his heart kicked up a gear. "Jeez, Randall. Bad guys won't knock. Get a grip," he muttered to himself as he climbed off the bed and answered the door.

Dominic and Derek waited for him. Randall smiled and invited them both in, but Dominic shook his head.

"I showed him the way. I won't stay."

Derek entered, and Randall stepped into the doorway, leaning up to kiss Dominic. "I'll see you later, right?"

Dominic smiled. "Nothing could keep me away. If you want to, either come find me when you're ready or message me, and I'll find you."

"Okay. Be careful."

"Always." Dominic kissed him again and strode off down the hallway. Randall closed the door and turned to Derek, who stood in the middle of the floor.

"Please, sit." He gestured to the chairs by the window. "Would you like something to drink?"

"No, I'm all good, thanks," Derek said as he sat. He pulled out a notepad and pen. "So, what's going on, Randall? I know you had to rearrange the appointment from Friday."

"To be honest, rearranging that appointment was only because my friend turned up on my doorstep unannounced. I wouldn't have made it in time." He chuckled as he made a tea for himself.

"I was planning on making another appointment this week, but last night…"

There were certain things he couldn't divulge to Derek, even with the confidentiality contract and an NDA. He would never take a chance like that, but he could talk about the incident in general.

"While Dominic and I were…busy at home last night, someone entered my home and left something for us to find. It's unnerved me." He sat opposite Derek, cradling his cup and inhaling the steam.

"I can imagine. I can tell you're leaving things out, but it might help to get it all out."

Randall gestured to the bed where his dishevelled notepad sat. "I've been writing for the last two hours. Journalling like you told me to. It has helped a little, but I still feel like I don't want to leave Windsor now. This place feels safe to me, even with what happened before."

"If someone violated your safety at your home, I'm not surprised. Did they catch whoever it was?"

"Not yet. They're working on it." Randall sighed. "It seems like it's part of a bigger situation that's happening. It's focused on someone else, but I'm on the edge of the…family if you like."

"Dominic's family?" Derek chuckled when Randall stared at him. "Dominic mentioned that something was happening with his family, and it seemed like you had been dragged into the situation because of your relationship with him."

Randall breathed easier, knowing Dominic had explained part of it. He hadn't wanted to give more information than Dominic would want him to, and it seemed Dominic had anticipated his struggle.

"Yes. It's not his fault or anyone from his family. It's the fault of whoever is doing it."

"That's right. How did you feel about the situation before the event from last night?"

Randall exhaled, trying to organise his thoughts into words Derek could understand. "Unsettled. I felt worried for the family, worried it might bleed into the royal family, worried it might not have anything to do with Dominic's family, but they were the ones suffering. So many thoughts."

"That's understandable. And have your feelings changed since last night?"

"Now, I'm scared. And angry. Whoever they were came into my house and ripped my security away. I can't go back there. I don't even want to leave Windsor Castle now."

"That is a common experience. It will ease with time and support. Do you have someone to go home with you when you first go back?"

Randall nodded. "I'm sure Dominic will. He mentioned getting additional security added to the house to make things easier for me."

"Good. Now, talk to me, Randall. What's worrying you most?"

Randall sipped his tea, delaying the answer that he'd acknowledged when he'd written his journal. "I'm worried Dominic won't want me if he thinks I'm going to be in trouble."

Derek nodded. "You're worried he's going to push you aside to keep you safe."

"Yes. I can understand why he would, but I don't want to be without him now we've found each other."

Derek smiled. "I don't think you'll have any problems with that."

"He's that type of person, though. He'll sacrifice himself to save others. It's why he's so good at his job."

"True. But I have the feeling he's also the type of person who'll keep everyone he holds dear close to him so he can protect them."

Randall thought about that. "He might," he said, though he wasn't completely convinced.

"He won't up and leave without talking to you, Randall. On that, I'm certain."

"How can you be so sure?"

"He told me."

Randall raised his eyebrows. "What?"

"He gave me permission to tell you this, so don't worry about me betraying confidences. As we were walking here, he said he had a feeling you would be worried about his plans, and he reassured me that no matter what happened, he wasn't letting you go without a fight. I have a feeling *he's* worried you'll push him aside." Derek winked. "I think you need to communicate, Randall. You're both scared about the same thing. You need to talk to each other and remove those worries so the things that really matter can be addressed."

Randall drank the rest of his tea, thinking that through. Adding worry upon worry about something that could be alleviated by talking it through with Dominic seemed silly now he thought about it. He inhaled and glanced at Derek, who was watching him closely.

"I'll talk to him."

"Good. Now, what else?"

Randall spent the next hour and a half talking through some other things that were circling in his head. There was no rhyme or reason for them, but he spoke them aloud, and Derek helped him to get perspective. By the time Derek left after booking another appointment for that week, Randall was exhausted. He sent a message to Dominic to tell him he was grabbing a nap and then collapsed onto the bed.

When he woke, he was cocooned in warmth, and he smiled into the pillow. "Hello."

Dominic pressed a kiss to his nape. "Hey. Did you sleep okay?"

"I did. What time is it?"

"Five-thirty."

"Oh, my god! I slept the day away. Poor Portia. I've left her all alone."

Dominic tightened his hold when Randall attempted to move. "It doesn't matter. You needed the rest. Nothing needs your attention at the moment, so relax. Portia has it all covered."

Randall turned over to face Dominic and settled back down. "How was your day?"

Dominic sighed. "Busy. We haven't had any DNA results back yet, but the note had the initial C on it."

"What do you think it means?"

"Well, thinking about the order they were received in. May had an A, my parents had a B, and you had a C. It sounds like they're putting you in order. A threat of what might happen." He shook his head. "There have also been a lot of comings and goings with Fletcher's gang. People we would prefer him not to be associating with."

"Like who?"

"Traffickers."

"You think he's going to try for May?"

Dominic swallowed hard. "Maybe." He sighed again. "If I'm honest, yes, I do. And if he gets her, there's no telling where she'll end up."

16

Dominic

Dominic sometimes wished he had more control over the king's calendar. He hadn't wanted to visit Edinburgh with Andrew, Kean and Kendal two days after the rose had been left in Randall's house, but he had a job to do. Being on high alert for the duration of their two-day visit would be tiring, and though they took shifts, it wasn't an easy assignment, which was why Andrew didn't schedule too many of them close to each other, thankfully. It also meant he was going to be tired for his date with Randall the following day. There was no way he was cancelling. No way.

The flight took around an hour and a half, which gave Dominic far too long to get worked up about the lack of progress from Commissioner Thomas's elected officers, Detective Addams and themselves. None of them had managed to find much other than Fletcher's gang was mixing with the wrong people—as usual. Commissioner Thomas was bringing in some of the gang members to get information from them under the illusion of asking them about their drug business. Dominic was hoping they could get some other information out of them, too.

"Everyone know what they're doing?" Dominic asked the team just before they headed out with the king to the first of the locations they were visiting during their time.

When he received nods and affirmations, he set them to their tasks. It was the same routine they'd always had—it had started when Simon had been their lead and Dominic hadn't felt the need to change most of it. A few things he'd tweaked, and they seemed to be working fine. The main thing was communication. If they didn't communicate, everything went to shit.

He inhaled and gave one lasting thought to those he cared about before pushing all thoughts of them aside so he could do his job without distractions.

The three events they had scheduled went off without a hitch, which was what he'd wanted—it's all they ever wanted—and they headed back to the Palace of Holyroodhouse, the official royal residence whenever the royal family stayed in Edinburgh. As with most of the royal residences, it was sizeable, but Andrew, Kean and Kendal rarely went further than their suite when they were there. It made Dominic's life a lot easier.

By the time he was in his suite, he was exhausted. He slumped onto the sofa, his head dropping to the back of it, and he had barely enough energy to pull his phone from his pocket.

RANDALL: *I hope you've had an easy-ish day. Think of me when you dream tonight. I'm looking forward to tomorrow. x*

Dominic's lips curved. His plans might surprise Randall, even with the little fish clue he'd given him. He hoped they could stay inconspicuous while they were there. It was not an easy feat when they were known by the public. They weren't famous by any means, but those who had seen them with the royal family would know who they were.

It was one reason he worried about having the bodyguard position in the first place. When Owen had put him forward for it, Dominic had tried to brush it off. Anyone who could dig deep enough—and the royal family had deep enough spades—would find what he'd done and cross him off the list quicker than he could say, King Andrew.

But they hadn't. They hadn't even brought it up in the interview process. No one had said a word to him about it, and he'd wondered if they'd even found it. He wasn't one to look a gift horse in the mouth, as his dad would say, so he hadn't mentioned it to anyone, thinking they'd bring it up if it was relevant. They never had. It had taken him a lot of courage to meet with Brett and explain his situation, and Brett had laughed at him. *Laughed at him.* Dominic had been gobsmacked.

"You think we didn't know?" Brett said, barely withholding another chuckle. "We've known even before Owen put you forward. We knew when Owen was employed. His interactions with you brought it to our attention."

Dominic stared at him. "But why...?"

"Because you were nineteen and stupid. Because you paid your dues. Because everyone deserves a second chance." Brett raised his eyebrows at him. "Bear in mind, though, if you hadn't had a clean record since that incident, you would've been kicked to the curb."

Dominic didn't know what to say. His heart raced as if he was training for a one-hundred-metre sprint, and he couldn't catch any of the snippets of thoughts swirling around his head.

Brett sighed and rounded the desk, settling his ass on the front of it and crossing his arms. "Look, Dominic. You are a good man. One stupid incident when you were a teenager is not something that should bring you down for the rest of your life."

"He wasn't so lucky," Dominic whispered, dropping his head.

Dominic had never told Randall what happened, but maybe now was the time. Face-to-face would have been better, but if he lost his courage, he wouldn't do it. And Randall deserved to know who he was in a relationship with.

He dialled, his heart racing as hard as it had been when he'd spoken to Brett.

"Hey, you. I wasn't expecting to hear from you tonight. Is everything okay?" Randall said, and Dominic could hear the smile in his voice, see it if he closed his eyes.

"Yeah, everything's fine. I was just sitting here, getting the energy to shower, and I realised I had never told you what I needed to." He sighed. "I always found an excuse to do something else rather than tell you about my past indiscretions."

"You don't have to tell me anything if you don't want to, but I'm here to listen if you do."

Dominic closed his eyes. "You're far too good for me, Randall. You should be pushing for answers so you know who you're sleeping with."

"I know who I'm sleeping with. A good man. A protector. A brother. A son."

Dominic swallowed past the lump in his throat that Randall's words created. "Someone who almost killed an innocent person."

Randall was quiet for a few seconds, and Dominic let that sink in. "Talk to me, Dominic."

"I was a teenager when I started getting interested in going to the gym, beefing up. I'd been teased as a child, and I wanted to be able to defend myself. Defend May if I had to." He exhaled long and quietly. "I overheard a couple of guys talking about a fight that was happening that weekend, and I figured out where it was taking place. I wanted to see what I'd learned in real-life action. Get an idea of how it would work should someone come at me."

He sighed. "I was so naïve. I sneaked in but got caught by the organiser, Ty. He let me stay and watch, though I wasn't allowed out of his sight. I didn't know why at that moment, but I was mesmerised. It was only after the fight finished that I realised it was an underground fighting ring, and Ty couldn't allow me to leave without giving me a few reasons to keep my mouth shut.

"He offered me a place to train, away from the gym. Real fight scenarios. I asked him time and again to have a go in the ring, but he wouldn't let me. Later, I found out he was keeping me hooked on what I couldn't get anywhere else. When I turned nineteen, he finally allowed me to fight. That first one was brutal, and I still have a scar on my neck from a stone I fell on. I won, though. And when he gave me my winnings, I couldn't resist the rush it gave me."

He fell silent, not knowing if he could get through the rest of the story. Randall didn't rush him. Dominic could hear him breathing on the other end of the line, and that gave him strength.

"I'd been fighting two or three times a week for about six months when I turned up for what I didn't know then was my last fight. I never knew who I'd be fighting until I turned up, so when a twenty-one-year-old guy wandered into the ring, I knew he'd be an easy takedown. And he was. He barely lasted five minutes, but the final punch that put him on the floor...broke his hip so badly he couldn't move. I found out at the hospital later that it severed his lower spinal cord. He was paralysed from the moment I struck him."

Randall's gasp hit his ears, and Dominic clenched the phone hard, curling onto his side on the sofa.

"What happened when he fell?" Randall asked.

"Ty told everyone to run, but I couldn't. I couldn't leave him there. Alone. I knew something was wrong because his legs weren't moving, and he was pulling himself forward with his arms. I called an ambulance and stayed with him. I wanted the doctors to know what happened so they could help him."

"There's that protector instinct."

Dominic huffed. "I didn't protect him. I destroyed his life. He uses a wheelchair to get around. He can't drive, can't walk, can't stand. I did that to him."

"I'd say you had only half the blame for that. He agreed to the fight."

"Yeah, but I hit him."

"How many times did he hit you during that fight?" Randall asked.

"A lot. He was quick but not as strong."

"Any one of those hits could've landed wrong, Dominic. And then you'd potentially be in the situation he is."

"Why are you defending me? I hurt someone. Put them in the hospital. Ruined their life."

"How do you know?"

Dominic frowned. "How do I know what?"

"That you ruined his life? Did you ask him?"

"God, no! The moment the police let me go, I left and never looked back."

"Rubbish. No, you didn't."

"What do you mean?"

Randall chuckled. "There is no way you left that hospital without saying anything to that guy."

Dominic licked his lips and wiped at his face, which was wet with tears he hadn't realised he'd shed. "How do you know?"

"I know you. You might've been a misguided teenager, but that incident would've moulded you into the start of who you are today. What did you do?"

Dominic paused. He'd never told anyone what he'd done. Not even Owen, Evan, his parents or May. Knowing Brett, he'd probably found out. "I emptied my savings and slid it into his bag at the hospital when no one was looking. I wrote him a note to say sorry."

"There's my Dominic."

Dominic's tears fell again. "I've lived a life of freedom while he's been stuck in a wheelchair."

"I think you'd be surprised at modern medicine. I'm sure he's not as stuck as you believe him to be."

"Maybe everything that's happening with May is fate making me pay for what I did."

"That's a load of shit," Randall spat. "If you were such a monster, you wouldn't have cared about the guy. Just like all those other assholes who ran away to save their own hides. You did the right thing."

"Maybe so, but it doesn't change that I hurt him."

"Yes, you did. But you also hurt yourself."

Dominic cleared his throat. "What do you mean?"

"If I know anything about you, it's that you would've closed yourself off from your family and friends. You would've made yourself suffer more than anyone else could've."

Randall wasn't wrong, and wasn't that a sign he was perfect for Dominic? "I spent two years in Scotland, training with someone who knew what I'd been through. He taught me restraint, resilience and respect. The three R's, he called them. It was only then I allowed myself to go home."

"Where you belonged."

"Why are you not horrified?"

"Because two of you entered that ring alive, and two of you left that ring alive. You learnt a valuable lesson and would suffer yourself before hurting another innocent person. You are not your nineteen-year-old self, Dominic. You're a protector. You always have been. You just had to find it in yourself."

Dominic didn't say anything. He couldn't. Hearing the way Randall saw him was too much for him, and he broke down. Something he had never done within hearing distance of anyone before.

When he finally calmed enough to hear and see properly again, he checked the phone to see Randall was still there.

"Dominic? Are you still there?"

"Yes," he croaked.

"You might not like me for this, but answer your door," Randall said.

Dominic shook his head, wiping at his face. "I can't. Not like this."

"You can. Trust me."

Dominic tried to make himself look presentable, but his face would show every tear streak and bloodshot eye. He climbed off the sofa and exhaled as he wandered to the door. He inhaled again and opened the door, his knees buckling when he saw who it was.

Owen and Evan enfolded him in their arms, and he broke again. This time around, he brought himself back because he knew he was the lead officer in charge and had to be on call. He settled further onto the sofa, where someone had guided him and stared through swollen, sore eyes at his best friends.

"What are you doing here?" he asked.

Owen chuckled. "Well, Christian decided to bring Oscar to Edinburgh as a surprise, so I had to tag along, and then this reprobate turned up on my doorstep as I was leaving. I thought it would be an awesome road trip surprise." He sniffed. "I didn't expect our arrival to be met with tears of joy."

Dominic shook his head and chuckled. "I'm assuming Randall called you." He glanced at his phone, which showed the call had ended. "I need to call him back."

"He said to tell you to call later when you're feeling up to it," Evan said.

Dominic stared at him. "How come you're here, anyway? I thought you were happy in Italy."

"I was. But I decided it was time to come home." He rolled his eyes. "Just in time for waterworks, I see."

"Fuck off," Dominic said.

Evan leaned forward. "On a serious note, though. Are you okay?"

Dominic sighed. "That's a loaded question if there ever was one. I am okay, yes. I was telling Randall about what happened with Diego. I couldn't keep it all in this time."

"It's about time. Have you ever let it out before?" Owen asked.

"When no one was around," Dominic said, not meeting their gazes.

"Stupid shithead," Evan said.

"I see Italy has done nothing for your language." Owen shook his head.

Evan leaned back and crossed his leg over his knee. "It's done plenty for my language. Just maybe not for the good. I can swear like a trooper in Italian now."

"Wonderful," Owen deadpanned. He turned to Dominic. "Brett has arranged for me to take over from you tomorrow if you're not feeling up to it. It's your call, though."

Dominic checked in with himself. Sometimes, the burden of carrying his sins was more than he could bear, but that evening, he was feeling lighter than he had in so long. After some sleep, he thought he would be fine, and he said so.

"Well, I'll be here, anyway."

"Thanks." He glanced at Evan. "Thanks to you both. You couldn't have come at a better time."

They spent the evening talking about what happened—properly, this time—and then reminiscing about what they used to get up to as kids. Evan told them about the people he'd met in Italy and how, despite him having lived there for seven years, it had never felt like home to him. Hence his return. Dominic hoped the man would find whatever it was he was looking for because some of the spark was missing as if it was trying to be snuffed out.

When Owen and Evan left in the early hours of the morning, Dominic sent a message of thanks to Randall and requested for him to call him in the morning, no matter the time.

But it wasn't Randall who woke him. It was Owen and Evan…by water bombing his bed.

"You fucking assholes!" he shouted, standing by his bed, dripping wet. "I'm sure the palace staff are going to love having to clean this up. Maybe I should tell them to make you two do it."

Owen held up his hands, waving him away. "We had permission."

"From who?" Dominic yelled.

"THE KING!" Evan and Owen shouted as they ran out of the room, the slamming of his suite door ringing through the space.

"Imbeciles," Dominic muttered as his phone rang. "Hey, sweetheart. How are you today?"

"I would ask the same, but Owen just messaged me to say you might be grumpy this morning. Any reason why?"

Despite his bedraggled appearance, the smile on his face wouldn't quit. "The assholes, pardon my language, water bombed me while I was sleeping."

There was a beat of silence before stifled laughter came through. "Oh, god, Dominic. I can just imagine what you three used to get up to."

"Oh, you really couldn't," Dominic said and proceeded to tell a few stories about his friends, and when Randall's open laughter rang through the line, his smile widened.

It was going to be a good day.

17

Owen

Owen paused at the end of the corridor, holding his sides and laughing at their antics. He hadn't thought to do anything like this since he started working for the royal family, but Evan had reminded him how much fun it was. Of course, being reasonable and sensible, Owen had asked Andrew if it was okay to make a mess of the place, and after explaining why it was necessary, the king had readily agreed.

"I truly wasn't expecting you to go through with it," Evan said, panting from their sprint.

"If it had been for any other reason than what it was, I probably wouldn't have." He sighed. "We need to do something to help him. He can't keep going like this."

"I think Randall's helping." Evan leaned against the wall and rested his head back, the long column of his neck exposed to the air.

Owen swallowed and looked away. "He is, yes. We should've done something sooner. I never realised he hadn't let it out. Not properly. Twenty years of holding all that in must be..."

"Hell?" Evan supplied, and Owen nodded.

"I know it's how he works, but still."

Evan pushed away from the wall and headed down the corridor. "It's far too early for this," he said, yawning. "I need more coffee."

Owen followed him through the maze and to the kitchen, where the staff were already elbow-deep in making breakfast for the soon-to-be-rising household. The property was still a royal residence; therefore, staff were all over the place, but it wasn't as strict as with Windsor Castle. The security staff were allowed to help themselves to food and drink whenever they wanted to. At Windsor, the staff preferred to do everything, even serve the guards. Owen wasn't sure which he liked best. He'd never turn away the chance for someone else to do the cooking, but grabbing his coffee whenever he wanted was a bonus.

When they both held mugs of the steaming nectar of coffee addicts, they headed for the gym. Despite Dominic's penchant for choosing karate and tai chi instead of boxing, Owen and Evan still "fought" regularly now Evan was back home. Where he belonged. Where he'd always belonged.

He would never admit to grieving for the loss of one of his best friends aloud, but alone, he could flay himself alive for his past mistakes. The main one was letting Evan leave when all he wanted to do was pull him into his arms again and never let go.

Unfortunately, his younger, stupider self had ruined the chances of that.

"Best of ten?" Evan said once they were padded up.

Owen nodded, pushing everything else aside other than thoughts of whipping Evan's butt at boxing. And if thoughts of whipping in a different scenario floated through his mind, he ignored them.

After forty-five minutes, sweat-soaked them, and they were breathing as if their lungs were on fire. A cold shower helped, and even though he told himself not to, he ogled his best friend whenever he wasn't looking.

Dominic's issue was far more serious, but Owen had a pretty big issue, too. One that wasn't jetting back to Italy any time soon.

Which was great news.

And terrible news.

Because how the hell could Owen keep pretending he'd not made the biggest mistake of his life when the one person who knew about it was with him every day?

18

Randall

R andall was excited about the date that afternoon. He'd already cleared it with Andrew that he could have the afternoon off. Andrew being Andrew waved him away, saying they would be exhausted from the trip back from Edinburgh anyway, so he might as well get some long-earned time off. Randall didn't see it that way, but he wasn't going to argue. He hadn't been sure if Dominic wanted to keep the date because of their conversation from the previous evening, but the light-hearted laughter of their phone call that morning had eased his worries.

Dominic had insisted on it being a proper date, so Randall finished work at noon and headed to his Windsor room to shower and change before Dominic "picked him up." He threw far too many outfits onto his bed—how had so many clothes made their way from his house?—before deciding on something simple—a dark purple polo shirt and black trousers. Then he paced the room, holding the fish and waiting for the knock on his door.

Where were they going? If they were going fishing, he was wearing the wrong clothes, but it didn't matter if they got wet or muddy; they'd clean. But if they weren't going fishing, what else did the fish signify? Sushi? He'd never had it, but he'd be willing to try it. The beach? They were a long way from the seaside. Maybe down to the river?

A knock interrupted his musings, and his heart galloped as he went to answer it.

"Hey. You look great," Dominic said with a smile.

"Thanks. You do, too."

It eased his mind that Dominic was dressed similarly to what he wore. While it didn't rule out fishing, it was less likely.

"Are you ready?" Dominic asked. Randall nodded, having already put his phone and wallet in his pockets. "Great. Let's go." He stepped back, allowing Randall to exit the room. "Oh, I brought another clue."

Dominic handed him another fish, this time a different type. The first had been a clownfish, whereas the new one was an angelfish. Randall frowned.

"I'm no good at puzzles," he said with a self-deprecating chuckle.

"You don't need to be. You'll find out soon." Dominic took Randall's hand and slid it under his arm so they were linked. Randall's cheeks heated, and he ducked his head, hiding his smile.

"I'm looking forward to this, even if I have no idea where we're going," Randall said.

They passed several people on their journey, each smiling at them, and Randall's head lifted further each time. Dominic wanted him. He didn't mind parading him down the corridors of Windsor, didn't care who saw them. It was freeing in a way Randall had never expected to feel.

Dominic opened his car door for him and closed it after Randall had climbed in. When they were on their way, Dominic asked, "How was your morning?"

"Busy." He chuckled. "That's my rote answer. It's never not busy. I wasn't sure if you were going to cancel the date," he admitted. "You've had a stressful couple of days."

Dominic inhaled and exhaled slowly. "It's been a tough couple of days. Hell, make that a tough couple of *weeks*. Everything has been up in the air, and I haven't known if I was coming or going." He glanced over at Randall before returning his gaze to the road. "But having you there, supporting me, believing in me, being there for me has been...everything."

Randall couldn't contain his smile. "There's nowhere else I'd rather be than right beside you."

Dominic took one hand from the wheel and reached for his hand, threading their fingers together. "Same."

"Are you going to tell me where we're going yet?" Randall asked.

Dominic chuckled. "Not happening. You'll have to wait. I will tell you we're going to London."

Randall brightened. He loved London, though he would never live there full-time. "And it has something to do with fish."

"It does."

Randall wasn't getting anything else out of him, so he changed the subject. "How are your parents?"

Dominic smiled. "Wishing they could see May again, but we don't want to chance them visiting Windsor Castle again so soon. Once could be brushed off as a visit. Twice could make someone look closer, especially as they haven't visited before."

Randall nodded. "I can understand that. Changes in routine are always red flags."

"Exactly."

"Could we engineer something so they could meet? I'd been thinking about asking if I could take May to Book Drunk."

Dominic sighed. "I'd love to say yes, but I'm not sure. We haven't noticed anyone observing the castle more than usual, but that doesn't mean they haven't been there, and we just haven't seen them. It's unlikely but not impossible." He tapped his thumb against Randall's hand. "I hate keeping her inside all the time, but I don't know what else to do to keep her safe."

"She understands, Dominic. She doesn't mind."

"I know she does. But what kind of life is this for her? She can't stay cooped up forever."

"She's willing to stay for as long as you think it's necessary. She's happy to be able to see and speak to you."

"It's still not fair, and it's all those assholes' faults. That gang needs taking apart."

Dominic took his hand back to concentrate on the road, and Randall used the time to go through everything he'd been told about May's case, which admittedly wasn't as much as he'd found out by himself.

The case had been dependent on May's testimony, and she'd made it without a quiver of doubt from what he'd seen. The gang members had been out for blood for weeks while the case was on, and May had been given protective security to keep her alive. Twice, she'd had a close encounter and had ended up in hospital, but it had seemed to spur her on all the more. The news reports of the case were full of opinions, both good and bad, but most gave her the credit she deserved for taking on such a gang—and winning. Unfortunately, it had made her a target, and she'd had to go into witness protection. It was either that or she would look over her shoulder for the rest of her life. Which was where she was now. They needed to get rid of the gang, once and for all, so May could live the quiet life she deserved.

Dominic parked the car in a long-stay parking garage and opened Randall's door for him. Then he took his hand and tugged him in the direction he wanted them to go. Their easy conversation took them through the streets, and when Randall spotted a sign for the aquarium, he had to withhold his squeal.

He couldn't have been completely blasé about it because Dominic chuckled.

"I take it you like the aquarium?"

Randall gaped at him. "*Like* the aquarium? I *love* aquariums. I've always thought about getting one for home, but as I'm hardly there, it seemed pointless."

"You'd still see them, even if you're only there for a short time."

Randall considered and dismissed the idea. "It wouldn't be worthwhile."

"I'll just have to bring you here more often."

They entered the white brick building amidst the tourist crowds, but Randall didn't care. They received some lingering looks, but whether that was because they were a gay couple or because they were the king's staff, he would never know. The brightly lit glass immediately took his eyes, behind which multitudes of fish swam. His feet took him in that direction, and he followed the path of the multi-coloured swimmers.

A hand at his back pulled him from his observations, and Dominic smiled at him. "Shall we see more?"

Randall nodded. As they weaved their way through the paths laid out by the aquarium's designer, they transfixed him with every step. Through glass tunnels where fish swam above them, to glass floors where they swam beneath them, to little glass domes which he could stick his head into and view a three-hundred-and-sixty-degree view of the landscape. It was one of the best experiences he had ever had.

Dominic paused their viewing so they could sit and have a snack and a drink, and Randall couldn't stop talking about what he'd seen. By the end of the visit, his cheeks were aching so much from how much he'd smiled.

"Thank you so much," he said as they walked back to the car.

Dominic slid his arm around Randall's shoulders. "You're very welcome. I'm glad I picked well."

"I don't think you could've picked better. I didn't consider the aquarium when you gave me the fish. I thought of fishing or sushi or the beach."

"Even though you love the aquarium?"

Randall nodded. "It never occurred to me that someone might bring me here. It's aimed at children, after all."

Dominic chuckled. "If it was aimed at children, there wouldn't be viewing pods at adult's height."

Randall considered that. "That's true."

They wandered in silence until they reached the car, and Dominic caged him against it, lowering his head to nuzzle at his neck. Randall's eyelids fluttered closed. "Where would you like to go now?"

Randall didn't hesitate. "I want you to meet my parents."

Dominic lifted his head. "Are you sure?"

Randall nodded. "I want them to see how amazing you are."

Dominic kissed him. "If that's your wish, show me the way."

During the ride, they talked about anything and everything, though they stayed away from the topics that would bring their joy down. When they parked outside his parents' house, he had a momentary blip of worry, but he pushed it down. It wasn't a Sunday, so they wouldn't be expecting him, but they were hardly likely to turn him away, especially when he had someone to introduce.

He grabbed Dominic's hand to walk up the driveway and knocked on the door. He heard his mother's less than quiet mutterings about cold callers as she came towards the door, and he smiled.

"Randall! I wasn't expecting you." Her gaze flitted to Dominic and then down to their joined hands. "I see we have someone to meet. Come on in." She left the door open for them and shuffled down the hallway towards the kitchen.

Randall pulled Dominic into the house and closed the door. "Too late now," he murmured with a grin.

Dominic lifted his eyebrows. "I wouldn't want to be anywhere else."

Randall's mouth twitched. "You might change your mind when you get the third degree."

"They can ask me whatever they want."

When they entered the kitchen, his mother was boiling the kettle. "Tea or coffee?" she asked.

"Coffee, please," Dominic answered.

"Take a seat. It'll be ready in a moment."

They settled on one side of the table, and Randall kept hold of Dominic's hand. He wasn't worried per se about his parents' reaction to Dominic, but he wasn't sure of their reaction either. Rose was set in her ways and had certain things she wanted for her kids. Ryan and Rae had already fitted their lives into her expectations, and Randall had been trying to do the same. He couldn't see anything wrong with his relationship with Dominic, and he hoped his parents didn't either.

Rose set a coffee in front of Dominic and a tea in front of Randall. "I'll get your father." She shuffled out of the kitchen, her arthritis having become more painful as the years wore on. She refused to stop her charity work, though.

"She's a woman of few words," Dominic said.

Randall couldn't help it. He burst out laughing, covering his mouth with his hand. It took him several long seconds to get himself under control, and he whispered, "You just wait."

"I just remembered that your siblings are called Ryan and Rae. Any reason for the 'R' names?"

"I like things to match, young man," Rose said as she re-entered the kitchen with Randall's father behind her. "If I could've changed Wade's name to something beginning with R, I would have."

Randall sucked in his cheeks, trying not to laugh again, but he couldn't stop the smile.

"That sounds reasonable," Dominic agreed.

Rose and Wade settled opposite them, and Randall was suddenly nervous.

"Aren't you going to introduce us?" Rose asked.

"Ah, yes. Mum, Dad, this is Dominic. Dominic, my parents, Rose and Wade."

Dominic reached a hand across the table to shake hands with his father. "Nice to meet you, Mr and Mrs Metcalfe."

Wade waved him away. "Just Wade and Rose. Don't stand on ceremony."

"Thank you. You have a lovely home."

Rose's expression lightened at the words, and she said, "It's the perfect house for growing kids." Her gaze shuttered a little. "It's a little too big for just the two of us now, though."

Randall stared at them. "Are you thinking of moving?"

Rose glanced at Wade. "Possibly. We need to let someone else have the joy of this house now."

Randall looked around them, and memories swarmed in. The window seat in the dining room that overlooked their garden, in which he'd spent many hours reading. His bedroom, where he'd had his big coming out reveal to himself. The living room where they'd spent many birthdays and Christmases opening presents and celebrating the good times.

Dominic squeezed his hand, bringing his attention back to the conversation. Dominic was talking to his parents about his job—as much as he could anyway—and Randall appreciated his frank words about what he could and couldn't talk about.

"Would you like to stay for dinner?" Rose asked, standing. "There will be plenty. The slow cooker is busy creating chilli as we speak."

Dominic glanced at Randall with a hungry expression—nothing to do with the bedroom, unfortunately—and Randall shrugged and nodded. "We'd love to," he said.

"Wonderful. Why don't you settle in the living room with your father and I'll finish up. It'll be around half an hour."

"Would you like any help?" Dominic asked, and Randall saw the moment he won more brownie points.

"Thank you for the offer, but I'm fine." Rose went to the counter and busied herself while they rose and headed for the living room, leaving her to her domain.

"Football or boxing, dear boy?" Wade asked once they were sitting again.

Randall saw Dominic flinch, but he answered, "Football. Although if there were other choices, I'd choose darts."

"Darts?" Randall asked, surprised.

Dominic smiled. "I'm pretty good."

"Well, it just so happens we have a dartboard in the back room. Maybe we can have a game after dinner," Wade said.

"Sounds good."

And just like that, Dominic had integrated himself with Randall's parents with an ease Randall had never expected. He should've, though. Dominic was an amazing person, and he would do anything for anyone should they just ask.

As he watched his father and his boyfriend play darts after dinner, he realised he'd fallen in love. Maybe he had always been in love with Dominic, but it was that clearly defined moment that made it crystal clear in his mind.

He was in love with Dominic.

And he was so scared he would lose him.

Two hours later, they were on their way back to Windsor, and Randall couldn't help teasing Dominic about sucking up to his parents.

"Maybe, but there is definitely something else I'd prefer to suck." Dominic glanced at him, and Randall felt the heat go through him.

"I'm sure that could be arranged," he whispered, ignoring the way his cock pressed against his trousers.

"It won't be arranged. It'll happen the moment we're behind closed doors. Whether that's yours or mine is up to you."

Randall said nothing and allowed Dominic to lead the way. He could've walked him straight into a snake pit, and Randall would've been none the wiser. His brain was lost in the images of them coming together, and his arousal soared with every step.

When the door slammed, Dominic shoved him against the wall and devoured him. There was no other word for it. Randall lost track of everything but wherever Dominic touched him. The tingling warmth where his fingers brushed his skin. The blistering heat where his lips pressed. The scorching inferno as his mouth closed around his cock.

And then nothing but pure pleasure tinted with a bite of pain as Dominic brought him to the edge over and over without letting him fall.

"Please, Sir! Please! Please!" he chanted, banging his head against the wall as Dominic released him from the edge once more.

"Once you're done with this, I have a cock cage with your name on it. I want you on the edge with your mind on me every minute of the day."

As Dominic swallowed him down again, Randall knew there was no problem with that because his mind was already on him in every spare second he got. All he needed to do was stop working, and his brain flew to Dominic, wishing they were together.

And then his thoughts disappeared because his master took him over the edge, flying him into a starlit sky of release.

After he returned to earth, Dominic swung him into his arms and carried him into the bedroom. Once he was lying on the bed, Dominic opened the drawer and pulled out a cock cage. "I've been waiting to use this on you. I think now is a pretty good time, don't you?"

Dominic posed it as a question, but it wasn't. Randall nodded. "Yes, Sir. Please, Sir."

The sensitivity of his cock as Dominic fitted the cock cage made him squirm, but when it finally clicked shut, there was a sense of relief. No more did Randall have to worry about his releases. That was Dominic's domain now. All Randall had to think about was obeying Dominic's orders.

And wasn't that the most freeing feeling of all?

19

Dominic

After two days of blissful peace, everything came crashing down around Dominic's ears. First, there was a news article about Dominic and Randall's date, with photos of them at the aquarium. Then Addams turned up. Again.

"Are you suggesting what I think you're suggesting, Addams?" He stared at the detective, pushing the man to repeat what he'd said.

Addams sighed and rubbed a hand over his face. "I don't like this any more than you do. But the fact is, the line of questioning by the officers led them to believe that May took something the gang said was theirs."

"And what is that 'something?'"

Addams didn't back down this time. "Drugs."

"No way! May would never touch the stuff."

"I'm not saying she's using or supplying it, Dominic, but they say she has it. And I need to speak with May about it. Without you getting all possessive about it."

Dominic ran a hand through his hair. "There is no way she's involved."

"Then we don't have anything to worry about, do we?"

As much as he hated the idea that May had anything to do with the drugs that the gang dealt, he had to admit Addams was right. They needed to know for certain.

"She knows you're here to speak to her. We can go now."

Addams nodded. "Thank you."

They headed towards May's room, and Evan met them at the door. Addams raised his eyebrows.

"You remember Evan Montgomery?" He said nothing more as he knocked and entered when May called for him to. Evan followed them in, and Dominic didn't stop him, even when he settled beside May and reached for her hand. He and Owen were as protective of her as Dominic was. Dominic stood to the side and crossed his arms while Addams took the seat opposite May.

"I'm sorry to bother you again, May, but I have further questions for you."

"It's okay. Go ahead."

It was hard not to notice the white-knuckled grip she had on Evan's hand, and even Evan frowned down at it.

"There has been some speculation about a haul of drugs that supposedly never made it to its destination. During the interviews with Fletcher's gang members, they pointed the finger at you. Can you tell me anything about it?"

May shook her head, staring at Addams with a slight frown. "I don't know anything about it. I never had anything to do with the drugs they were pushing. The minute I knew Paul was in with them, that's when I got the police involved."

Dominic's heart pounded, and he wished Addams was gone.

Because May had just lied.

"Did you hear anything about drugs being missing during your involvement?"

May sat straighter. "I wasn't *involved* with them. I was gaining evidence, as the police requested. I didn't touch anything. It was just about the intel."

Addams nodded and closed his notebook. "Okay, thank you." He stood. "That's all I needed."

If that was all he needed, why had he driven over when it could have been done over a phone call? Dominic nodded, hugged his sister and headed back down the hallway with Addams. He waited, knowing Addams would say something.

"Personally, I think the gang is just trying to get the heat off their backs by pointing the finger at May, but I have to follow up on it."

"I know." He didn't have to like it.

Addams held out his hand. "Thanks for escorting me."

"Anytime."

He watched Addams leave and then headed back to his sister. When he was within reach, he heard raised voices and paused.

"—you hiding, May? I don't believe they were pointing the finger at you just for shits and giggles," Evan said. "What aren't you telling us?"

"Nothing!" May shouted. "I've told you everything!"

"Don't forget that we've all known you since you were a baby. You've never been good at hiding things. Not from us."

At that, Dominic entered the room. "He's right."

May swung around. "You're all paranoid. I've done nothing."

Dominic just stared at her, waiting her out. May threw her hands up in the air and opened her mouth, but Evan's hand closed around it, startling her. He put his other finger to his mouth and let go of May. Dominic frowned as Evan dropped to his knees by the sofa Addams had been sitting on. Evan pulled at something under the table and held it up. A little black device that had a red pulsing light.

The same kind of device that Paul had planted by Dominic's doorbell.

"Okay. I believe you. It must just be the gang trying to clear their name." Dominic rolled his fingers in a "keep talking" movement.

"I wouldn't put it past them to lie about everything," May said, and Dominic glared at her. She shrugged.

Evan handed the bug to Dominic. "Let me take her for a walk in the gardens to cool off. We can talk more about this later when tempers are not so fraught."

"Fraught?" Dominic mouthed, rolling his eyes. "Good idea. I'll visit the security room to see if Brett has any more information. Let me just grab this first." He picked up a metal sugar canister and, apologising silently to the household staff, tipped the contents onto the tray. He gently attached the bug to the inside. He kept the lid off for now and said, "Right, come on. Get some fresh air."

He opened the door, and everyone filed out. The moment he closed the door, he put the lid on the sugar canister and sighed. Keeping his voice low, just in case, he said, "Go for that walk. See if you can't knock some sense into her." He kissed May's cheek and pivoted towards Sec HQ.

When he knocked and entered, he held up a finger to his mouth, and the room fell silent. He held the canister out to Felix and mouthed, "Another bug."

Felix nodded and grabbed it, taking it to the same computer he'd used for the last one. Everyone kept still and quiet while he worked; the only sound was the occasional click of the computer. Dominic moved closer, watching him work. Seven minutes later—yes, he counted—Felix reached a hand out, and Brett put a glass of water in his hand. As before, Felix dropped it inside.

"Done. It's going to somewhere on St Alban's Street."

Dominic sighed. "Just down the road. I bet it'll lead to Addams."

"Where did you find it?"

"Evan found it under May's coffee table when Addams left. I don't know how long it's been there."

"Not long," Felix said. "The battery life on that one was minimal. Maybe twenty-four hours."

"So he just planted it." Dominic shook his head. "Why?"

"To catch May out if she spoke candidly to you?" Brett said. "I'm surprised at him, though. He could lose his job if we take this further. Bugging Windsor Castle. He'd be thrown from the window before anyone blinked."

"I'm not sure what his game is. Something isn't sitting right. How come he's doing all the investigating and questioning when Commissioner Thomas's officers are interviewing suspects? I know he was involved with May's case five years ago, but surely, this is different now?"

"I'll look into him for you. See if we can find out what his endgame is. Maybe he just wants the case closed so he can go back to his mundane life," Felix said with a chuckle.

"Maybe," Brett said, but Dominic could see he didn't agree. Dominic wasn't sure he did either. "What was he asking about this time?"

"A haul of drugs. It went missing at the same time as May's testimony. He thinks she had something to do with it."

"And you think...?" Brett stared him down.

Dominic stared back. "She's not being truthful." He couldn't lie to them. Not when they were helping him and when he had the royal family to think of.

"You think she was involved?"

"Not with the gang, no. And I doubt she would use or sell drugs. But if she had access to some, she might dispose of it to put a middle finger up to the gang."

"Smart idea," Felix said. "Do you think that's what she's done?"

Dominic shrugged. "I really don't know, but I intend to find out." He headed for the door. "I'll speak to her after my shift."

Brett waved at him. "I'll find cover. Go sort this now. It's important."

Dominic nodded. "Thanks."

"Take this with you." Felix threw something towards him, and he caught it. "It's a signal jammer. Use it whenever you're talking about stuff you don't want overheard."

He thanked him and headed towards the gardens, finding May and Evan sitting on a step, talking. He stayed back until Evan waved him forward. He switched on the jammer as he settled beside them.

"I have a signal jammer with me. It's not perfect, but it might help."

"May has something to tell you," Evan said.

"I assumed she would have. May?"

She sighed. "The missing drugs?" She met his gaze. "I hid them."

Dominic closed his eyes and shook his head. "May. Do you realise how much trouble you're in? What happened?"

She leaned forward, resting her elbows on her knees. "When the police came to arrest Paul, he told me to stash the car. He wouldn't tell me why; just told me not to look in it." She smirked. "Me being me, I found the drugs. I already knew what I was going to do once Paul had been arrested, but that solidified things. I wasn't naïve. I knew they'd come after me when I testified, so I hid it and used it as blackmail."

"Bloody hell, May!" Dominic said.

"When they came after me for testifying, I told them I would return their drugs if they left me alone. At the time, I had no idea how much it was worth."

"How much?"

"One million street value."

"Fucking hell! You've been sitting on one million pounds worth of drugs for five years! Where have you been hiding it?"

"It's safe."

"You need to tell us," Dominic said.

May shook her head. "If I do, they won't need me."

Dominic slid his arm around her shoulders, pulling her close. "They won't get you, May."

She sniffed. "They didn't leave me alone, so I never told them where it was."

"So this is why they've been looking for you after all this time. I thought it was revenge, but they want their drugs back." Dominic exhaled. "How did they get their hands on so much?"

"That I don't know," May said. "Paul didn't have time to explain. And he obviously didn't mention it to the police at the time."

"Okay, let's forget about it for now. I'm turning the jammer off in case someone needs me." He switched it off, and almost immediately, his phone rang. "Hello?"

"It's Addams. Fletcher Pinton is dead."

"You bring me happy news, Detective. Thank you."

Addams huffed a laugh. "Maybe so, but the new leader is out for blood, not tears."

"What do you mean?"

"If you think what Fletcher was doing was bad, you wait until you've met Carlos. He doesn't want anything but the deaths of those who he perceives have wronged them. There's no jury or trial with him. It's execution first and questions later. That is unless he can sell someone for more money."

"Fuck. Did Carlos kill him?"

"We don't know. I've just been notified that Fletcher's body was found in an alley. I don't have more details yet."

"Can you let me know when you do?"

"Of course."

The call ended, and Dominic sighed. "Chop the head off the Hydra, and three more replace it," he muttered.

"What's wrong?"

"Fletcher is dead."

May brightened. "It's over?"

Dominic snorted. "No. Apparently, it's just beginning." He explained what Addams had told him. "I need to get back to Brett again. Evan, can you keep her company for a while longer?"

"Sure thing. We still have that movie marathon to start," he said, bumping shoulders with her.

"Thanks." He caught May's chin. "We'll figure this out. I promise."

"I know you will."

He stood. "You are going to have to tell me eventually, you know."

May nodded. "I know."

He jogged up the steps and all the way to Sec HQ. "Have you heard?" he asked when he entered.

"Fletcher Pinton is dead. Carlos has risen," Brett said.

"Do you know anything about Carlos?"

Brett shook his head. "Felix is still searching, but so far, nothing has come up. We don't even have a last name for him."

"I wonder if he was the one who had something to do with Yousef's death."

"What makes you think that?"

Dominic leaned against a table and crossed his arms. "Something about what Addams said. 'He's out for blood, not tears.' Torturing someone sounds more bloody than what Fletcher was capable of, now I think about it."

"So, Carlos has been working outside of what Fletcher wanted, maybe?" Felix said.

"We have to keep May safer now than ever. Carlos will attempt to sell her if he gets to her." He explained about the hidden drugs.

"Brave but stupid," Brett said. "We need to know where they are. We might need them as a bargaining tool."

Dominic shook his head. "She won't give it up unless she believes they won't want her anymore. She thinks she would be able to talk her way out of it if she's the only one who knows where it is."

"Talk to Carlisle Police. That detective on the case of the shooting at May's house. They might have something they don't even realise they have. And talk to Addams. I want to see Yousef's case files."

Dominic nodded. "I'll get on it."

He chose a desk and settled in, working on finding the information he needed from the different sources. Addams agreed to send Yousef's files over to him, saying he'd love a second pair of eyes on it. But it was when he called Carlisle Police that he paused.

"He's what?"

"Detective Maloney was found dead yesterday from a self-inflicted gunshot wound to the head. The medical examiner estimated the time of death as being four days ago."

"And nobody found him before yesterday?"

"He'd taken a week's holiday," the detective snapped. "We're not miracle workers."

Dominic winced. "I apologise. I didn't mean to sound callous."

The detective sighed. "No, I'm sorry. Emotions are running high. Maloney was a good guy. None of us saw his struggles."

"And it was definitely self-inflicted?"

The detective fell silent before saying, "You think otherwise? Because I'll gladly keep the case open if this was foul play."

"Honestly? I don't know. But something seems off. Can you keep the case open for a few days until I have more thoughts on it?"

"I can give you two days, but then I'll need to close it unless you have something for me."

"Thanks, Detective."

Dominic ended the call and let his brain follow the trails as if it were following breadcrumbs. He needed to talk this out. "Brett? Have you got a minute?"

"Actually, no. Christian is due to go out. What do you need?"

"A sounding board."

"Owen? Or Colt? Or Nick?"

"Okay, thanks."

"Fill me in when I get back," Brett said, exiting the room.

Dominic called Owen. "Are you busy?"

"Not now. Just got back from the event with Freddie. Locke is taking the first shift."

"Can you come to the briefing room? I need your help." He called in Nick, too.

Within minutes, Owen, Nick and Dominic were sitting around a table while Dominic outlined what he'd found. When he started throwing in other titbits of information, Nick stood and cleared the whiteboard, writing down everything Dominic said. Once all the pieces of information were on the board, they started hashing it out.

Owen rested his ass on the desk. "So, Yousef is dead, Maloney is dead, and Fletcher is dead. Carlos has taken over and is trigger-happy, Paul is in the wind, and Gavin is still locked up. The gang has been observed hanging with traffickers and drug suppliers, and they are known for selling said drugs. Addams has not been any help in figuring out who, specifically, is after May. Carlisle Police can't figure out what May said she saw at her house, and they don't know who killed Maloney yet. No one is bothered about who killed Fletcher, but the best guess is it's this Carlos guy who no one knows anything about. How am I doing?"

Dominic groaned. "That about sums it up."

"There is one thing that links all of these together," Nick said.

"What's that?"

Nick raised his eyebrows. "Who, you mean. May."

"She doesn't have anything to do with these deaths."

Nick crossed his arms. "I'm not saying she did them. I'm saying she's the only thing linking them together that we can see. We need to figure out what else links them. Let's go through each one and see where May fits in, and then we can add in anyone else who is in the peripheral. That's the only way we're going to find who else is involved."

Dominic sighed and rubbed his hands over his face. "You're right. Sorry."

Owen squeezed his shoulder. "We'll figure this out. Hopefully, before Malachi Sanders prints any more mistruths." He rolled his eyes.

"Let's start at the beginning. Tell us about May's relationship with Paul and the case," Nick said, settling into a chair with a notebook and pen.

Both Dominic and Owen gave him as much information as they could remember, and then they poured over the case files from Addams. They worked forward, making notes to track where individual people were on certain days and years, depending on where their thoughts went. They worked through May being found and calling Dominic, the roses, and up to the present day.

It took them seven hours to work through it, and when it was done, the whiteboard looked like a spiderweb.

"I think we need to visit Gavin," Owen said.

Dominic nodded. Why not ask the man who was at the centre of the case five years ago? Maybe he was orchestrating this entire thing from prison.

"Let's go."

"Hold up," Brett called from across the room, the man having returned during their discussion. "I just got a call from Carlisle

Police. Two men have been pulled from the River Eden. It sounds like the men May described from the car."

"So that makes five fatalities. All surrounding May's case. I don't like those odds," Dominic said.

"Me either," Brett said. "See what Gavin has to say. If nothing else, he might have information on Carlos."

20

Randall

When Dominic told Randall he was going to visit the gang leader in prison, his first thought was concern. Despite knowing there would be security guards and that Dominic was more than capable of looking after himself, he hated the idea of him being in there if something went wrong. But he pulled up his big boy pants and ignored his trust issues. Trust of other people, that was. Not Dominic.

Instead, he spent the few hours he could with him before he had to leave early the following morning. A few blissful hours.

"That's it, sweetheart. You can do this," Dominic crooned.

Randall panted to the ceiling as sweat poured off his skin. He tugged at the ties roped around his wrists and squirmed against the tethers around his ankles, spreading him out for Dominic's use. His cock gallantly twitched as the vibrations in his ass increased, but the cock cage prevented him from coming, sending glorious tingles of pain through his groin.

His lover had taken him as close to the edge as he could more times than Randall could count after two hours, and his body was on the brink of exhaustion, but somehow, Dominic kept him suspended and in need.

"Just one more for me." Dominic nibbled at his nipples, laving his tongue over the tips as they ripened for his use. "That's it. Almost there."

The vibrations increased further, and Randall bucked against his restraints. "Please, Sir!"

Dominic rose to his knees, his hand leaving his ass and the butt plug. "Tiny bit more, sweetheart." His fingers fiddled with the cage enclosing Randall's cock, and hope blossomed in his chest. Would he be allowed to come now?

Dominic's hand returned to the plug, and the vibrations increased again, shooting a mix of pleasure and pain throughout Randall's body. As he neared the edge once more, his ragged voice tore through the room.

"Please. I can't take anymore. Please, Sir," he sobbed as pleasure rose.

His heart pounded when Dominic didn't reply, and Randall braced himself for the painful comedown of not coming. But then Dominic removed the cage, and his cock filled so quickly that his head went dizzy. All it took was for Dominic to tap the plug, and Randall flew.

He lost all of his senses apart from the feel of the pleasurable pain streaking through him. He lost track of time as he floated in the bliss.

When he finally rose from the depths of pleasure, he was untied and cocooned in a warm embrace. He blinked his eyes and rubbed his cheek against Dominic's chest, and a straw poked at his lips. He sucked, and cool, sweet liquid filled his mouth. Closing his eyes again, he concentrated on the sweet apple flavour as he swallowed. Fingers slid through his hair, soothing him, and he smiled around the straw.

"Are you okay?" Dominic asked when he removed the empty glass.

"More than," Randall mumbled, too tired to do much else. He doubted he could move at all after that marathon.

"Glad to hear it. I grabbed some fruit. You need to eat because that was an intense scene."

"Never have truer words been spoken. I feel amazing, though. Thank you."

Dominic chuckled and held a grape to his lips. "My pleasure."

Randall gasped and tried to lift his head, but he was too tired. "What about you?"

Dominic huffed a laugh, holding out a strawberry. "Don't worry about me. The sight of you flying over the edge had me painting your body with my release."

Tingles went through Randall at the words, though he had no hope of climaxing anytime soon, and he wished he hadn't missed such a sight. "I want to see that next time," he murmured when he'd finished his fruit.

"Done."

Dominic fed him until the fruit was gone and then held a glass of water for him to drink from. Randall settled back in where he was comfortable once he was done and sighed.

"You take very good care of me."

"It's the least I can do. You give me so much." Dominic scooted down the bed until they lay with their heads on the pillows and face-to-face. "This is the wrong time to do this, but...I'm falling in love with you, Randall."

Randall's eyes burned as tears threatened. "I'm not falling," he whispered. "I've fallen." He chuckled through his tears. "I never thought I'd have this, but then you charged in, took everything I had and gave me something priceless in return." He cupped Dominic's cheek. "You. Everything about you makes me happy. A few weeks ago, I dreamt of having this with you but believed I would never get it. You've changed everything, and I can't wait to see what we can achieve together."

Dominic kissed him, and Randall slid his arm around his neck, holding him to him. When it gentled, they rested their foreheads together.

"I love you, Randall. You've just proved to me I wasn't falling, either. I had already fallen in love with the brilliant, beautiful and brave person you are." Dominic traced his fingers across his face. "I love you," he whispered again.

"I love you," Randall replied.

They shared another kiss and then wrapped themselves around each other.

"Please wake me before you leave," Randall said.

"Okay."

It seemed like ten minutes since he'd said the words when Dominic roused him. It was still too early for Randall to go to work, but when had that stopped him? They showered and dressed together, and Dominic left him with a searing kiss that Randall hoped he would feel for the rest of the day.

Despite it being five o'clock in the morning, he headed to his office and got stuck into the work that never ended. His phone ringing jerked him from his concentration, and he smiled, expecting to see Dominic's name. Instead, it was an unknown number. He always hesitated to answer when he didn't know who it was from, but once, when he had, it had been his sister calling from a new number.

"Hello?" he said.

"Randall? Is that you?"

He recognised the voice but couldn't place who it was. "It is, yes."

"It's Tom. Dominic's dad? Do you remember me?"

Randall slumped back in his chair, smiling. "Of course I do. How are you, Tom?"

"Not too bad, not too bad. I'm sorry to bother you, but Dominic gave me your number in case I needed it. I wondered if you could help me?"

"I'll do what I can, sure."

A sigh came across the line. "I don't want Dominic to know about this at the moment, but we've received some letters, and we want to get some advice without worrying him unless there's no option."

"What kind of letters?" Randall sat upright, instantly alert.

"The kind that threatens my son."

Randall's heart rate doubled, and he went through several options he had. Whoever he told about it would immediately tell Dominic, and Tom didn't want him involved yet. How could he deal with this without him knowing?

"Have you called the police?"

"No. I don't want anyone involved that doesn't have to be. It might not mean anything at all, but I'm not certain, especially with everything going on with May."

"I understand." He didn't like the idea of not telling Dominic, but he could at least gather the evidence for him while he was gone. "Let me get my things together, and I'll come over. We can figure out what to do then."

"Thank you so much, Randall. I really wasn't sure who else to call."

"It's okay. I'll be there as soon as I can."

As Randall ended the call, he wished he knew what the best course of action was. Dominic would want to know, but what use was worrying him when he had to concentrate on his interview with the gang leader?

It was still early enough that he didn't have to be in the office, which made him realise just how worried Tom was about the letters, so he left a note on his desk in case anyone came looking for him and headed for his car.

When he pulled up at Dominic's parents' house, he didn't feel as uneasy about being there alone as he thought he would. And when Tom opened the door and hugged him, he couldn't help the smile that crossed his face.

"I'm glad you're here. Would you like a drink?"

"Tea would be wonderful, thank you."

Once they were settled on the sofa, Tom and Chance broached the subject that had brought him there.

"We received the first letter four days ago. No stamp, no postmark, nothing. It must've been hand-delivered, the same as the rest. We've received a letter every day since," Chance explained.

Tom gestured to the coffee table. "We've touched them, obviously, but no one else has."

Randall had thought ahead and pulled some latex gloves from his pocket. Once he'd put them on, he picked up the first letter. Rather crudely put together, each letter was what he considered old-school and had been cut from magazines, newspapers or leaflets.

Wouldn't life be wonderful if a certain son was gone? It would for me. Tick, tock.

A shiver ran down Randall's spine. He picked up the next one.

Early retirement might be an option for a bodyguard. On the clock.

And the next.

Who needs him when he's always gone, anyway? Where's his head?

And the final one.

I'll save you the stress of him dying on the job. On the chopping block.

Randall pressed his hand to his mouth, hoping to keep his breakfast down. Tom squeezed his shoulder.

"If you read the last sentences of each note, it reads, 'Tick, tock on the clock. Where's his head? On the chopping block.' To say I'm worried is an understatement."

"I can understand that."

Randall was at a loss as to what to do, but he had to speak to Dominic about it, just not right then. He'd tell him when he got back.

"I have to tell him," he told Dominic's parents. "This might pertain to the ongoing case or something completely different, but he needs to know. I will, however, wait until he's back this afternoon before I mention anything."

"I don't want to worry him," Tom said.

"He would prefer to know. With everything else that's happening at the moment, this is just a drop in the bucket." Tom raised his eyebrows. "I can't say anything, unfortunately, but I will say that you need to keep your eyes open. If you notice anything unusual, let us know immediately."

"Is he in danger?" Tom asked.

Randall smiled. "He's the lead bodyguard for the king. He's always in danger, but he's qualified, he's smart, he's strong, he's brave. He has everything he needs to keep himself and others safe."

Tom's expression eased, and a smile graced his lips. "You love him."

Randall's cheeks heated, and he dropped his gaze before admitting, "I do."

"I'm glad. He loves you, too."

"I know. I don't know why, but he does. I'm not letting go of him."

Tom chuckled. "I should hope not." He sighed as his gaze dropped to the letters again. "I'm his father. I want him safe."

"I know you do. We'll work on making that so," Randall said.

He left after some more conversation and a snack of a blueberry muffin. As he drove towards Windsor, he went through all the information Tom had given him about the letters and tried to cross-reference it with what he knew about May's case and anything else that was happening. There were so many loose ends and seemingly unrelated aspects to it all. He couldn't even begin to unravel it all.

With the letters burning a hole in his bag, he settled in to work to pass the time until Dominic returned and he could tell him what his parents had told Randall.

Unfortunately, he received an unexpected and somewhat unwanted visitor.

"Detective Addams, what can I do for you?"

Randall glanced behind him, but there didn't seem to be a guard with him, which was unusual.

"Morning. I was looking for the security room, but I've got myself turned around. Would you mind pointing me in the right direction, please?"

"Of course." Randall was about to give him directions when he decided better of it. "In fact, I can take you there." He rounded the desk and gestured to the door. He didn't like the detective being so close to the king's office.

"Thank you." They'd been walking for around thirty seconds before Addams said, "While I have you, though, do you mind answering a few questions?"

It was then Randall knew this wasn't a chance "wrong turn," and he'd engineered it. "If I can."

"What do you know about May's case?"

"Only what is in your report. I'm not privy to certain security aspects." He didn't look at the detective because that wasn't strictly true. He had as high a clearance as anyone bar the royal family.

"What is your opinion of May Ainsley?"

Randall swallowed hard. "She is a kind, generous person who has time for anyone."

Addams was quiet for a moment. "Carlisle Police didn't find any evidence of anyone having entered her house like she claims."

Randall waited for the question, and when it didn't come, he said, "Okay?"

"The gang have pointed the finger at her, saying she took something that belonged to them. Do you think she's capable of that?"

Randall shook his head. "I doubt that very much. She's not a thief. I can imagine the gang are trying to take the heat from their own heads by making you look elsewhere."

"That's possible, yes."

They turned the corner on the last stretch to the security room. Randall would be glad when the detective wasn't his concern any longer.

"One last question," Addams said when they paused outside the door. "What's your relationship with Dominic Ainsley?"

"What concern is that to you?"

Addams shrugged. "I'm curious."

Randall debated with himself. Should he reveal their true relationship? Dominic hadn't told him to keep it quiet, and he couldn't see the harm in admitting it. "He's my boyfriend."

Addams nodded, his mouth curving. "I thought as much. A recent thing?"

"Fairly."

Addams nodded again and gestured to the door. "Thank you for the escort."

Randall knocked and waited for the call to enter before he opened the door. "Detective Addams lost his way," he announced when Brett looked up. He didn't miss the scowl that crossed Brett's face.

"I'm glad he found his way back. Thank you, Randall."

"My pleasure." He turned to leave, but Addams' voice brought him back.

"Thank you for the chat."

Randall stared at him and then exited the room. The quicker he got away from that guy, the better. There was something about him Randall didn't like, but he couldn't put his finger on it.

The rest of his morning went as planned, with no extra-curricular activities cropping up. With Portia's help, they finalised the last few details for the upcoming joining and made a start on wedding number two. By the time they were done with all these wedding preparations, they could advertise themselves as wedding planners.

Just before lunch, he had a delivery of the item he'd been waiting for. With a skip in his step, he trailed down the hallway to May's room and knocked.

"It's Randall," he announced.

The door opened, and May dragged him inside with a grin. "It's been far too long since I've seen you."

Randall chuckled. "It's been a day at most, May."

"Yes, but you're my new best friend. I get to tell you all about the things Dominic got up to as a kid."

"I'm sure you have all the gossip."

May tucked her legs beneath her on the sofa and gestured beside her. "Was there something in particular you wanted, or do you want to gossip?"

"Well, actually... I got this for you." He handed the box to her.

She frowned at it and then at him. "You don't need to get me things, Randall. I'm happy as I am. But thank you."

"I think you'll like this one. At least if I got it right."

May frowned again but tore into the wrapping. Her gasp said it all, and Randall smiled. "Oh, my god, Randall. It's perfect!" She ripped at the box, trying to get to the contents as quickly as she could. When she held it in her hands, her face lit up, although tears rolled down her cheeks. "Thank you so much."

"I hope it's the right one."

"This is similar to the camera I had before, so it's perfect." She sighed. "Let's hope I can remember how to do it."

"I'm sure it's like riding a bike."

They spent an hour talking about Dominic—gossiping, for want of a better word—with Randall letting her use him as a muse for getting back into the rhythm of taking photos. He'd had his photo taken more times in that hour than he had in his entire life, he believed. But as he wandered back to his office, he couldn't stop his smile.

If only the news he had for Dominic could be happier.

21

Dominic

The prison was as dank and dark and depressing as Dominic had expected it to be. They were shown into a small room where Gavin Lowry already waited, shackled to the chair and table. Dominic had brought Felix and Nick with him, leaving Hudson, Greg and Ford to cover the king in their places should they need to.

"To what do I owe the pleasure of the king's guards?" Gavin sneered from his seat, still as smarmy and greasy-looking as before.

Dominic settled in the chair opposite him while Felix and Nick flanked him. "You don't seem at all repentant for what happened five years ago."

Gavin snorted. "Why should I? I did nothing wrong."

Dominic laughed. "So, dealing drugs and attempting to kill my sister are not wrong?"

"Not in my book."

"Fair enough." Dominic leaned back and crossed his arms over his chest. "What went missing five years ago?"

Gavin shook his head. "I see someone's been talking." Dominic said nothing. "Drugs. A lot of them. Paul was supposed to deliver them to our client. They never arrived."

"Because he got arrested."

Gavin huffed a laugh. "Yeah, but also because your bitch of a sister hid them. I had a man coming to fetch them when I heard about Paul. Guess what, though? They weren't where Paul left them."

"You think my sister hid them."

"I know it was your sister. She contacted Fletcher, blackmailing him into leaving her alone. Fletcher refused to bend. Rightly so."

"It's a long time to hold a grudge."

Gavin waved his hand, his chains rattling. "Five years is nothing. I'm in here for twenty-five. When I get my revenge, I'll be relaxing for the next twenty."

"You're admitting to plotting revenge?" Dominic asked, hoping it was that easy.

"Yeah, man. I can plot all I want. I can't do anything from in here." The twinkle in Gavin's eyes troubled Dominic.

"Your reach is further than these walls."

Gavin smirked as he tried to cross his arms, unsuccessfully. "I'm no longer the leader of the gang. Fletcher is."

Dominic smiled and raised his eyebrows. "Really?" He glanced at Felix. "That's not what I heard."

For the first time, Gavin hesitated. "Why's that?"

"Last I heard, Fletcher was lying in the morgue. It seems there's a new player in town."

Gavin worked his jaw. "And who's that?"

"Carlos." Dominic had been paying close attention to Gavin, so when his eyes flared slightly, he knew Gavin knew him. "Friend of yours?"

"I wouldn't say 'friend,' but he's not one to be trifled with. Fletcher obviously took the wrong route."

"Maybe he shouldn't have been in that alley," Dominic said. "He might've survived had he not been."

"Swings and roundabouts, man. Life in the gang is quick to change. You have to keep up."

"Unlike you, who didn't even know your right-hand man was dead. What does that say about your so-called leadership? Oh, yeah. You just said you weren't the leader any longer." Gavin looked away. "What can you tell us about him?"

"Why would I tell you anything?"

Dominic leaned forward. "Because you're scared. And if the name Carlos scares you, that means you're not as invincible as you thought. I wonder how long it will take for him to get to you."

"There's no hiding from Carlos. He's got fingers in all sorts of pies. If he wants me dead, I'll be dead. I'm more useful to him alive, though."

"Oh, yeah. Why's that?"

"Because I have the contacts he doesn't."

Dominic chuckled. "Are you sure about that? Have you heard who the gang is dealing with lately?" Gavin said nothing. "Traffickers. Wasn't your sister taken by them?"

"Fuck that! There's no way they're dealing with them. They wouldn't."

Dominic held out his hand, and Nick put a photo in his hand. He turned it around and placed it down. It showed the men leaving the property Felix had found from the first bug and shaking hands with several known colleagues of Gavin's. The curses flowing from the man's lips were nothing short of epic. He shouldn't have found it amusing.

"What the fuck are they doing?" Gavin muttered.

"I'm assuming they're following orders. Carlos's orders."

Gavin slumped back in his chair. "Swings and roundabouts," he muttered. "Fuck." He sighed and straightened. "Even if I'm a dead man walking, you're not getting anything from me. You and May deserve everything you get."

It didn't escape his notice that Gavin added him into the equation and not just May. "You don't want us to stop Carlos so he doesn't come for you?"

Gavin snorted. "You can't stop Carlos. He doesn't play by anyone's rules but his own. Never has, never will."

"Good to know. Thanks."

Dominic stood.

"What? That's it?" Gavin said.

Dominic glanced at him. "What else do I need? You've said you won't talk, so there's no point in us being here." He headed for the door again.

"Good luck," Gavin said. "And if I end up six feet under, I'll be sure to save you a space for when you deal with Carlos."

"Well, I'm not sure how much use that was," Nick said as they exited the prison.

Dominic grinned. "Well, we know Carlos is not someone to underestimate. We know the plan is not just to target May. They're targeting me, too, for some reason."

When they got back, Felix told Dominic what his contact had given him on Addams.

"His record is pretty clean. The only thing that showed up was a failed drug test from eight years ago. None since. They put it down to having a faulty test when he came up clean in the follow-up. There's nothing else official on there."

"Unofficially?" Dominic asked.

Felix sighed. "Unofficially, he gives everyone the creeps. Even the higher-ups. Feeling uncomfortable around him, him always hovering around, wanting the scoop, that kind of thing."

"I wonder if that's a similar feeling May always gets around him?" Dominic shrugged. "Maybe I just don't like him because he seems to want to take May down. As if she had something to do with the gang."

"Did she?" When Dominic glared at him, Felix held up his hands. "Hey! You need to consider the question instead of blindly letting your feelings get in the way. I know she's your sister, but you don't know everything about her. I guarantee it."

Dominic exhaled. "I know. But I also know she wouldn't touch drugs or anyone involved in them."

"Okay. That's good." Felix clapped his back. "Get some rest. I think you're needed back on shift this afternoon."

Dominic groaned when his phone rang as he aimed for May's room. "Hello?"

"Ainsley, I'm calling to see if you have any further information for me."

Dominic sighed. "I wish I did, Detective. We're still working on things from this end, but I know you can't keep the case open indefinitely."

"I can't, no. One thing, though. I can always open it again later if something comes up."

"True. Sorry I don't have better news."

He huffed. "I'm not sure if I want there to be any news or not. I've known Maloney for years, and I would never have said he was depressed. Unhappy with his job, yes. Depressed enough to kill himself, no. At least, I didn't think so."

"I'm sorry for your loss. I'll keep you updated if I find anything."

"Thank you."

Dominic tucked the phone back into his pocket. He had so much whirling around in his head he could hardly make heads or tails from it, but at least having Felix and Nick helping him brainstorm was good. Three brains were better than one.

He pulled his sister into his arms when she answered, needing to hold her close for a long second before switching on the jammer he now carried with him.

"What's that for?" she asked with a chuckle.

"I went to see Gavin. He's still holding a grudge."

May rolled her eyes. "I'm sure he is."

Dominic sighed. "This isn't just about you. Gavin let slip that they're after me, too. I don't know why, but I'm going to find out. This will be over soon. I promise. And I'll get you that house in the countryside you've always wanted."

May smiled. "My dreams might've changed a little since you last saw me."

He raised his eyebrows. "What to?"

"I liked living in Carlisle, but I don't want to be so far away from family anymore. I want to find somewhere similar. Somewhere I can be anonymous but build a life."

He noticed the camera on the table behind her. "Where did you get that?"

She beamed. "Randall."

Of course. The man who thought of everything.

"I want to do photography again. While I was in Carlisle, the need had dimmed, but since I've had this camera in my hands, I can't stop wanting to use it. To see the colours, the images, everything."

He kissed her temple. "Have you been to the gardens today?" She shook her head. "Then let's go. I haven't got long until my shift, but I have some time."

As they walked through the gardens of the castle, May lost herself in taking photos, and Dominic happily watched her. She looked younger and older at the same time. She looked older because they'd lost five years together but younger because the weight of her life lifted whenever she brought the camera to her eye. He hadn't realised how much something he considered a hobby would help ease her burdens. He would have to thank Randall for thinking of such a gift.

"Where are your thoughts? Because they're not here," May said, returning to him.

"I was just thinking that you look free whenever you have the camera to your eye."

May nodded. "I am. When I look through the lens, I can see what I want to see. The beauty in the world. I don't have to witness the bad. I can make the world a nicer place because of what I choose to take photos of."

"Dreams," he murmured.

"Dreams," May agreed.

She showed him the photos she'd taken. "Are you considering doing this full-time?" he asked.

May shrugged. "I don't know. I love it. I really do. I just don't know if I'm good enough yet."

"They look good to me."

"You're family. I won't trust your opinion." She laughed at his pout.

"Seriously, though. If it's something you might be interested in, I'm sure we can find someone who can help. We have contacts everywhere, including within the royal family."

May smiled. "I'll think about it. I've got plenty of time." She lifted the camera to her face and snapped a picture of him. "Now take me back to my room so you can see lover boy."

Dominic shoved her shoulder and then tucked her under his as they wandered back the way they came. He left her to her photos and jogged down the corridors. He paused before he entered Randall's office, not wanting to slam the door open like usual and scare another year off his life. Instead, he opened the door slowly and knocked gently. Randall glanced up, a crease between his eyebrows until he saw Dominic, and then he beamed and shot from behind the desk. Dominic caught him as he threw his arms around his neck, and he lifted him clear off the ground.

"I was so worried about you," Randall whispered into his neck. "I hated the thought of you being there."

"I know," Dominic said, rubbing his hand up and down Randall's back. "I'm back. I'm okay."

Randall's feet rested on the floor again, and Dominic kissed him, leaving no inch of his mouth undiscovered. He only stopped when the door hit him as it opened again, knocking him forward.

"Oh, god! Sorry."

Dominic smiled. "Nothing to worry about, Your Highness."

Kendal waved him away. "I'm still not used to that. I do wish you'd call me Kendal."

"Sorry, Your Highness. It's next to impossible."

Kendal chuckled. "I'm sure it is." They sighed. "Do you happen to know where my liege is?"

Dominic smiled inwardly at the nicknames the king and his partners had for each other. He glanced at Randall, who nodded.

"He's in Prince Freddie's suite."

"Thank you, Randall. You're a lifesaver." They waved, glanced at their joined hands and exited.

"Don't they have each other's phone numbers?" Dominic asked.

"They do," Randall said, resuming his seat behind his desk. "But you know Andrew doesn't check his phone often."

"Ah, yes."

Randall rested his elbows on the desk. "What did you find out?"

"Not a lot, really. He didn't know about Fletcher or that Carlos had taken over. He seems resigned to death. Wouldn't give up much else, although he did insinuate that this is not just about May. It's about me, too. I don't know why, though."

Randall paled at that, and Dominic cursed his tell-all attitude. He reached across the desk for Randall's hand. "I'm sorry. I shouldn't have just thrown that out."

"It's okay. I was just thinking earlier that you were in a dangerous job, and injuries were inevitable. Doesn't mean I have to like it."

"Speaking of the job. I have to start work. I've had guards covering for me for a few days, and I need to give them a break. We don't have much to go on at the moment, so I can let it rest for now."

"Before you go. I had a visit from Addams this morning." Dominic's hackles rose even before Randall continued. "He asked my opinion about May, what I knew about the case, and whether we were in a relationship."

"And you told him...?"

"She's amazing, only what's in the case file, and yes."

Dominic smiled and then frowned. "I didn't realise he was coming back for more questions."

"I don't think anyone else did either. He didn't have an escort. I'm assuming the guards at the gate just let him in because he'd been here so much. I escorted him back to the security room and into Brett's capable hands."

"I'm sure he had a few choice words for the detective," Dominic said.

"I can imagine." Randall inhaled. "There is another thing, too." He wrung his hands, staring down at them rather than at Dominic. "I went to see your parents this morning."

Dominic's eyebrows rose. "Okay. What's the problem?"

"Tom called me, asking me to visit because they've been receiving threatening letters." Randall glanced up at him. "All about you."

"What the hell! Why didn't they tell me? Why you?"

"Tom didn't want to worry you if it was nothing to worry about."

"Fucking hell, Randall!" Randall flinched, and Dominic knew he was being harsh but couldn't help it. "What the hell do you think you're doing?"

"I was trying to help."

Dominic paced, running his hands through his hair. Visions of gang members breathing down their necks when Dominic couldn't get to them whirled around his head. Worst-case scenarios filled his head with blood, injuries and death. If something happened to them, there was no telling what Dominic was capable of. His brush with Diego's injuries would be nothing compared to what havoc he could wreak should someone hurt his family.

"Did you even think about how it would make me feel?"

Randall's expression blanked. "I didn't think you would have a problem with me visiting your family without you. I know now I was wrong."

Dominic growled, no other sound available to get his emotions across. "I have no issues with you visiting my parents, Randall. What I do have a problem with is you having no regard for your safety. You didn't consider taking someone with you, even when you knew they were being targeted with letters. Where's your brain at, Randall? You know what's going on around here. Think!"

Randall settled into his desk and shuffled papers. "I can take care of myself."

"Oh, like you did with Ernest?"

It was a cheap shot, and Dominic regretted it the moment he said it, but he couldn't acknowledge that right then. He needed to get away. "I'll be back later."

He left the office and strode towards Prince Freddie's suite. He didn't make it because he met the king and his partners, as well as Prince Freddie and Prince Damon, as they headed towards him.

"Your Majesty," Dominic said, trying to calm his rioting emotions.

"Everything okay?" Andrew asked.

"Just a little upset. Nothing to worry about."

Andrew stared at him for a moment before continuing down the corridor. "We're heading to my office for a phone appointment."

"Understood."

Dominic stopped beside Ford and thanked him for covering for him. Ford broke off when they reached the corridor for Sec HQ, but Dominic and Nick continued. As they entered the office, Dominic didn't dare look at Randall. He knew he was in the wrong, but while his emotions were still raw and bubbling, he couldn't apologise. Besides, he needed something more than to just say "sorry."

"I'll wait outside," he murmured to Nick, and his eyes widened. He never stayed outside when he could spend time with Randall.

As he settled into the chair outside of the offices, he stewed. He sent a message to his dad.

DOMINIC: *Next time, come to me. Don't put Randall in the middle.*

It didn't take long to receive a reply.

DAD: *Randall is only in the middle if you put him there. He was being kind and doing what I asked of him. If you are going to be mad at someone, be mad at me. Don't go upsetting Randall.*

Too late.

22

Nick

Nick stared at the door long after Dominic had closed it with him on the other side. No one minded being stuck in the corridor, especially when Randall always included them when he made drinks or snacks, but it was almost unheard of for Dominic to stay out there. More so when he was supposed to be in a relationship with Randall.

He glanced at the personal assistant, whose face was pale with several tear tracks. What the hell had happened between them?

Whatever it was needed rectifying immediately. He wasn't having those two people, who had the most amazing relationship Nick could remember anyone but the royal family having, split up if he had anything to do about it. His parents weren't relationship material, and he would never emulate them. Dominic and Randall, however? They were what he would strive for when he found someone worthy of his time. His relationship goals.

He pretended to ignore the sniff coming from across the room, but he kept an ear out in case there were more. He hated people crying and would do anything to make them stop. Instead, he pulled out his phone and typed in a name he hadn't been able to stop searching for. Malachi Sanders.

Telling himself he was researching to see what the guy was up to worked to a degree, but when three hours or more of his internet history was from reading article after article from the reporter, he should admit to having a problem.

He re-read the article about Dominic and Randall's date the previous week, including several tasteful photographs of the couple looking loved up and happy as they wandered around. Malachi's desire to cover the royal family, no matter what they were doing, was annoying as hell. At least, that's what he kept telling himself. Somehow, that damn reporter had found them no matter where they went, and Nick wanted to know how. He must be getting inside information from someone, and that would mean there was a security breach somewhere.

Maybe he should speak directly to the reporter to find out. He doubted he would spill who his contacts were, but it might scare him enough to back off a little. Especially if Nick gave him something worthy to use instead.

He'd need to clear it with Brett for obvious reasons, but he perked up at the idea.

"Coffee, Nick?" Randall asked, and Nick glanced at him. He looked better already, as if a weight had been lifted, and Nick smiled.

"Yes, please." He never wanted to turn down coffee—even if he did sometimes. Having coffee as blood was not healthy, and that was what he'd end up with if he drank too much.

He never understood how anyone could drink tea, no matter how it was made. As he sipped the nectar of the gods, he sighed. Nothing better than coffee.

Except sex.

And even then, there was a fine line.

23

Randall

The moment the door closed behind Dominic, Randall's tears overflowed. Only for a minute, though. He sniffed, wiped his face and set to work. He could understand Dominic's concerns, but his vocalisation of them left something to be desired. Randall wasn't in the wrong; he knew that. But he could understand why Dominic was scared for him. For them. With everything that was going on at the moment, no one knew what could happen. And these letters were another pin on the board of someone focusing on Dominic and his family.

When the king returned with his partners and Freddie and Damon in tow, Dominic stayed out in the corridor, which broke Randall's heart. Not because he thought it was the end of them but because Dominic was hurting, and there wasn't much Randall could do to help except be there when he decided to come back to him.

He might be unsure in the way of relationships, but he was old enough to have seen and experienced other people's relationships from the outside, so he could see what was happening. The moment Dominic's emotions were under control, he would be back. And if he wasn't, then Randall would go to him. This was not the end of them. He refused to even consider that possibility.

His phone pinged.

TOM: *I'm sorry if I've caused a problem between you and Dominic. That was never my intention. I'll speak to him, and he'll see sense. Thank you for your help, though. I do appreciate it. Make sure you come for dinner again soon, okay?*

Randall smiled and sent a message back, saying that he didn't need to apologise and that he would love to have dinner. That entire family had enough compassion and love for the world that they would suffer themselves to ensure others were happy. It's about time they had some peace.

His office phone rang. It was going to be someone important because only those people had that number. "Good morning, His Majesty's Office. How can I help?"

"Randall, is that you, dear?" an older woman's voice floated down the line.

He smiled. "Yes, Mrs Lafferty. How are you?"

"Not too good at the moment, Randall. The Prime Minister would like an urgent meeting with His Majesty if that's not too much trouble."

Randall checked the calendar, though he had the thing memorised. "That's not a problem from here, but I'll need to double-check with the king. Can I ask what it's about?"

"There's gossip around that there are problems afoot with one of your guards and his family. The Prime Minister would like to discuss rather than speculate."

Randall's heart pounded. How dare they? He breathed through his anger. "There's always gossip, Mrs Lafferty. You know that."

"Yes, my dear, but we know that there is always some truth hiding amongst the rumours, don't we?"

Randall couldn't begrudge her concerns or the Prime Minister's, so he put her on hold and interrupted the king's meeting. Damon opened the door and let him in.

"—don't have any concerns about Australia leaving the commonwealth if that's what they want." Andrew glanced at him, eyebrows raised. Randall nodded, a sign that he needed to talk to him. "Logan, can you give me just a moment? I just need to answer a question from my assistant real quick."

"Sure thing, Your Majesty."

Andrew muted the call. "What's wrong?"

"The Prime Minister is asking for an immediate meeting about 'a guard's' situation. I'm assuming they mean Dominic. Rumours abound."

Andrew cursed and nodded. "As soon as I've finished here, we can meet if that's what he wants."

"Thank you."

"Make him come to me, though, Randall. I'm not moving from this office."

"Understood, Your Majesty."

Randall went back to the Prime Minister's assistant. "Mrs Lafferty, the king is free in an hour and a half if the Prime Minister can attend then?"

"Wonderful. He'll be there. Thank you, Randall."

"Not a problem, Mrs Lafferty. I hope you have a better rest of your day."

He ended the call and blew out a breath. Should he mention something to Dominic about it? No, he'd wait and let Andrew have his meeting first.

When Andrew exited his office an hour later, he said, "I'm going to meet him in the Drawing Room, Randall. I can't stand another minute of my office, after all."

"I'll let the guards know to take the Prime Minister there when he arrives, Your Majesty."

"Thank you." Andrew glanced at Nick and then at Randall with raised eyebrows. Randall's cheeks heated, but he said nothing. "I'll be back later."

"Yes, Your Majesty."

Nick followed him out, and Randall hoped Dominic would pop his head in, but he didn't. Randall's shoulders lowered, but he went back to work.

An hour later, he received another message.

DOMINIC: *I want to say I'm sorry in person rather than over the phone. Can you meet me at your house so I can show you the new security features I've had installed for you?*

Randall smiled. He hadn't realised Dominic had been sorting that for him. They'd spoken about it, but they hadn't made any firm plans to do anything about it. Randall had been staying at Windsor instead of trying to face his home.

RANDALL: *Of course. What time?*

DOMINIC: *Four o'clock?*

Randall didn't finish work until five o'clock usually, but there was nothing on the calendar that needed his urgent attention. It could wait until the morning.

RANDALL: *Definitely. I'll be there.*

DOMINIC: *See you then.*

Randall felt lighter for the rest of the afternoon, and even when Andrew handed him something else that needed doing, he squeezed it in before he had to leave. As he drove to his house, he couldn't stop smiling. He hated being at odds with Dominic, and it didn't happen often, but he needed to explain why he'd visited Dominic's parents without thinking of his safety. The truth was something Dominic wouldn't like—he hadn't thought about it. It had never crossed his mind that he needed to be careful because of what was going on. He didn't see himself as someone important in the grand scheme of things, but Dominic obviously did.

He parked the car but didn't see Dominic's car. Maybe he was running late. He stared at the house and wondered if he could enter the place alone without causing himself palpitations or passing out. He decided to walk around to the back of the house and see if there was anything visibly different that he could see.

The back gate wasn't as secure as it could be, and Randall easily let himself into the back garden. Nothing seemed any different, so maybe the work had only been done on the inside. He didn't want to enter the house in case he set off alarms he didn't know about, so he turned to go back to his car and wait, but something hit him in the head, and a figure in black was the last thing he saw.

Randall groaned as he woke, reaching a hand to touch his throbbing head, but something stopped him from moving. With effort, he blinked repeatedly to focus. He was sitting in a chair, his wrists, elbows, ankles and knees taped to it. He jerked and wriggled, trying to free himself, but he was stuck fast. The only thing he managed to do was make his head pound harder. Who the hell had hit him, and what the hell did they want?

He stopped moving, out of breath from the exertion, and studied his surroundings. The room he was in was empty and had a window boarded with intermittent wooden slats. There was a single uncovered and unlit lightbulb hanging from the ceiling but nothing else that he could see. The light was dim, so either the window didn't let enough light in, or it was getting later in the day.

How long had he been out? Did anyone know he was missing?

Dominic's words from earlier in the day came back to him. *What I do have a problem with is you having no regard for your safety.* Yet again, Randall had run off without thinking about his safety. Even though the message said it had come from Dominic, had it really? Could someone have cloned his phone or made it look like it came from Dominic's number? Randall wasn't tech-savvy enough to understand if it was possible.

Randall sighed and bowed his head, conserving what little strength he had. With every movement, his head hurt, but he didn't feel dizzy, only nauseated.

He had no idea how much time had passed when the door opened and someone entered. Randall lifted his head, blinking through the pain, and watched someone in black clothing and a black ski mask walk towards him.

"Good afternoon, Randall. Nice to see you awake now."

The voice wasn't one Randall recognised, but he could identify the lack of heart behind it. It was cold and mean, which didn't bode well for him. It was a man's voice, though, unless they were using voice-changing equipment.

"Who are you?"

"If I wanted you to know, I wouldn't be wearing a mask now, would I?"

Randall tried to catalogue the man's build and anything else that might help him to figure out who it was, either then or later.

"You are a bargaining chip, nothing else. If you behave, you will leave here unhurt." He huffed. "Well, no more hurt than you already are."

Randall stared at him. "What do you want?"

"That's easy. I want Dominic."

"Why?"

The man walked behind him, and Randall braced for something, though he didn't know what. "That's of no concern to you." He came back around to the front and crossed his arms over his chest.

"I won't help you," Randall said.

"You already have. You don't need to do anything else other than sit here nice and pretty and wait."

Randall's chest heaved. What had he done? Why couldn't he have listened when Dominic spoke and remembered everything he said to him? He should've told someone where he was going. As things stood, no one knew he had gone home to meet Dominic. They only knew he left early. How the hell was anyone going to find him?

"Dominic will be here soon, and you'll be reunited. However brief that might be."

The guy headed for the door.

"He won't fall for your trick."

His kidnapper paused. "There's no trick, Randall. He just needs to come and fetch what he's lost. That's all." He left and closed the door behind him.

"What he's lost? What the hell is he talking about?"

Randall closed his eyes and lowered his head, resting as much as he could. When the time came, he needed to use whatever energy and strength he had to get away. He needed to find Dominic before he fell into this trap.

When would anyone notice he was gone? It was Sunday, after all. No one was expecting him to be at work until eight o'clock the following morning. He'd had an argument with Dominic, so he wasn't expecting him to reach out until he wanted to. How long would that be? He would miss dinner with his parents, and although he would usually let them know if he wasn't attending, it wasn't unusual for him to miss it.

Time passed, and his kidnapper came back in. "Here's a drink for you." He held a bottle of water.

"I'm not drinking anything from you. How do I know what you've done to it?"

The man unscrewed it, and Randall heard the click of a brand-new bottle, but he still wasn't convinced. The guy then took a drink of it. Randall didn't want to, but he was so thirsty. And what more could the guy do other than drug him? If he was being used as bait, he wouldn't kill him. Yet.

Randall lifted his head as the guy held the bottle to his mouth. He drank his fill, and the guy stepped back once he was done. For once, Randall's politeness didn't win out. He refused to say thank you.

"Why do you want Dominic?" he asked again.

The kidnapper stared at him through the mask, his dark eyes showing no emotion at all. Randall couldn't tell if his eyes were brown or not. The limited light could be playing a trick on him.

"He has something of mine."

Randall frowned, and his breathing increased as his heart tried to jump from his chest. "Are you Carlos?"

The guy stared at him, saying nothing. Then he reached for Randall, making him flinch, and caught his chin, tilting his face to see his forehead. "I'll get something for that." He let go and left.

Randall blinked. What the hell was that all about? He was tied to a chair, unable to move, but the guy was making sure he drank and tending to his wound. What kind of kidnapper was he?

The one thing that kept a spark inside Randall was that he hadn't let him see his face, which meant one of two things. Either Randall knew him and could identify him, or the guy would be letting Randall go in the end. Or both. He'd received no reaction from the guy when he asked if he was Carlos, but did that mean he was or wasn't? So many questions and Randall's head hurt too much to concentrate.

The door opened again, and the guy returned with a first aid kid. Without any fanfare, he cleaned the wound and put a plaster on it. Then, he held out a packet of paracetamol. "Do you want some?"

Randall snorted. "Tablets? From a complete stranger? I don't think so."

The guy shrugged, and something about the move looked familiar. "Your loss." He pocketed them and tidied up the first aid kit, heading for the door.

"I know you, don't I?" Randall asked.

The guy chuckled and left.

Silence descended again, and Randall tried to get free, but the tape was too thick to break. He doubted he was stashed anywhere that would matter if he shouted; otherwise, the guy would've put a gag on him. He was thankful for that small mercy.

More time passed, and the room grew darker until there was no light at all. It made him think they were somewhere where streetlights didn't reach. The countryside, maybe. Was the guy still waiting for Dominic to turn up? Had he even contacted him yet, or was he waiting?

The guy entered again, this time flicking the light on, and Randall blinked at the sudden brightness, however dim the bulb truly was. He held another bottle of water. They repeated the actions from before, and Randall drank the water. His stomach churned from lack of food, but he'd manage. He definitely wasn't taking the chance to eat anything. Water was fine. Anything else was pushing his luck.

"You're taking good care of me, considering you kidnapped me," Randall said.

The guy shook his head. "I have no problems with you. My issue is with Dominic. You are a means to an end, but not one I plan on hurting." He stared at him. "Unless there is no other option. When Dominic arrives, you will be free to go."

"I don't understand."

"You don't need to. You just need to stay here until I'm done with you, and no harm will come to you."

"But it will to Dominic?"

"Not if he gives up what is mine."

"And what is that?"

The guy chuckled and headed for the door. "Try to rest."

Randall snorted. "Yeah, sleeping in a chair is so comfortable."

The man paused. "I could lay the chair down if you'd prefer."

Randall frowned. "You are a contradiction."

"No, I'm not. You base your knowledge of kidnapping scenarios on the movies and books, I'm sure. Not everything you read or see is truth." He closed the door.

Randall exhaled. He had no idea what else he could try. There was absolutely nothing in the room. Not even a stray nail he could try to cut the tape with if he scooted the chair closer. Nothing. He couldn't even slump in the chair and rest his head. Resigning himself to having to wait, he did just that.

Hours passed, he was sure, and the lightbulb flickered intermittently. Randall hoped it wouldn't go out. There was nothing worse than being in an unfamiliar place in complete darkness.

He strained his ears for any sound, but there was nothing. Nothing to see, nothing to hear.

As the light in the room increased, Randall craned his head to look at the window. Yes, light was beginning to show between the slats, meaning it was Monday morning. Soon, someone would know he was missing and would come looking. But how the hell were they likely to find him when he was sure it was somewhere he would never dream of going?

The door opened, and his kidnapper held another bottle of water. At least he seemed to be truthful about keeping Randall unhurt. When he finished his drink, the guy said, "It's nearly showtime. I'm doing this for your benefit." He held out some tape.

"The more you pull at it, the more it'll hurt when it eventually comes off. Close your mouth and roll your lips inwards. It'll hurt less when they take it off."

"Why? You don't seem like a monster. Why do this?"

"I've already told you why. But I won't hurt those who don't deserve it." He chuckled. "Unless money is involved. Ready?"

Randall did as he suggested—though why, he had no idea—and the guy taped his mouth. He could still breathe through his nose, which was another small mercy.

"You'll see Dominic soon, okay?"

Randall nodded, and the guy left. Who the hell was that guy?

24

Dominic

Dominic had plenty to apologise to Randall for. Not only for going off at the deep end when it came to him visiting his parents but for not trusting him to keep himself safe. He knew—he *knew*—Randall wouldn't purposefully put himself in danger, but Dominic's instincts for protection were not something he could switch off.

With that in mind, he headed for Randall's office. He hadn't spoken to him all night, even though he'd sent messages to say he wanted to see him because he wanted to give Randall the space he needed after Dominic had been an ass. But it was early on Monday morning now, and he wanted to see him. No, *needed* to see him.

He knocked and carefully entered Randall's office, but he wasn't there. Dominic frowned and checked his watch. It was seven o'clock, and although Randall's official starting time was eight o'clock, Dominic had never known him to arrive later than seven. He was usually earlier.

He checked the kettle, touching it to see if it was warm. It wasn't. Randall hadn't been there yet, then. Should he wait for him?

Dominic stood in the centre of the room, hands on hips and studied his surroundings. No, he needed to get this done sooner rather than later, and waiting for Randall to turn up was wasting time. He wanted Randall to have a good start to his week, not a crappy one.

He strode for Randall's room and knocked. No answer. He knocked again and called his name. No answer. Turning the handle, he found the door unlocked, and he called his name again. It was empty. He frowned. Where was he? Had he gone home? Dominic's heart raced. He hadn't had time to see to the additional security features he wanted to add to Randall's house, which meant if that person who sent the roses was still waiting for them, Randall could be in danger.

He jogged through the corridors to the exit and climbed into his car, aiming for Randall's house with barely a second thought. When he pulled up at his home, Dominic sighed when he saw Randall's car. He climbed from the vehicle and breathed deeply a few times to calm his rioting emotions. Able to understand why Randall wanted time away from Windsor—and him—he slowly approached the door, hoping Randall was up. He rang the doorbell and waited. No answer. He knocked. No answer.

Did Randall not want to speak to him? Is that why he wasn't answering his calls, messages and his knocking? Should Dominic give him the space he seemed to want, or should he fight for him?

Dominic stepped back from the door, walking backwards to his car but keeping his eyes on the house in case he saw a twitching curtain indicating that Randall was watching. But there was nothing.

He sighed and turned to his car, opening the driver's door. As he did, his phone pinged, and he grabbed it, hoping for a message from Randall. It wasn't. It was an unknown number. He opened it with a frown.

UNKNOWN: *Time's awastin'. Your precious boyfriend has been taken for a ride. If you arrive quickly enough, you might be able to save him. If not... Well, you won't like what happens. Come alone.*

An address finished the message, and then a photo downloaded. Randall was sitting in a chair, head hanging forward, as if unconscious.

"What the fuck!" Dominic said. He zoomed in on the picture, taking in the details he hadn't seen before. The tape tying him to the chair. The blood on his forehead and shirt. The seemingly empty room behind him. "I'm going to take you to the bottom of the Thames myself, you asshole!" he shouted, uncaring if the neighbours were listening.

He climbed into his car and sped towards Windsor. He was going to need supplies when he got to the place. Undoubtedly, it was a trap, and he would need firepower to ensure they got out alive. If there were any other wounds on Randall, he wasn't going to kill the guy; he was going to inflict the same wounds on him before he died. Over and over again. As many times as he could until he felt it was enough to repay what he'd done to Randall.

He slowed as he reached Windsor, not wanting to alert anyone else to the issue, especially as the message said he had to be alone. He wasn't taking any chances with Randall's life.

He smiled at the people he passed, trying not to show anything more than his usual stoic, happy self, and headed for the weapons room. He grabbed a couple of smaller guns he could stash in his waistband and covered it with his T-shirt, then he took his replacement gun—the usual still missing—and put it in the holster, as was his routine. He glanced at the vests but decided against one because he wanted to be able to move freely.

Knowing he should check in with Brett but not wanting to potentially raise any red flags with him, he chose to go without saying a word. If nothing else, he would be able to save Randall, even if it meant the end of his own life. Hopefully, he'd be able to take this fucker down with him.

He programmed the address into his phone and frowned. The property was a small house on a large acreage. There was nothing around the house, not even hedges or trees. It was as if someone had built a house in the centre of the field so the occupants could see the entire perimeter from inside. It was a good idea, but it limited Dominic's chances of creeping up on whoever it was. It wouldn't matter. They knew he was coming anyway, so the chance of surprise was non-existent.

Aiming the car in the direction he needed, he set out for the location. It would take him twenty-two minutes, according to his phone, but there was no way he was going to make Randall stay there for longer than necessary. By the time he got close, it'd been fifteen minutes, and he made himself slow down to keep an eye on his surroundings.

Turning onto a dirt road, he drove out of the trees and saw the house in the distance, even though he was still a mile away from it. He couldn't be stealthy, so he didn't try. He drove up the road, stopping on the stones near the house. He waited for a few seconds, then climbed out, leaving the engine running—they might need a quick getaway.

He palmed his gun and held it in front of him as he scanned the property, looking for anything to indicate that someone was in it. When no shots were fired, he continued up the steps to the door. Controlling his breathing was difficult, but he worked his way through the house, room by room, trying to find where Randall was being held. Despite the property being small, it had quite a few rooms.

He wandered down the hallway and opened the last door on the right. His gaze immediately took in Randall, still taped to the chair but alert and with tape over his mouth. Tears flowed down Randall's face, and Dominic's heart broke, but he needed to concentrate. He took another step inside and paused.

A man in a mask, wearing nothing but black, stepped out from the shadowed wall. Dominic froze. He had a gun pointed at Randall, and Dominic couldn't take the chance that if he shot the guy, the guy would reflexively shoot the gun.

"Who are you?"

"It's nice to see you, Dominic." He didn't recognise the voice. "I'm glad you could join us. I'm sorry it won't be a long reunion, but it is a reunion all the same."

Dominic adjusted his aim to shoot seconds after the guy did, but pain blossomed in his leg and his shoulder simultaneously. He fell to the floor, smacking his head on the doorframe as he went down.

Randall's muffled scream was the last thing he heard.

25

Randall

R andal's heart skipped several beats as he saw Dominic fall, and though he couldn't be heard, he screamed with all his might as tears flowed down his face. Dominic wasn't moving. He couldn't be dead. Yes, the guy had shot him twice, but Dominic was a survivor. There was no way he was dead. No way.

"Okay. It's time to go," the guy said.

Randall shook his head, trying to see past him to where Dominic lay on the ground.

"Co-operate, and you'll survive this and be able to tell others where he is. It's either that, or I leave you with his dead body, and no one will find you. Your choice."

Randall couldn't think. He couldn't leave Dominic on the floor alone. He shook his head again.

The guy chuckled. "You don't actually have a choice. There is a plan, and you can't stay here."

He fumbled with Randall's wrists, removing the tape from each arm and then taping both wrists together. Randall should've fought him, but his gaze was stuck on Dominic's unmoving body.

He couldn't be dead. He couldn't. Tears streamed down his face as the guy pulled him to his feet. More tape was tied around his waist and wrists, so he was unable to lift his arms. He was dragged towards Dominic.

Now, Randall did struggle, wanting to see how Dominic was, but the closer they came, the more blood Randall could see. He cried harder. There was no way Dominic survived that. His legs buckled when reality hit home, and he could barely move. The guy kept him doing so, though. They stepped past Dominic and out of the door. They'd barely moved two steps before the guy stopped.

"Oh, I almost forgot."

He pulled something from his pocket, unfolded it with one hand and threw it on the floor beside Dominic. He fumbled with something else, but Randall's attention was on Dominic, wishing him to move. Any sign that he was alive.

"There. Mission accomplished."

He tugged Randall into motion again. It didn't make sense. The guy had said Dominic had something of his. Why kill him?

"You probably have questions, but I won't answer any of them, even if you could voice them. Your only concern right now is to find your way home from where I leave you." The guy pushed him against a wall and pulled a ski mask from his pocket. "Time for darkness."

Randall struggled, but it was no use. He had nothing on the guy, and within seconds, the mask was over his face, blocking out the light. His kidnapper dragged him forward, and Randall tripped over his own feet, though the guy kept him upright. He felt cool air on his skin and then the sound of an engine. He was stopped, and the engine cut out, and then they were moving again. He heard a car door, and he was shoved. He fell into what he believed was the boot, which was confirmed when his legs were bent, and the boot slammed shut.

He sobbed. He couldn't help it. Dominic was dead, and this guy was going after others. Randall had nothing to give anyone who asked. He didn't know a damn thing. Not where he'd been held, not where they could find Dominic, nothing. He froze. Yes, he did.

Taking a calming breath, he listened as the engine started, and they bumped down a road. And he counted, trying to imagine the second hand on a clock and keep the rhythm of time was hard, but he did the best he could. If he could estimate how long he was in the car before the guy dropped him off, maybe they could get an approximate distance. The kidnapper had told him to figure out where Dominic was, after all.

When the car stopped, he estimated they'd been driving for eleven minutes. He tensed when cool air rushed over him. Hands grabbed him and threw him to the ground.

"I'll be kind," the guy said, and Randall felt his wrists loosen from his body. "Good luck finding your way home."

He heard a slam, and the car drove away. He tore the mask from his face as quickly as he could, but all he could see was dust kicked up in the car's wake. He couldn't see a numberplate or make or model of the car. He slumped back to the ground as sobs overtook him. He pulled the tape from his mouth and cried.

He had no idea how long he'd been there before he got himself together. Dominic needed him. Even if he was dead—which was highly likely because he hadn't been moving—Randall needed to get him home to his family. With difficulty, because he had nothing to cut the tape on his wrists with, he clambered to his feet and looked around him. He could see houses in the distance and lots of trees, but nothing remotely recognisable. He studied both ways down the road, neither looking extremely comforting, but chose the same route the car had gone. It didn't matter if it took him further away from Windsor; he just needed to reach someone who could help him.

The air was cold, both because of the early hours of the morning and because they were in autumn and heading for winter. He shivered as he stumbled down the road, hoping a car would come along, but nothing did. Swallowing against his dry throat, he tried not to think about Dominic, but he couldn't help it. He would do everything in his power to get him home. Dominic would've done the same for him.

He reached a crossroads with road signs and let out a breath. Despite being around twenty miles from Windsor, he at least knew where he was. He crossed the road and headed towards home, one step at a time.

He'd made it roughly a mile before he saw a car. He wasn't sure if he should trust whoever it was because he had no idea who the kidnapper had been, but he needed help. He waved them down, and they slowed to a stop and opened the window just a little.

"Everything okay?" the woman asked, and Randall could see the apprehension on her face.

"Hi, I'm sorry to bother you. My name is Randall, and I'm the king's personal assistant. I was kidnapped, and I need to get back to Windsor. I can see your hesitance, and I understand if you'd prefer not to help. If nothing else, could you remove the tape from my wrists, please?" He held up his wrists.

The woman gasped, her hand covering her mouth. She still hesitated, and although Randall needed help, he wouldn't force someone to help him if they were scared.

"It's okay. Thank you for stopping."

He tried not to show his upset and continued down the road, leaving the car behind. He'd gone a few steps when her voice stopped him.

"Wait! Let me help."

He paused. "You don't have to. I completely understand. You don't know me."

"But I do," she said, coming closer. "I just searched your name and the king, and your picture came up. You're telling the truth."

Randall let out a sigh, his shoulders lowering. "Thank god for the internet."

She gestured him towards the car. "I have some scissors in my bag." She helped him into the passenger seat and then used her nail scissors to cut the tape. They couldn't get it all off, but at least his hands were free, and he could move more easily. "Where do you want to go?"

"As close as you're going to Windsor Castle, please."

"I'll take you all the way. I was only going food shopping, anyway. Nothing that can't wait." She climbed into the driver's seat, and they started down the road. "I won't pry in what I'm assuming is royal business, but are you okay?"

Randall huffed a wet laugh. "Not really, but I will be."

"My name is Alicia. If there's anything I can do, please let me know."

"Thank you, Alicia. We might need to take you up on that."

The ride to Windsor, while brief, was quiet, and Randall lost himself in the memories of Dominic's body falling to the floor as the shots entered his body. He barely restrained the sobs that wanted to escape, but he didn't want to put all that onto this brave, selfless woman as well as his presence, so he kept quiet.

At the gates to Windsor Castle, Randall climbed out, taking Alicia's contact details in case they needed them later. When the guards saw him, several raced towards him, helping him through the gates. They encouraged him to sit down, but he finally raised his voice.

"I need to see Brett. Now!"

Several stepped back, but one nodded. "I'll call ahead and help you inside."

"Thank you, Aiden."

Every bone in Randall's body ached, but he walked through the corridors of Windsor with purpose. When pounding footsteps reached his ears, despite knowing he was safe, his instincts were to curl and hide. He stood his ground, though, and when he saw Brett, Felix, Andrew, Kean and Kendal, plus many others, he almost dropped to the floor. Aiden, the kind guard from the gates, caught him before he hit.

Andrew reached for him. "What happened?"

"Dominic's dead," Randall sobbed into Andrew's chest. "He shot him right in front of me."

Andrew tensed. "Who did?"

"I don't know!"

"It's okay, Randall. It's okay."

Randall pulled back, ashamed at his show of sadness when things needed to be done. He wiped his face, took a breath and said, "I was kidnapped last night and held until this morning. It was a guy, but he wore a mask, so I don't know who it was. I didn't recognise his voice. He must've sent something or spoken to Dominic because he turned up this morning." He inhaled, trying to get through his words before he broke down again. "Before Dominic could shoot him, the guy shot Dominic. He fell to the floor and didn't move. The guy dragged me from the house, put me in the boot of a car and then dropped me on a remote road. I walked and found someone to bring me here."

"Do you know where you were?" Brett asked.

"Not exactly. The woman picked me up near Henley-on-Thames. Before that, I walked about a mile, and then the guy drove for roughly eleven minutes before dropping me. That's the best I could do."

Brett squeezed his shoulder. "That's great, Randall. We'll find him."

Randall couldn't smile because he could've done more, but he appreciated the gesture all the same. Kendal slid an arm around his back and urged him forward. Where they were going, he had no idea, but he didn't care. All he wanted was for Dominic to be found.

When he was encouraged to sit down, he glanced around him and saw the security room. A glass of water was pushed into his hands.

"I know you're tired, Randall, but we need to try to figure out where he could be. We're getting nothing from his phone, so he either didn't take it with him, or it's broken."

"Brett, security footage shows Dominic entering Windsor and going into the armoury about three hours ago," Felix said. "He left around ten minutes later."

"Could you track his phone before it went down?"

Felix shook his head. "I think he turned it off. It disappeared the moment he left Windsor."

Brett cursed. "Okay, let's work on what you said, Randall." He brought up a map on the screen. "You said the woman found you in Henley-on-Thames. Can you be more specific?"

Randall studied the map. "So this is the route she took to bring me back, so if we go backwards, it would be...approximately there." He pointed. "I got her phone number in case we need information from her. Her name's Alicia."

Felix nodded. "I'll call her." He left the group.

"Okay. Can you see anything on the map that is familiar?" Brett said.

Randall frowned. "As I walked, I hit a crossroads. It had a sign for Windsor, saying twenty miles, but that was it. I walked straight across the crossroads following the sign, and that's where Alicia found me."

"Great." Brett zoomed in on a small piece of road after Felix came back to him and told them where Alicia had picked him up. "This is the crossroads. You said you walked for about a mile?"

Randall shrugged. "It was approximate. I'm not brilliant at judging distance when I'm walking."

Brett followed the road on the screen and stopped. "This would be around a mile from the crossroads."

Randall leaned forward. "It looks about right."

"Felix, can you get an area which is around eleven minutes from this point?"

Felix clicked a few buttons, and a circle appeared on the screen, covering some of the map. Randall stood and stepped closer.

"Can you tell us anything about the place you were held in?"

Randall shook his head. "I was held in a room with a boarded window and taped to a chair so I couldn't look."

"What about sounds?" Brett asked.

Randall closed his eyes and wobbled when the first thing he saw was Dominic's body. He inhaled when hands helped him to sit down. Then he concentrated. What did he hear? "Birds, but nothing else. It was so quiet." He scrunched his face. "It smelt of hay. Horses!" His eyes opened. "It smelt of horses, but I didn't hear any."

"Fantastic, Randall. Anything else?"

He closed his eyes again. "I never went up or down any stairs, but I could've been kept on the ground floor. It wasn't a big house. There were stones outside. They crunched as we walked." He shook his head. "I can't think of anything else."

"That's great, Randall. That helps."

Andrew stepped closer. "Why don't we get you something to eat and a change of clothes while they work?"

Randall shook his head. "I can't. I need to help."

"You have," Brett said. "We'll find him."

Randall stood. "Don't leave without me." Brett opened his mouth. "No! Don't you leave without me."

Andrew cursed, and Randall glanced at him. Andrew met his gaze, and Randall's heart sank. "What?"

Andrew handed his phone to Brett. Randall moved closer to see it. It was a picture of Dominic as Randall had last seen him, but with a piece of paper on his chest with a black "#1" on it. Randall gasped, tears brimming again.

"*That's* what he threw down." Randall exhaled. "We stopped just outside the room, and the guy threw something down before we left." He cleared his throat. "There's a lot of blood," he whispered.

Kendal wrapped him in their arms, and Randall cried. "We'll find him," they murmured.

26

Dominic

Pain forced Dominic to wake, and he groaned and reached for his leg, making his shoulder and head scream in agony. He collapsed back down again, breathing heavily, trying to figure out what happened. Where was he? And why was he hurting?

He blinked to clear his vision and glanced around him. A dusty, empty room with dim lighting greeted him. He rolled to his side, biting back a shout as pain shot through him. Paper crinkled beside him, and he glanced at it, seeing a black #1 written on it.

He paused. Shot. Images flashed through his head. He'd been shot. Twice. He closed his eyes, and a hazy image of the gunman and someone else flickered behind his eyelids. Who were they? The gunman came into focus. Muscular, tall, dressed all in black. A dull, black gun pointing towards... Randall!

Memories rushed forward, battering his brain as he sorted them into order. The gunman had kidnapped Randall and pointed a gun at him. Dominic had been too slow to stop him.

He shook his head. No, that's not right. The gunman had moved his gun at the last minute, aiming for Dominic instead of Randall.

He'd been hit in the shoulder and leg and hit his head on his way down, leaving Randall without any help.

Dragging himself upright, he leaned back against the wall and removed his belt. He tied it around his leg, hoping to stem any more blood loss, though from his wooziness, he wasn't doing great. He couldn't do anything about his shoulder right then. Gritting his teeth, he pushed himself to standing, pausing when his head swam, and he breathed through his nose until the nausea finished rolling through his stomach.

He limped through the door, checking the house a lot slower than he wanted to, but he couldn't help it. When he found no sign of anyone, he exited the house, almost tumbling to his knees as he descended the steps. He leaned against his car and opened the driver's door.

He smacked his hand against the roof. "Fuck!" Someone had taken his keys.

He studied his surroundings, but it was as empty as it had been when he'd turned up. Wincing with every movement, he reached for the phone he'd turned off and stashed down the side of the seat. Luckily, it was still there. He'd turned it off as soon as he'd left Windsor because he hadn't wanted anything to get in the way of him rescuing Randall.

Big mistake.

He wasn't as competent as he thought he was.

Cursing, he switched the phone on and waited, leaning heavily on the car. When the phone had started, he called Owen.

"If you're calling me from the grave, you better have a good excuse for running off half-cocked without backup," his best friend said.

"Owen," he gasped.

"Fuck, Dom. As awful as you sound, it's damn good to hear your voice."

Dominic frowned. "Why?"

"We had photographic evidence plus an eyewitness to say you were dead, my man. I need to let them know."

"No! Wait!" Dominic cleared his throat, breathing through the pain.

"Explain."

Dominic inhaled. "Whoever that guy is, he's working on the assumption I'm dead."

"You sound it."

"I feel it." He blew out a breath. "He's going to make his next move. We need to figure out what it is without anyone finding out I'm alive."

"What you need is medical attention."

"That can wait."

"Where are you?"

Dominic gave him the address. "Don't let anyone know."

Collecting as much energy as he could, he shuffled back towards the house. There had to be something left behind. There had to be. He managed two rooms before he had to sit down and wait, and it wasn't long after when he heard car tyres. He pulled one of the guns he still had on him—he assumed the guy had not bothered disarming him because he'd thought he was dead—and aimed it at the door.

"Dominic!"

Owen's voice was a relief, but he held the gun up until he saw his best friend. When Evan came into view as well, he couldn't help but chuckle.

"I should've realised you couldn't keep your mouth shut," he complained, his hand dropping to his lap.

"Bloody hell. Couldn't you have dodged the bullets?" Evan said, dropping beside him with a first aid kit. "I haven't got what I need to fix you up properly. You need to go to hospital."

Dominic shook his head. "Not happening. This is heating up. He has to be making his move now that I'm supposedly out of the way."

Evan cursed as he checked Dominic over. "The bullet went straight through your shin, and from the amount of blood I see, it's not hit anything too important."

"Wonderful," Dominic deadpanned. "That makes it hurt so much less."

"Your shoulder, however, is fucked. You're going to need surgery on that one, I think."

Dominic grimaced. "It's not the first time I've been hit in the shoulder."

"Exactly my point. You've got an injury on top of an injury. You're going to need it looked at."

"Tape it up for now. We have work to do."

Evan cursed up a storm, but he did what Dominic asked. Dominic knew he had to get it looked at, but he wasn't wasting time with that when they needed to figure out what the hell was going on.

"Do you know anything about the guy?"

Dominic shook his head. "Nothing. He was muscular, tall and fully dressed in black, including the mask. I didn't recognise his voice." He tensed. "Fuck! How is Randall? Why didn't I ask about him sooner?"

Owen put out a placating hand. "He's fine. He's been checked over, and apart from being hungry, his head wound was fine. He'd had a scan, and everything came back okay. He's shaken, though. Even more so because he thinks you're dead." Owen glared at him. "You better get your excuses in order because when you see him, he'll be in the right to clock you one for not telling him."

"I know. And I will. I'm just glad he's okay. Did the guy just let him go?"

Owen explained what happened and the message Andrew received. "Everyone believes you to be dead, and they're out for blood. Brett is searching for you based on what Randall could remember. He tried your phone, but you had it turned off, you asshole."

Dominic winced when Evan tightened the bandage around his shoulder. "I know. I thought I could handle him. He was much better prepared and trained than I was expecting."

"Did you remember nothing?" Owen bit out.

Dominic sighed. "Prepare for the worst."

"Exactly." Owen shook his head. "Look, we can't stay here just in case he comes back. As much as we have more people on our side—probably—if what you think is true, he's probably heading for Windsor."

"Agreed."

Evan climbed to his feet and steadied Dominic as he rose. "Who do you think he's going for?"

"May."

"She's at Windsor. How is he going to get to her?"

Dominic shrugged. "I don't know. He has to have someone working on the inside. Someone is either going to get to her or to get her out of there, somehow."

They shuffled towards the front door. "Who do you think?"

"I really don't know."

Evan helped Dominic into the back seat where he could rest his leg along the seat, and then Owen drove them towards Windsor.

"I have somewhere we can hunker down, but when we get there, we're calling Brett. We can't do this alone," Owen said.

"Okay," Dominic said. He rested his head back. He was all out of energy.

They roused him when they arrived, and he climbed from the car, Evan helping him into the back door of the property they were using.

"Whose is this?"

"Mine," Owen said. "Evan's been staying here with me."

Dominic stared at him once he was sitting. "When did you buy a house?"

"A few months ago. I've been doing it up. It's only recently been finished."

"Why didn't you tell me?"

Owen raised his eyebrows. "You've been busy."

Dominic sighed. "Sorry."

Owen waved him away and pulled his phone out. He put it on speaker. "Hey, Brett."

"Owen, where are you? We need all hands on deck here."

Owen smirked. "I've been fetching another pair for us to use, but we have to keep it quiet."

"Who?"

Owen held out the phone.

"Hey, Brett," Dominic said.

Silence. Then, a long exhale. "Fuck, it's good to hear your voice, Dominic Ainsley. How are you?"

"I'm okay, but we have a problem."

"No shit, Sherlock. Who did it?"

Dominic sighed. "I have no idea, but we need to assume they think I'm dead. It might work in our favour."

"Where are you?" Brett asked.

Owen answered, and Evan held out a glass of water to Dominic, along with some paracetamol. He downed the medication and the entire glass. It would take the edge off his pain, but he'd still need medical attention as soon as this was over. For some reason, he had a feeling this would end sooner rather than later.

"Brett's on his way over," Owen said. "How are you holding up?"

Dominic took stock. "As well as could be expected."

Owen didn't look convinced, but Dominic didn't care. They had work to do, and he wasn't going anywhere while there was still a danger to May and Randall.

His friends plied him with food while they waited for Brett, and then they all settled down and went through what they knew.

"He's going after May," Dominic said. "He has to be. If he's Carlos, he has to be going after her. She's been his main focus throughout all of this."

"What if he's not Carlos?" Brett said, being the devil's advocate.

Dominic thought that through. "Well, Fletcher is out of the picture, as are the guys from Carlisle. Gavin is still in prison. Would someone else from the gang be trying to overturn Carlos's reign?"

"It's a possibility. Is there anyone else you can think of who might be working behind the scenes here? It seems unlikely—although not impossible—for the gang to be bothered about tying up loose ends in Carlisle when they'd already managed to flush her back home."

"I'm missing something," Dominic muttered. "What else links everything that's happened?"

"The only things I can think of are you, May, your parents and the gang," Brett said.

Evan held up his hand. "What did the police get out of the gang when they arrested some of them? Did they have any information?"

Brett shook his head. "Not a great deal. Most were terrified of Carlos and refused to speak ill of him. No one would identify him, and we've not managed to get any surveillance of what the guy looks like."

"Can't they be arrested for who they've been associating with?"

Brett chuckled. "Wouldn't that be nice? No, although we have pictures of them with known felons and traffickers, we have no evidence to prove they are actually 'dealing' with them."

"That's a load of bullshit," Owen spat. "Of course they are."

"One new piece of information we did find out was that one member had studied computers during his stint in prison and had become quite adept at creating bugs, hence those we found."

Dominic stared at him. "Both of the bugs?"

Brett nodded. "Both were of similar creation, and Felix said they were made by the same person."

"So how did Addams get hold of one?"

"I'm assuming from a similar place others do. The gang sells them for a bit of side cash."

"Who the fuck is Carlos?" Dominic growled. "I want this fucker on a platter."

"Don't we all," muttered Owen.

Brett paced the living room. "So, if he's going after May, how will he do it?"

"Either he has an in within the castle, or he's going to figure out how to get her out of it," Dominic said.

"Let's go through the options, then. How will he do either of those?"

"What reason would she leave the safety of the castle when she knows she's safer inside?" Evan said, then shot upright. "Your parents!"

Dominic grimaced and nodded. "It's the only thing I can think of.

"We already have two guards keeping an eye on them. They're at home and have been so all morning," Brett said.

Dominic stood, wincing and inhaling when pain powered through him. "I want to speak to May...and Randall, too. They need to know. I can't put them through it any longer."

Brett nodded. "I agree. But we need to do it stealthily enough that no one else finds out." He glanced at Dominic. "I can't persuade you to sit this one out, can I?"

Dominic found a laugh from somewhere. "No chance."

"In which case, you need patching up again."

Dominic waved him away. "I'm fine."

"The blood has seeped through those bandages. You need them changing. That's an order."

Evan entered the room with another first aid kit. "This has better supplies than the one I brought with me."

As he worked on Dominic's wounds, he cursed and muttered about visiting a hospital, and Dominic would, but only once the situation was sorted.

It didn't take long for Dominic to be deemed as good as he could be, and they weaponed up. Between the four of them, they should be able to get to May's suite and keep her safe until they created the trap for whoever was orchestrating this when they made their move.

Despite the pain lancing through him, he insisted they walk the short distance to where they were entering the castle—the secret subterranean tunnels that had mostly been sealed up. These were the same tunnels that Randall had problems with when that asshole Ernest had used him at gunpoint to summon the king. This time, they were going through to Andrew's office rather than Randall's, as his had been irreversibly sealed.

Sweat poured down his spine and temple, soaking into the mask they'd decided he should wear to hide his identity when they reached their destination, and Brett was the first to enter, holding his gun up in case something had changed in the short time he'd been gone. The office was empty, as they'd expected it to be. They swept Randall's office, similarly empty, and Owen inspected the corridor before indicating for them to continue.

They carefully worked their way through the long hallways towards May's suite, keeping Dominic in the centre so that, even without his mask, it would've been more difficult to recognise him. They startled several staff members, who rushed to get out of their way. They didn't worry about them announcing the news that people were infiltrating the castle because they knew Brett by sight. They would, however, be aware that something was wrong.

Although Brett hadn't announced Dominic's rise from the dead, he had let Felix know that some of them were working their way through the castle to May and had asked him to keep things normal and not let anyone else but the guards studying the security cameras know.

When they reached the corner around which May's suite was, they paused. Dominic could hear voices, raised and angry, and it took all the training in him to keep still when he recognised Randall's terrified voice.

He couldn't hear what anyone else said, but the scared yet strong tone of his boyfriend had pride racing through Dominic. No matter what anyone said, Randall had some crazy strength inside him.

"You're not taking her anywhere," Randall said.

27

Randall

Randall couldn't ever remember being so grief-stricken as he was right then. It had been a long morning, and he couldn't even go through the motions of trying to work. He'd settled into his room after Kendal had taken him there, but his mind was all over the place. With Dominic dead, what else did Randall have? Whereas, before he'd considered a future with Dominic, he'd envisioned a long life alone, now he couldn't think of spending so many years without the man standing beside him, holding his hand as they finished their years on earth.

He sniffled and wiped at the tears flowing down his cheeks. How were May and Dominic's parents holding up? May was still in danger, but if Randall knew the royal family at all, they wouldn't turf her out just because Dominic was no longer working for them. She would need some support, though.

Clapping his hands to his thighs, he rose and headed for the door. He wasn't much use to anyone at the minute, but maybe he could help May by just being there for her. Even if they were both silent in their grief.

He shuffled along the corridors, eyes on the floor so he didn't meet anyone's sympathetic gaze. It would be more than he could take while the wound was still raw. Much like the head injury he had. He'd have a scar for sure, but at least he'd survived, which was more than he could say for Dominic.

"—need to get you to safety. The royal family can't protect you. They couldn't protect Dominic," a man's voice pleaded.

"He would've wanted me to stay here and let them help," May said, her voice shaky and strained.

"For fuck's sake! They're no use to anyone. The fact that I've got this far goes to prove that." The tone changed completely from cajoling and pleading to mean and cold.

Randall froze, chills spreading down his spine. He recognised that voice. He'd listened to it enough to know the man who'd kidnapped him. He rounded the corner slowly, not wanting to believe what he'd heard. It was true. The man who'd kidnapped him was now holding onto May's arm, tugging her towards Randall.

Detective Addams.

As pain blossomed from his heart and through his body, Randall realised he might be the only one between May and her fate at Addams' hands. No matter the outcome, it was the least he could do for Dominic. With a deep inhale, he stepped away from the wall.

"You're not taking her anywhere," he said. His voice, while loud, was shaky, but he refused to bow down to him after what he'd been put through. After what this asshole had done to Dominic.

Addams lifted his head and stared at him, and Randall could see the uncertainty on his face. Would he try to pretend he was helping May, or would he drop the act and face the truth? Randall was hoping whoever was monitoring the cameras noticed something was wrong and sent people to help.

"Well, well, well. The so-called boyfriend has appeared," Addams said. Randall tried not to shiver at the coldness in his voice. "I thought you'd be licking your wounds after seeing what I did to Dominic. You're obviously not as in love with him as you pretended."

Randall glanced at May, her face reflecting the same pain that he was sure was on his own but also a hint of anger. He hoped she didn't do anything to antagonise Addams.

"You're Carlos," he stated.

Addams smirked. "The one and only." He lifted his arm, and a gun appeared.

Randall stared and swallowed. "Why are you after May?"

"She has what is mine."

Randall frowned. "You said that about Dominic, too."

Addams nodded. "Dominic was a means to an end. It made it possible to get closer to May because it showed she wasn't safe with the royals. He did have what I wanted. May. And May has the physical items I want."

"The drugs," May said.

Addams nodded again. "It's my payment for services rendered. I just needed you to tell me where it was."

"Services rendered?" Randall asked, detecting movement behind Addams and May and not wanting to draw attention to it.

"You're very inquisitive." Addams tilted his head, lowering his gun a little.

"It's in my job description. It's how I know what needs to get done. I can't help it."

Addams raised his eyebrows. "Fair enough. I have some spare time. Yes, services rendered. They requested I remove Dominic from the picture. As it benefited me, I did so."

"You were requested?"

"I'm very good at my job. And at cleaning up after myself. I have many years of practise at what police officers look for."

May gasped. "You cleaned up my house!"

Addams smirked again. "What better way to make people second-guess your statement of events?" He focused on Randall again. "Anyway, sorry to love you and leave you again. But at least you're not stranded this time." He lifted his arm and pointed the gun at Randall again, and icy fingers clasped at his heart.

"I don't think so, Addams."

Randall must've been hearing things, but the next thing he saw was Addams reaching for his shoulder and falling to the floor, and a muffled shot echoed around the space. May raced to the other side of the hallway, giving Addams a wide berth and threw herself into Dominic's arms.

Randall stared. It sure looked like Dominic, but he must have a twin or something because Randall had seen Addams shoot Dominic. Dominic fell to the floor and didn't move. Dominic had blood pouring from his body. Dominic wasn't responding to anything.

Dominic was dead.

Wasn't he?

He watched Brett and Owen handcuff Addams none too gently and lean him against the wall.

"I fucking shot you!" Addams shouted at Dominic. "Twice!"

"You need to aim better. Neither shot hit anywhere vital."

Dominic's voice washed over Randall, and he transferred his gaze to the man again. Dominic was already looking at him, and Randall stared.

And stared.

And stared.

His supposedly dead boyfriend wandered towards him, and the closer he came, the more he looked like Dominic. Tears blurred his vision as Dominic's arms came around him. The moment his scent reached Randall's nose, he broke down and clutched at his back. After several long minutes, he ran his hands over Dominic's body, cataloguing limbs, winces and groans.

Then he stopped, twisted around and stomped over to Addams. "Asshole!" he said, kicking his leg.

Addams' growl of pain was music to Randall's ear, and he stalked back to his boyfriend amidst chuckles. Dominic wrapped his arm around Randall again, and Randall snuggled into his chest, closing his eyes.

"I can't believe you're alive," he murmured.

"I'll be truthful. I thought I was dead, too. Plus, I still need to get checked out at the hospital," Dominic said.

Randall gasped and moved back, batting Dominic's good shoulder. "Go! Now! In fact, I'll take you."

"Listen to him," May said. "I want you checked out."

Dominic shook his head. "We need to talk to Addams."

Brett stepped forward. "Eric and Viola are escorting him to lock up. We can talk to him later after he's stewed for a while. Besides, we need to get the go-ahead from Commissioner Thomas. You have time to get seen to."

Dominic sighed. "Okay, okay." He slid his hand into Randall's. "I'm in your capable hands."

Randall closed his eyes and inhaled and then smiled and tugged Dominic towards the exit. "Hospital time."

They left everyone behind, even May, after a quick hug from her brother, and then Randall held tightly to the miracle that was Dominic all the way to his car. He opened the door for him, helped him to sit and fastened his seatbelt because his shoulder complained. All the while, he was smiling broadly because Dominic was alive!

"I'm so glad you're okay," Randall said as he drove towards the hospital. "I'm sorry you're in pain, but I'm so happy you're alive."

Dominic reached across and squeezed his thigh. "I know. I am extremely happy to be alive, too. Can I just say how proud I am of you?"

Randall frowned. "Why?"

"You stood up to Addams. You told me not long ago that when someone pointed a gun at you, you'd do anything they asked. Addams pointed a gun at you, and you were asking him questions. That's not the Randall you thought you were."

Randall nodded slowly, considering what Dominic said. "I wanted to."

"But you didn't. And that gave us time to come to your aid."

"I couldn't believe my ears or eyes when you stepped around that corner," he whispered. "I thought Addams had shot me, and I was in heaven, waiting for you."

"Not yet, you're not."

Randall parked the car as close to the entrance as he could, uncaring if he was in the wrong parking bay. He helped Dominic out of the car, and when they entered, a nurse and doctor appeared immediately.

"I'm Doctor Leonard Knightley. We were told of your impending arrival. Let's get you into a wheelchair and a room."

Dominic sat in the chair with an audible sigh and unhidden wince, which just proved how much pain he was in. He grabbed Randall's hand as the nurse pushed them towards their destination.

They were hustled and bustled from room to x-ray to scans and back again, doing all kinds of tests, for which Randall greatly appreciated their thoroughness. Dominic, however, was teetering on the edge of grumpy from all the poking and prodding.

"How long is this going to take?" he said for the tenth time in as many minutes.

"I see you're as patient a patient as the king is," said Commissioner Brady Thomas as he entered the room. Dominic moved to stand, but Brady waved him away. "Stand down, soldier. I'm here for more than one reason, but one is in the king's stead. I told him it wasn't wise to visit just yet."

"I won't be here long, so he doesn't have to worry," Dominic said.

Brady raised his eyebrows at Randall, who hid his smile behind his hand. "No one has spoken to Addams yet. Brett requested it wait until you could be present, though depending on what the doctor says, I might have to say no to that." Dominic opened his mouth, but Brady continued. "However, as he's locked away somewhere he can't contact anyone, we have some time to play with. Not much, mind."

"Understood, sir," Dominic said.

"Talk to me, both of you. Tell me what happened."

Dominic glanced at Randall. "I think you should start. Your story began yesterday."

Randall settled onto the bed beside Dominic and explained what happened about the message from "Dominic" asking him to meet him at his home and being knocked out. He described Addams' behaviour and appearance during his captivity, which made a bit more sense now they knew it was Addams, the events of Dominic's arrival and supposed death, being left in the countryside and finding his way home.

"Have they checked you out since then?" Brady asked.

Randall nodded. "They gave me the all-clear, though I was told to make sure I see a doctor if I felt dizzy or nauseated." He stared at Dominic. "You should continue because, until the last bit with May and Addams, I was hiding in my room."

Dominic slid his good arm around Randall's back, resting his hand on his stomach as he spoke. Randall nearly clocked him on the bad shoulder when he mentioned turning his phone off, but he refrained. Barely. If Brady's mouth twitch was any sign, he'd seen the promise of a backhand in Dominic's future. When he mentioned holing up in Owen's house, he couldn't help interrupting.

"Owen has a house?"

Dominic chuckled. "He does. He's been doing it up, and now that Evan is here, he's helping, too."

"I always thought Owen would keep his bachelor pad."

Dominic nodded. "Me, too."

Brady cleared his throat, and Randall covered his cheeks. "Sorry."

Dominic continued until he reached the point of the story when he'd heard Randall's first words, so Randall took over. After they'd finished their story, Randall realised it was unusual for a questioning to take place with someone else at the same time. Usually, they would interview one person at a time. When he mentioned it to Brady, he shrugged.

"I have faith that you will tell the truth; otherwise, you wouldn't hold the positions you do within the royal family."

A knock sounded, and a doctor bustled in. Brady stood. "I'll leave you to it. Let me know as soon as you have news, and we'll do what we can about Addams."

"Thank you, Commissioner," Dominic said.

As the door shut behind Brady, the doctor started talking. "Well, we have good news and bad news."

Randall glanced at Dominic, who said, "Bad news first."

"You need surgery on your shoulder. The bullet that entered smashed up some of the bones pretty badly. We need to repair it as soon as possible. To be honest, I don't know how you're still moving it."

Dominic huffed a laugh. "Sheer force of will. The good news?"

"Your leg is surprisingly fine. The bullet missed every possible dangerous place and went straight out the other side. Other than blood loss, it'll heal with time."

Dominic sighed. "No work for a while, then."

The doctor smiled but shook his head. "Sorry, no."

"Didn't think so." Dominic leaned back on the bed, staring at the ceiling. "I'm sure Brett can use someone in the office for a while."

"We'll schedule you for the surgery as soon as—"

"Is there any rush for the shoulder?" Dominic interrupted.

"Ideally, yes. These shattered fragments could easily cause more damage the longer it's left. I can maybe give you a day if you don't use it at all, but then it must be done."

Dominic nodded. "Give me that day. Strap my shoulder however you need to be happy, and I promise I will be back here in twenty-four hours."

The doctor narrowed his eyes on him, and Randall bit his lip to stop his laughter. "Be sure that you do." He sighed. "I'll send a nurse in to sort your shoulder, but if you use it even once, you must come straight in. Any of those fragments could potentially get into your bloodstream and cause irreversible damage."

"Understood."

Randall wasn't particularly happy about Dominic's choice, but it was his choice, after all. The hospital insisted he take a wheelchair with him—and use it—to ensure less stress on his leg and shoulder.

"Mr Ainsley? I'm glad you're okay. Can you tell me what happened?" Malachi Sanders stood on the edge of the path outside the hospital as Randall pushed Dominic towards the waiting car.

"I got shot, Mr Sanders. It happens." It was more than he should've said, but he was getting annoyed at the constant "popping up" of the reporter.

"Who shot you?" Malachi asked.

Dominic glared at him, but Randall helped him into the car and shut the door before Dominic could say anything else. He stared at the reporter as Randall put the wheelchair in the boot and climbed in. Malachi stared back, unblinking, though when Randall pulled away from the curb, Malachi's shoulders lowered.

When Dominic reached the security room, they were let in with a resounding cheer from the occupants.

"Nice job, Dominic," Colt said, shaking his hand. He glanced at Randall. "I hear you were the hero of the hour."

Randall's cheeks heated, and he waved him away. Brett came over.

"I'm surprised they let you out so soon."

Randall snorted. "They're not happy about it. As long as he doesn't use his arm *at all*," he stressed the words and glared at his boyfriend, "he can have one day before surgery on his shoulder."

"I'm going to be out of action for a while, Brett."

"I know. We are always short-handed in here, so we're happy to have you, and your job will be waiting for you when you're fit and healthy again."

"Thanks, Brett."

"As soon as Commissioner Thomas gets here, we'll start," Brett said, tapping Felix on the shoulder. "Can you let him know?"

"Already have done."

Brett smiled at Felix, whose cheeks darkened, and Randall hid his smile. He had always wondered about their relationship, but there was never any gossip or clues about it. He'd love for them to start dating, though; he thought they'd fit extremely well together.

By the time Brady arrived, everyone was raring to have a go at Addams. Dominic asked Randall if he wanted to watch the interrogation, but he chose not to. He'd had enough of the guy, and instead, he kissed Dominic goodbye and—after insisting that someone take charge of making sure Dominic did as the doctor had ordered—headed for May's suite. Evan and Owen had been sitting with her, but they were probably smothering her by now. It was time for a chick flick, ice cream, chocolate and tissues.

Kicking the boys out of May's suite was invigorating, and they chuckled as the men grumbled but left. No one was overly worried about there being another infiltration because Addams seemed to be the head of the snake, but a guard was staying outside of May's room, anyway. At least until they had confirmation from Addams.

"I have around twenty hours. What are we starting with?" Randall said.

May laughed, though it was a little watery. "*Love Actually.*"

"Good choice!"

As they settled in to watch the half a dozen couples get their happily, and not-as-happily, ever after, they chose their poison—ice cream for Randall, chocolate for May.

The only way that night could get any better was if Dominic was with him, but his boyfriend had work to do.

28

Dominic

Being relegated to a wheelchair was not how Dominic wanted to appear to Addams, especially after having stood on two legs to apprehend him, but he had to do what the doctor ordered; otherwise, Randall would kill him. He needed to be there because he wanted to know what Addams' motivation was. Dominic had heard what he'd told Randall, but he wanted more detail, as did everyone else.

Commissioner Thomas was with them, as were Brett, Felix and one of Brady's detectives. Dominic was a little more leery of police officers now, but he understood not all of them were assholes—Addams' behaviour had changed Dominic's opinion.

When they entered the room Addams was being held in, Dominic saw he wasn't exactly comfortably situated, and he barely withheld his smile. Addams had tape around his waist, wrists and ankles, just like Randall had when the asshole had kidnapped him. What went around came around.

Addams sneered at him as Dominic was pushed in. "I see you're not as strong as you believe yourself to be."

Dominic smiled. "At least I'm not bleeding out." He checked on Addams' injuries, which had been seen to, but not enough to make him not wince whenever he moved.

"It's illegal to keep me here," Addams said, and every one of them laughed.

"It's illegal to kidnap, injure and kill other people, too. I don't think we have anything to worry about," Brady said. "You have a lot to talk to us about before we'll even consider giving you anything you may ask for."

Addams glared at him. "I won't give you everything."

Dominic raised his eyebrows. "Why not? It's not like you to keep quiet. You told Randall quite a lot of things that we already have on record. You may as well pick up where you left off and finish your gloating about how incapable we are. I'm sure we'd love to hear how we can improve."

Addams snorted. "Everything. You're far too trusting."

"How long have you been involved with this?" Brady asked.

Addams stopped squirming—it was as if he was trying to make himself bleed out quicker to stop the line of questioning, but Dominic was sure they would let him rather than stop their questions—and chuckled. "Seven years. After my positive drug test, I knew I had to do something. I started talking to Gavin. We came to an arrangement."

"When did you take on the persona of Carlos?"

"Straight away. It is my name, after all."

"What is?"

Addams shook his head. "And you call yourself investigators. I told you, too trusting. My name is Carlos Miguel Adan. Carl Michael Addams is the English version. It made it easier for me to get people to trust me if I wasn't seen as an 'outsider,' and then when I made the arrangement with Gavin, I went by Carlos. Back to my roots, you could say."

"Why not take over the gang earlier than you did?" Brett asked. "Why now?"

"Because things weren't getting done. They were taking too long. Asking too many questions. Getting themselves fucking jailed." Addams rolled his eyes.

"But you were front and centre with the case that got Gavin and Paul sent to prison," Dominic said. "You were heading the case."

"I had to keep up appearances. You should know better than anyone what doors open when you know or work with the police. Being a detective was an in few people can boast about."

"Why get rid of Fletcher?" Dominic asked.

"He had the gall to threaten to spill everything to you. I couldn't let that happen. Gavin, too. He knew too much about me. He could easily have used that to help his appeal." Addams stared at them and threw his head back, laughter echoing around the room. "You've not been notified of his death yet, then. They're slacking."

Dominic didn't like how forthcoming Addams was being, especially when he originally said he wasn't going to say much. He glanced at Brett, who leaned closer. "He's biding his time by talking to us. Why?"

Brett shrugged. "No idea, but let him run his mouth as much as he wants. We'll deal with whatever consequences come from it."

Dominic didn't like it, but he acquiesced.

Brady leaned against the wall, crossing his arms over his chest. "What do you know about Yousef Azizi?"

Addams smirked. "He held out longer than I expected him to."

"You tortured him?" Brady asked.

Addams nodded. "With help. Although those guys needed to learn how to be more careful with a scene. There was no way I had time to clean up their mess."

"So, you killed them, too," Dominic guessed.

"After they failed to capture May, yes. They were sloppy. Clean-up was necessary. Including that stupid car everyone remembered. I needed people to second-guess May's version of events. Who would listen to someone who wasn't sure they saw and heard what they thought they had?"

"How did you become so adept at cleaning scenes?"

Addams chuckled. "After visiting so many crime scenes over the years, I learnt what detectives found and looked for. It's easy to clean up when you know where to look for potential clues."

"And after those men ended their usefulness?" Brady asked.

"I broke their necks and dumped them in the river. I knew they'd wash up eventually, but there would be no trace of me."

"But there was speculation, wasn't there?" Brett said. "Detective Maloney found something, didn't he?"

Addams clenched his jaw. "That asshole was far too clever for his own good. He saw me, and despite trying to talk my way out of it, he didn't like my answers. It was a necessary precaution."

"I wouldn't call killing people in cold blood a 'necessary precaution,'" Brett snapped.

Addams stared at him, and Dominic wondered how he'd hidden this part of himself for so long. He just had to look into his eyes and see the coldness in them. Even his voice sounded different. Meaner, less caring than when he'd been speaking to them as a detective.

"What about Paul?"

Addams smiled. "I'm sure you'll find him soon. If you think about it, I'm doing you a favour."

"So, you've disposed of anyone who could identify you as being involved?" Brady asked.

"Yes."

"Not everyone," Brett said, looking at his phone. "I've just had word that the police have arrested some traffickers and gang members that were waiting for a 'delivery.' I wonder if that has anything to do with why you were after May?"

Dominic watched Addam's reaction to the news, and Addams' eyes and mouth tightened briefly. "They were, but not until May had told him where the drugs were hidden. Right?" More tension. Dominic changed the subject. "What was the deal with the roses?"

Addams frowned. "I had nothing to do with that."

"Who hired you to go after me?"

Addams shrugged. "No idea, and I don't really care. I will say, however, that I tried tracking them, and it was impossible. I don't care because it was fun to terrorise you and your family." He smirked at Dominic, making him want to punch him.

"If you didn't have anything to do with the roses, what did you do?"

"Everything else." He laughed. "Going after May, sending those awful letters to your parents—that was a rudimentary tactic—and kidnapping your boyfriend. That was the icing on the cake."

"If you had nothing to do with the roses, why did you choose to go in the order you did: May, my parents, and then Randall?" It couldn't be a coincidence.

"That's what my 'employer' requested, and I didn't see a reason to deny the list. It made no difference to me. I would still get what I wanted. All of you willing to do anything to make it stop."

Dominic stared at him, and the silence dragged on. "Why?"

"Why what?"

Addams sighed. "Have you not been listening?"

"To what? You listing your so-called achievements? That's not why you did all this."

Addams sat forward, or at least tried to. The tape stopped him, and he gritted his teeth against the pain he undoubtedly felt. "I wanted the drugs."

Dominic exhaled. "You did all of this for drugs?"

"Do you know how much those drugs are worth?"

"You were going to sell them?" Brady asked.

Addams shook his head and then tilted his head back and forth. "Some of them. But those drugs would set me up for years. I wouldn't need to deal with assholes like Gavin and Fletcher anymore. I could use what I wanted whenever I wanted."

Brady rose from his lean. "How did you get away with the mandatory drug tests the police insist upon?"

Addams chuckled. "My brother loves me."

Brady shook his head. "They would've known it was from a different person. Even if he was your brother."

Addams smirked. "Yeah, but when I changed my DNA information within the system, it wouldn't be flagged up as wrong."

"You've gone to a lot of trouble for these drugs," Brady said. "And look where you are now."

"Yeah, but not for long. I'm a patient man. I'll get what I want, eventually. I've waited five years already."

"Why now?" Dominic asked. "Like you said, you've waited five years. How long were you going to wait?"

"My plan had been another two years. Then I was going to go after her and find where they were. My 'employer' changed my timeline to my advantage. As did your argument with Randall."

Dominic frowned. "How *did* you know about that so quickly?" He glared. "You bugged the office, didn't you?"

"You're heading for prison, Addams," Brady said.

"None of this will stick. It's all circumstantial."

"Not when we've got your confession on video."

Addams paled, and he glanced at the ceilings. "There are no cameras in here. I can spot them a mile away."

Brady stepped closer to Addams and pointed at the button on his shirt. "You missed this one, though."

Addams cursed. "All that will show is how you treated me. That will get things turned in my favour."

"Not if we only use the audio."

Brady moved towards the door. "I'm done. Montgomery, take him into custody when these fine men have finished with him."

"Yes, sir."

"I have more information!" Addams said.

"I don't need it," Brady said and left.

Addams swallowed hard. "This must be related to the king, Dominic. Not what I did, obviously, but my employer. They have to be focusing on the king. I can't see any other reason for who they're targeting."

Dominic faced Brett. "I don't have anything else for him. Do you?"

"I would like to know why you took Dominic's gun?" Brett glanced at Dominic. "The gun he held was yours. There were two bullets missing."

Dominic growled and glared at Addams. "You shot me with my own fucking gun!"

Addams smirked. "I needed it to point to someone else. That's all."

Brett clapped Montgomery's shoulder. "Feel free to keep him here until you have the others to help you. I'll leave two guards outside until your team is here. Don't listen to him."

Montgomery chuckled. "I'll wait outside with your guards. I'm too tempted to punch him."

Dominic held up a fist and bumped it against Montgomery's. "Welcome to the team."

As they exited, Addams called out, "This isn't the end! I promise you that!"

The words sent a shiver down Dominic's spine, but there wasn't much they could do about it. If something was heading their way, they'd deal with it. Like they had done every other time something had been thrown at them. After all, they'd spent the last few years dodging bullets, bombs and death threats from within the king's own family. They could deal with anything as long as they had a united front.

Brady waited for them in the corridor. "I was expecting you to be in there longer."

Brett shook his head. "He didn't know anything else. You can get more detailed information from him about the things he'd admitted to. He does think it's a threat against the king, though."

Brady nodded. "It's not impossible."

Brett agreed. "Anyway, now that's done, you can go back to hospital and get your shoulder sorted out."

Dominic grimaced. "I have another seventeen hours before I have to be back."

"Just because they gave you twenty-four hours doesn't mean you should use them all. Go back now. The quicker you get it done, the quicker you'll be back to work."

Dominic sighed. "Fine. Let me find Randall. But get someone to check for that bug."

"Already on it," Felix said, proving once again he was a mind reader.

Three days later, Dominic was chomping to get out of the hospital. He'd been given updates through Brett, Felix, Andrew and Randall, but he needed the doctors to finally agree to his release so he could join the investigation. He paced the hospital room, his arm still immobilised after the surgery, but his feet worked just fine, with the odd twinge from his shin.

"Sit down before you wear a hole in the floor," Randall said from his perch in an armchair by the window. He had a laptop open in front of him and was working on his phone while chastising him.

"It shouldn't be taking so long," Dominic grumbled.

"You're getting out sooner than they wanted you to. Deal with it."

Dominic raised his eyebrows, but Randall's attention wasn't on him. Not all of it, anyway. "Yes, sir." Randall's mouth twitched, and Dominic smiled, wandering over to his boyfriend. "I bet you'll be happy to be back at your desk rather than using this makeshift one."

"Without a doubt. I can work anywhere, though."

"I'm sure you can."

Randall put his phone down and stood, nestling into the space that was his new favourite position, so he'd told Dominic—under his right arm with his head resting on Dominic's good shoulder. "I can't wait for you to be out of here, too. Even though we can't sleep in the same bed, I'll be happy to be with you in the same room."

Dominic pressed a kiss to his hair. "We can sleep in the same bed. We'll be fine."

"No, we won't. I'm not damaging your shoulder any more than it is already. You've been shot twice in that same place. It needs rest. Just like you do."

"All I've done is rest for the past three days."

"And all you'll do is rest for many more. You're not going back to work before your body is ready."

"Sir, yes, sir."

Randall chuckled. "I like the sound of that."

A wave of heat went through Dominic, and he couldn't wait until he was able to do all the things to Randall that he'd been promising during his recovery. He still had a long way to go with being able to do anything strenuous, but he was good at adapting. He could figure out new ways of doing things. Lots of things.

It took another hour, but finally, he was able to get out of the hospital and back to Windsor. During the journey, he'd argued with Randall about working but had finally got his way after promising him he wouldn't do anything physical. He left Randall with a searing kiss that his groin didn't enjoy not seeing to a happy ending, and headed to Sec HQ.

As he entered, he received a standing ovation, and he inclined his head. "Thank you." He worked his way through the room towards Brett. "Where are we?"

"How did you get permission to be here?"

Dominic chuckled. "I was told as long as I didn't go gallivanting off, I could do desk work."

Brett raised his eyebrows. "How long will that last?"

"As long as possible." Brett stared at him. "I promised Randall."

"Good. Okay, so Addams has been in jail without bail since you went into surgery. We have someone watching him twenty-four-seven to reduce the chance of incidents, both from others and himself. The drugs have been recovered and disposed of. We've spoken with the traffickers, most of whom have been arrested and charged. We are about to speak to the gang members to find out exactly what they know about Carlos, aka Addams."

"I want in."

Brett checked his watch. "Two minutes. You lasted two minutes."

Dominic snorted. "I'm not doing anything physical. We're just interviewing them."

"Still. Two minutes, Dominic?"

Dominic shrugged, then wished he hadn't. "I'll be fine."

"As long as you don't shrug." Brett called to Felix, "We'll be adding one more to our party."

"Already had the minute he turned up," Felix called back.

"Thank you," Dominic shouted to him.

Brett had things that needed doing before they left, so Dominic took himself through the transcribed interviews with the traffickers. They didn't seem to know anything about anything other than Carlos was the one they dealt with, and everything was done through texts and calls that they'd been able to trace to a burner phone Addams had been using. At least, one of the burner phones. It seemed like he had one per person he dealt with. Like Paul, who had yet to be found, but Dominic believed him to be dead.

He did contact the detective in charge of Maloney's death. "Detective, I have news."

"Please tell me you found the fucker?"

"We did. He's in custody as we speak and won't be bailed. He's going straight to jail." He explained some of the pertinent details of the case, and the detective agreed to send the details about his case so it could be tied up in a bow to present to the court when the time came.

Two hours later, Brady, Montgomery, Brett and Dominic sat in a room as the first gang member joined them. Brett took point.

"Tell us what you know about Carlos."

They got next to nothing they didn't already know. The one thing that did crop up was an address they didn't know about. Dominic argued to be allowed to join them in visiting it, but Brett put his foot down.

"I'll stay in the car."

"No, you fucking won't. I'm not stupid," Brett argued.

"I promise."

Brett glared at him but changed direction, and Dominic allowed himself a small smile. As they approached the property, Dominic frowned.

"This is the address?"

Brett nodded, his mouth tight. "I didn't recognise the road name."

Dominic climbed out of the car and stared up at the property. Then he turned around and faced the property on the opposite side of the road.

Randall's property.

"He was this fucking close all this time?" Dominic muttered.

29

Felix

When Felix found out that the address the gang members had given them was opposite Randall's house, fire raced through his blood. He felt like an old-fashioned tea kettle on the stove, whistling away at top temperature, waiting to blow over. It wasn't easy for him to explode, but this was pushing all his buttons, and the cumulative weight was stoking his anger.

He got in contact with Commissioner Thomas. "Good afternoon, sir. Brett would like permission to enter that property. Both Brett and Dominic are waiting outside."

"Is there something to show it might need to be investigated?" Brady asked.

"Well," Felix gritted his teeth, "it's opposite Randall's house, sir. It seems far more likely to be something nefarious than pure coincidence. At least, to us."

Brady hummed. "Okay, tell them to enter with caution if they're not willing to wait for my men. I will have someone over there as soon as I can to back them up."

"Yes, sir. Thank you."

He relayed the information to Brett.

"Can you see anything on the maps about the property?" his boss asked. "We want to go around the back, but we don't want any surprises."

Felix clicked a few buttons on his computer and enlarged the image. "There's a shed at the far end of the garden, but the rest of the space is pretty open-plan, other than a large tree in the far corner. There's a conservatory on the back of the house, too."

"Thanks. We'll go check it out."

As Brett ended the call, Felix's stomach churned. The odds were in all their favours that one of these days, they wouldn't return from an outing like this. Normally, their jobs were to guard certain royal family members, but more often, lately, they were investigating. Felix didn't mind the shift, although he would truly miss protecting Oscar if that ever happened, and he enjoyed putting the puzzle together, but when it came to worrying about his family—his work family—he was unable to shut it off.

The never-ending plots against the crown wore on him, though he would never leave unless he was either too old or couldn't do the job anymore. Besides, he couldn't leave the one person who meant more to him than anything else in the world. He knew he would fail a test if someone asked him to choose between a member of the royal family and Brett, but he couldn't help it. And maybe that was reason enough for him to change jobs. Could he truly protect the royal family well enough if he couldn't guarantee he'd make the right choice if the crunch came to it?

He sighed at the screen and waited for a callback from Brett or Dominic to say it was all clear. Unease snaked through him the longer they took, but finally, his phone rang.

"All clear," Brett said, and Felix exhaled inaudibly. "Someone has definitely been staying here, but there's nothing to show who it might be. My guess would be Addams, but we're going to leave it as we've found it. Brady has arranged for someone to use Randall's house as a spy tower to see if anyone comes back."

Felix grinned at the spy reference, Brett's preference for James Bond-style films, something they clashed about frequently. Mainly because Felix pretended he didn't like them, and it caused long, drawn-out discussions about their unique storyline.

"Okay. I'll log it down," he said.

"Thanks. I'm bringing Dominic back. Asshole was adamant he was coming with me, and now he's pissed. He needs tying to a fricking chair."

"Handcuffs might work better," Felix said.

Brett coughed. "Maybe."

Felix snickered. Brett had never outright said anything, but Felix believed he was interested in the BDSM lifestyle. Whenever the royal family spoke about it, and whenever they visited the club as security, Brett's eyes wandered around them. Watching. What Felix wouldn't give to find out for sure.

30

Randall

The moment Dominic had told Randall about Addams' property being opposite his, he knew he wouldn't be returning to the house other than to pack everything up and move somewhere else. His parents had been overwhelmingly supportive of his relationship with Dominic and had even offered to help Randall find somewhere else to live, but Randall declined. He didn't want a house that his mother wanted him to have. He wanted something that felt right. Something he could see himself living in for years to come. With or without Dominic.

Yes, he'd already considered asking the guy to move in with him because he loved him that much. It had nothing to do with convenience and helping Dominic recuperate from his shoulder injury. But broaching the subject was something that Randall was nervous about. He didn't know why, but he couldn't seem to get the nerve to do it, even though it had been on the tip of his tongue for days.

"Oh, for god's sake, Randall," May said. "Just ask him. I know he'll say yes. He's my brother. I know him."

"And he's my boyfriend. He's not my husband or anything."

May stared at him. "Why would he need to be your husband for you to be more comfortable asking him to move in?"

Randall shrugged. "I don't know. It's something my mother always used to say. I'm not saying he has to be my husband, but…"

"You want him to be."

Randall's face heated. "Yes," he whispered.

"Then fucking ask him that, too!"

He threw his hands up in the air. "We've barely been together a month. I can't ask him yet."

"Why?" May picked up the ice cream tubs and put them on the coffee table, ready for their agreed-upon weekly movie marathon.

"Because."

May raised her eyebrows. "You sound like a child."

"Shut up."

"Is that any way to speak to my sister?" Dominic said as he entered the suite.

Despite the threat towards May being neutralised, she had asked to stay within Windsor for a few more weeks to make sure. The king had readily agreed for her to stay for as long as she wanted, but May had given herself two more weeks, and then she would move to a new house or back with her parents. She needed to feel free again. Randall had helped a little by introducing her to Nadine, who had gushed over May's photography skills.

Randall gasped, clutching at his throat, hoping with everything inside him that Dominic had not heard any more of their conversation. "She started it," he croaked, and Dominic raised an eyebrow. So much like his sister, regardless of not being blood-related.

"I can imagine that." Dominic pulled Randall into his arm, pressing his lips against his head. "Everything okay?"

Randall nodded and buried his face in Dominic's neck, needing to inhale his scent to calm his nerves. He glanced at May, who made a "go ahead" motion with her hands. Randall glared at her, but she slipped out of the room, leaving him to make a split-second decision. Something he was never good at.

"Dominic?" Dominic hummed his acknowledgement. "Do you want to... Will you... Well, would you like to..." He stammered through several starts to his sentence before Dominic claimed his lips in a searing kiss. His body responded immediately, having been denied for the last couple of weeks because of Dominic's recovery, and he held tightly as Dominic ravaged him.

Whimpering when Dominic pulled back, Randall blinked as Dominic spoke. "Tell me. Right now."

An order Randall couldn't resist. "Will you move in with me?" he murmured.

Dominic smiled. "I'm already packed and ready to go. Yes." He kissed him. "I." He kissed him again. "Will." He devoured him. "But first, we need to take this somewhere far away from my sister."

Randall chuckled even as his cheeks heated, and he lifted his face to Dominic again. "Later. I promise." When Dominic narrowed his eyes at him, he added, "I promised May a movie marathon, as you know. I'm not letting her down."

The person in question entered the room hesitantly as if she was unsure what she would come back to. "So, can I call you my brother-in-law, yet?" she asked, and Randall closed his eyes, his cheeks heating even further, enough to probably cook bacon at that point.

Dominic tightened his hold, and his lips brushed against his ear. "Was that all you wanted to ask me?" he murmured.

Randall swallowed. "No," he whispered. "But not yet."

"Yes, yet. Ask me."

Randall shook his head, but Dominic tutted at him. "Open your eyes and look at me, sweetheart." Randall did and saw a smile on his boyfriend's face.

His mouth opened before he had the chance to think it through anymore. "I want to marry you."

Dominic chuckled. "That's not a question."

Randall blinked. "It's not?"

"That was, but not the one I was expecting. Shall I make things easier on you?" Randall nodded. "Randall Metcalfe, will you marry the man in front of you despite his present less-than-ideal physical status?"

Randall's mouth twitched, but his heart raced. "I would love to."

"Good." Dominic lowered his mouth. "I don't care how long we've known each other. My instincts are telling me you're the one for me, and I'm listening to them. They've always put me on the right path when I've listened to them." He kissed him to the sound of May's cheering.

"Movie marathon cancelled. Get out of my room and go...do whatever you need to do to cement that question and answer."

Randall laughed into Dominic's mouth, breaking the seal of their lips. He pulled back and cupped Dominic's face. "I love you."

"I love you."

Dominic kissed his sister's cheek on the way out of the door, and she closed the door in their faces with a laugh. Randall steered them silently towards the room he had always used. It had become their home away from home. When they entered, Dominic slammed Randall back against the wall and took his mouth once more. Randall held onto Dominic's belt loops as the taste of his boyfriend—fiancé—registered. A taste he would never tire of.

Whenever Dominic kissed him, he always lost his mind, but since his injuries, Randall now made sure to keep his right hand locked around the belt loops while his left hand roamed around.

It was the best way to keep him from unexpectedly hurting Dominic. And Dominic's tongue in his mouth...well, that was mind-dizzying enough for him.

With the tension ratcheting up, Randall reached for Dominic's shirt buttons, unfastening them one at a time. They were the only shirts he could wear while he was healing, but Randall enjoyed being able to dress and undress him himself. As more and more tanned skin appeared, he pulled his mouth away, descending to Dominic's chest, mindful of his actions.

They hadn't touched each other sexually for two weeks—although Dominic had tried on several occasions—but this time, Randall knew what position would be best and how to do it so Dominic wasn't exerting himself too much. For once, Randall would be completely in charge.

He gently slipped the shirt from Dominic's shoulders, throwing it over the chair next to them, and took Dominic's hand, pulling him to the bed. Stopping him beside the bed, Randall sat and worked on Dominic's trousers. Again, he was careful, watching Dominic's expression as well as his body language to ensure he wasn't causing undue pain. The injured leg was healing well, and although it caused him some pain, Dominic had said it was bearable as long as he didn't stand for too long.

Randall removed the trousers and threw them in the direction of the chair he'd used previously, uncaring if they reached it or not. What caught his attention was the tent in Dominic's boxers. He slipped his thumbs into the waistband and pulled it over the engorged shaft. Fluid leaked from the tip, and Randall licked his lips, wanting it in his mouth, but he needed to wait. He helped Dominic to keep his balance as they removed the underwear, but once Dominic regained his tentative balance, Randall licked around the head of his cock. Dominic gasped and slid his fingers into Randall's hair.

"Fuck, sweetheart. It's been far too long since I felt this."

Randall hummed around his length in agreement, sucking him deeper and deeper until his throat contracted around it. He pulled free, panting, and stared up at his man. Tension lined his face, and Randall stroked his length.

"On the bed, please," he said.

Dominic raised his eyebrows, and although Randall wasn't used to being in charge in the bedroom, he lifted his chin and pointed to the bed. Chuckling, Dominic did as requested. Randall aided in getting him comfortable before stepping back.

"Where...?" Dominic started, but when Randall's fingers started on his own shirt buttons, his sentence remained unfinished.

He would admit to dragging it out a little longer than necessary, just to see the darkening of Dominic's eyes as he bared more of his skin.

"The next time we do this, we're putting your moves to music," Dominic muttered.

Randall's cheeks heated, but he didn't decline. It might make him less self-conscious if there was. When he pitched his underwear behind him, he rounded the end of the bed. Grasping Dominic's bad leg in his hands, he carefully lifted and repositioned it so he could crawl between his legs. He encircled his cock once more and took him straight into his mouth, needing to feel the silkiness of his heat.

"Fucking hell, Randall. You're so good at that." Dominic's words were more a growl than anything else.

Randall allowed him to thrust with gentle movements into his mouth, but the minute he put too much force behind it, Randall stopped him. Not because he didn't want him to do it but because Dominic's leg wasn't up to that kind of movement yet.

"Randall," Dominic warned.

"You know my conditions. It's not like we haven't spoken about this many times."

Dominic sighed and exhaled towards the ceiling. "Okay."

Randall's cock bobbed as he moved, and he hissed whenever it brushed against the covers.

"Let me taste you," Dominic said.

Randall shook his head. "Not this time. But you can watch this." He climbed off the bed and reached into the bedside table, pulling out the lube. As self-conscious as he was, he couldn't help but want to make a show for him, so he knelt facing the foot of the bed and squeezed some lube into his fingers. He braced himself on one hand and reached behind him with the other, arching his back. When his fingers skimmed across his pucker, he hissed and did it again. Massaging the lube into his entrance, he pressed one finger inside, coating his channel. He repeated it, pushing more lube inside him before sliding two fingers as deep as he could.

"Fucking hell. You're gorgeous."

Randall's skin heated as he slid three fingers in, pumping and scissoring them to stretch himself enough to take Dominic's cock. Fingers slid alongside his own, and Randall bit his lip, needing more. He pushed back a little, and Dominic's finger entered with Randall's, stretching him further. The burn was only a bite of pain, nothing he couldn't put up with.

"Enough. I need you," Dominic said, and Randall removed his fingers but stayed where he was, eyebrows raised. Dominic sighed. "If that's okay with you."

It was meant as a question but didn't sound like one. Randall chuckled and shook his head but obliged. After all, he wanted Dominic as much as Dominic wanted him. He turned around to face his lover and carefully straddled his hips. They'd already spoken about not using condoms any longer and had been tested, so that would be the first time Randall felt him bare, and he couldn't wait.

Randall lowered himself to his hands, one on either side of Dominic's head, away from his shoulder, and brushed their lips together. Then he lifted back up and reached between them for

Dominic's cock. The first nudge of his shaft against Randall's hole had him tightening his grip, and Dominic hissed in response. Randall pressed on, bearing down as Dominic slid deeper and deeper until his ass rested against his thighs. He paused for a long moment, enjoying the feeling of being full. He closed his eyes and dropped his head back, making a gentle circle with his hips.

"Fuck," Dominic said. "I won't last long if you keep doing that."

Well, that was good because that had been his plan. If he got Dominic's first orgasm out of the way, Randall might be able to coax a second one out of him. Randall kept his hands from resting on Dominic's body, not wanting to put too much pressure on him, and used his leg muscles to lift and drop him. It wasn't as easy as when he could brace himself, but he refused to hurt him. He would be feeling the burn in his thighs before they were done.

He sped up a little. "Oh, fuck. That feels good," Dominic said.

Randall couldn't say anything, his words taken by concentration. His thighs were already burning, but he wouldn't let Dominic do more work. The moment he thought that, though, Dominic began thrusting his hips. Randall froze.

Dominic's gaze immediately found Randall's. "What's wrong?"

Randall raised his eyebrows. "Stop moving, or I'll stop moving."

Dominic narrowed his eyes, and Randall could see him calculating what it was worth, but he allowed the order. He relaxed back, and Randall began the up-and-down motion again. He could feel himself climbing towards the apex and wanted Dominic to come first or even at the same time. He flicked a finger over Dominic's nipple, and Dominic's stomach clenched. Lines bracketed his eyes, and Randall changed his movements so it was more of a roll of his hips rather than an up-and-down motion. It made his head spin, and if Dominic's curses were anything to go by, it was a good thing.

"That's it, Randall. Ride me, sweetheart. Make yourself come."

Randall panted and kept up the steady rhythm, Dominic's cock brushing his prostate with every stroke. Dominic's hand wrapped around Randall's dick, and Randall's climax barrelled out of him with no warning. He tried to control his movements, not wanting to hurt Dominic, but his brain went offline as his body exploded.

When he came back around, Dominic had his eyes closed, but his face was free of pain. Randall knew it wouldn't last, but he kept up his movements until Dominic's body relaxed, and he slipped free from Randall's ass. Carefully, he climbed off and slid between Dominic's legs again, taking his shaft between his lips and cleaning him as thoroughly as he could before it became too sensitive for him. Then he rested his cheek against Dominic's good thigh and sighed.

"Bloody hell, Randall. When I said ride me, I didn't mean hard enough for my brain to turn to jelly." He chuckled.

Randall smiled and manoeuvred himself by Dominic's side, pressing his lips to his cheek. "That was the idea, wasn't it? Or have I been orgasming wrong every time?"

"That's not what I meant," Dominic said. "And you know it. I wanted to see you come."

"And I wanted to make *you* come. We both win."

Dominic pulled him close, but before they got too comfortable, Randall reached for the covers to pull over them, keeping the cold from invading when their bodies finally cooled. He closed his eyes and sighed.

"I love you, Randall. And I can't wait to make you mine."

"I thought I was making you mine," Randall argued.

"You are, but I am, too."

Randall drifted, but his thoughts were full of wedding plans. This time, it wasn't the princes' weddings that occupied his mind; it was his own. It wouldn't be anytime soon, but he couldn't wait to start planning it. One thing kept returning to the forefront, though, and he voiced it to Dominic.

"You do realise when we get married, we're going to have to invite the royal family. Our wedding won't be a small thing."

Dominic kissed his head. "I wouldn't have it any other way. They're family."

Randall smiled. "They are."

Just as Randall headed towards sleep, a beep sounded. Dominic moved to rise, but Randall woke fully and stopped him.

"I'll get it."

He left the bed to rummage through their clothes and handed Dominic's phone to him. He climbed back into bed but sat cross-legged instead of lying down. Dominic's expression clouded and then cleared.

"Everything okay?"

Dominic nodded slowly and passed the phone to Randall.

BRETT: *News. Addams is dead. Someone got to him in custody. We're waiting for more information as to who. I'll keep you posted.*

Randall's brain and body weren't sure what to do. Was he happy? Sad? Relieved? He wasn't sure, but he was glad Addams couldn't hurt anyone anymore. He handed the phone back to Dominic and saw him watching him.

"At least he can't hurt anyone now," he said, voicing his thoughts.

"Very true." Dominic frowned down at the phone as he closed it.

"What's bothering you?"

"Addams had an 'employer,' as he called it. We still don't know who that was and what *their* endgame is. We're blind all over again."

Randall nodded and snuggled in beside him again. "We've weathered plenty these past few years. If nothing else, it's taught me we can survive. Whatever comes our way, we'll deal with it."

Another message came through, and Dominic cursed. "Let's hope you mean that."

"Why?"

BRETT: *Bad news? Andrew just got a message from an unknown number:*

Number one might still be alive,

But who is weak within the hive?

Tick, Tock, Tick, Tock.

A shiver went down Randall's spine, but Dominic nudged him back and took his mouth in a soft kiss. "I love you so much."

"I love you. Always and forever."

31

Dominic

Four weeks later

Randall settled onto the bed beside Dominic, wringing his hands, and that alerted him straight away to his fiancé's unease. Dominic slid his arms around his shoulders and pulled him closer.

"Spit it out, sweetheart. Your pulse is reaching speedboat level."

Randall exhaled. "I have a surprise for you."

Dominic chuckled. "And you're worried about whether I'll like it? I like everything you give me." He winked.

Randall ducked his head and laughed. "This is something outside of the bedroom, sorry."

Dominic sighed as if he was upset, but he kissed Randall's temple, where the scar was from his ordeal with Addams. "I'll love it. I know I will."

"Then you need to get dressed. We have somewhere to be."

As much as Dominic wanted to press Randall for clues to the surprise, he didn't. It felt like something big, and he didn't want to minimise Randall's efforts. Instead, he made small talk during the journey, telling him what May had been doing to her new apartment, even though she'd only moved in two weeks ago. She was already removing the wallpaper and kitchen cupboards, redesigning everything to how she wanted it.

Dominic and Randall had found a new house, still on the outskirts of Windsor, where they both preferred to be, but it had a large back garden surrounded by trees with a porch on the front and back of the house. They'd moved in the week before May had moved into her place, and they hadn't changed anything. But they would be. Randall wanted the property to be painted green, like his old house, and Dominic would give him whatever he wanted. Even if he had to pay someone to come and do it for him rather than do it himself like he wanted.

It was Randall's birthday that week, and Dominic had big plans. He just needed to make sure Randall was out of the house so he could get it set up. It was a good job that he had plenty of strong friends because Dominic still could barely lift anything with his damaged shoulder. It was still healing, so everyone kept telling him when he complained about it.

When Randall parked the car near the curb, Dominic looked around. It was a residential area, and he couldn't see anything that might be a surprise for him.

"Where are we?" he asked.

Randall licked his lips as he switched the engine off. "We're going to meet someone."

Dominic frowned at his evasive answer but didn't press. He climbed out of the car, an easier feat than it used to be now some of the pain had diminished from his shoulder. He didn't need someone to help him any longer. Randall stepped beside him and gestured towards the house.

"We're going here."

They stepped towards the two-storey house, and the front door opened. Dominic froze, staring up at the man moving towards them in a wheelchair. The man was older now, but Dominic would never, *ever* forget what he looked like.

Diego.

They stared at each other for a long time before a smile cracked on Diego's face.

"You need a sit-down, punk?" Diego said, and the words cracked through Dominic's fog to slam him back twenty years.

The involuntary huff that bubbled out of him startled Randall. A smile crept across Dominic's face. "I'm good. I'll let you have a nap, though," he retorted, tears brimming.

Diego barked a laugh, throwing his head back and turning his chair towards the door again. "I can't believe you remembered our first words to one another," Diego said. "Come on in."

Dominic stared at the door he disappeared through.

"I'm sorry if I overstepped," Randall said. "I just wanted you to see that he wasn't wallowing in self-pity and what-ifs. He's living his life. An amazing life, actually. Helping others like him. He doesn't hold a grudge against you, Dominic. He never has."

Dominic wiped his hand over his face and inhaled. "I hadn't wanted to check on him in case his life was a mess. That would've made my life feel... I don't know." He swallowed. "Unfair, maybe."

"He has a great life, Dominic. Talk to him, and you'll see what he's accomplished."

Dominic reached for Randall, holding him close as he closed his eyes and breathed just for a minute. Then he exhaled and pulled back. "Let's go see what he's done." And what he could do to help, though he didn't say it. Diego might never understand just how much what happened changed the course of Dominic's life, but Dominic did.

Randall smiled, and Dominic knew he was the luckiest man alive.

"Be careful!" Dominic growled as Owen and Evan carried the birthday gift into the house.

"Fuck off, Dom," Owen cursed at him. "This isn't exactly light."

"Or small," Evan panted.

It was the day before Randall's birthday, and while he was at work, Dominic wanted to make sure everything was perfect for when he came home. He hadn't been able to think how to get and set up the aquarium so that he could see it on his birthday because that would've meant all the humping and dumping of it happened during the night. And no one would appreciate him for that.

Owen and Evan carried the huge-ass glass aquarium into position on top of the made-to-measure cupboard and then helped Dominic set up the electrics for it. When he first decided on purchasing an aquarium for Randall's gift, he hadn't realised how much other stuff he would need to get, too. He didn't begrudge Randall at all, but there was just *so much stuff.* Filters, pumps and lighting were just the start.

Once the electrical part was set up, his best friends moved it back against the wall and promptly dropped onto the sofa and groaned.

"Where's our pizza?" Evan said.

Dominic lifted his eyebrows. "I thought you were going to have that for dinner with us tonight?"

Evan opened one eye. "You really want us here when Randall sees what you've bought him. Okay, so be it."

He had a point. Dominic headed for the kitchen. "I'll make pizza."

Five hours later, Dominic wore a hole in the carpet as he waited for Randall to arrive. He'd texted to say he was on his way home, and Dominic couldn't wait to see his reaction. Not wanting to stop Randall from having things the way he wanted them, Dominic hadn't finished the set-up. He'd filled it with water, but everything else was up to Randall.

Hearing the car in the driveway, he inhaled and exhaled. The butterflies in his stomach took flight, and he watched the door handle. The moment he entered, Randall dropped everything he was holding, threw his arms around Dominic's waist and tucked his face into his neck. The same thing happened every time he saw him, and Dominic smiled.

"Hey, you. Did you have a good day?"

Randall pulled back, smiling. "It went well. I missed you, though. I had to see Nick's face all day—" His words dropped off, and his eyes widened as he glanced past Dominic's shoulder. "What is that?" he whispered.

"Happy birthday, sweetheart," Dominic murmured against his temple.

"It's an aquarium," Randall said. "In our house."

Dominic grinned. "It is."

Randall stared some more, and Dominic's stomach swirled. Did he not like it? But the moment he thought that, Randall squealed and tore himself from Dominic's arms and over to the glass fish house.

"It's an aquarium!" Randall said.

Dominic chuckled. "I filled it with water because that took ages, but I've left everything else on the side so you can choose where to put everything. Then we can fill it with fish when you're ready."

"We have to make sure the pH level is correct before we can add fish," Randall muttered as he went through the offerings of plants and ornaments.

Dominic hadn't been sure what he would like, so he'd spent a fortune on getting a variety. He had maybe gone a bit overboard, but they could swap them out so the fish didn't get bored. Right?

He settled on the arm of the sofa, watching as Randall unceremoniously shoved his sleeves up his arms and set to work on designing his aquarium. After half an hour, he was still going strong, so Dominic ordered dinner. After he put the phone down, arms slid around his waist.

"Thank you, Dominic."

He pivoted within his arms and smiled down at him. "You are very, *very* welcome."

"I can't wait to see what fish we can put in it. Each fish has to have a certain amount of water for it, so we can only have a certain number of them. Maybe we could get some zebra danios or tetras. They're so shiny. I'm not so sure about goldfish. There are too many connotations with winning them at fairs. Oh, I would love some of those guppies."

Dominic smiled as Randall continued to list the fish he would love to own. Fish that Dominic had no idea about. Yes, he'd done research, but not on the breeds of fish. That was Randall's domain.

To give him a chance to breathe, Dominic kissed him, and when he sank into his arms, pliant and needy, he pulled back. Randall followed, but Dominic held him steady.

"You have plenty of time to decide."

Randall blinked at him. "Decide what?"

Dominic chuckled. "Do you want a shower before dinner arrives?" Randall nodded, so Dominic turned him around and pushed him towards the stairs. "Go. I'll call you when it's here."

He waited in the doorway to the living room to ensure his fiancé didn't get distracted by the aquarium again and then settled on the sofa to wait. It seemed he liked it. He'd chosen well.

After dinner, Randall showed Dominic exactly what he thought of his gift.

It was a good job Owen and Evan had gone home. Randall was extremely appreciative.

32

Randall

Eighteen months later

"**W**hat do you mean, you're not doing the best man thing?" Geoff said as they sat eating Indian takeaway in Randall's living room.

The aquarium was lit, and the rest of the lights in the room were on low, so it stood out. Randall loved it, but he focused on Geoff's words.

"We have so many people we want to include in the wedding, it just seemed the better option to keep things simple. Dominic and I will bring the rings ourselves, and everyone can sit and relax and enjoy the wedding and reception without having to worry about forgetting anything or standing up to make a speech. We just want everyone there with no expectations." Randall clenched his fists. "Even with how much focus has been put on it with the reporters and social media, we still want things low-key and as small as possible."

"You're marrying the Lead Protection Officer of the king. How small do you think you can get when you have the royal family attending?" Geoff said with a laugh.

Randall exhaled. "We're trying, okay. It's not my fault they're famous." He chuckled. "They all offered to stay away, but we want them there."

"But no best man?"

Randall's mouth twitched. "No. No best man. For either of us."

"Damn." Geoff sighed.

"What's wrong?" Randall's heart sank. If Geoff wanted to be his best man that much, Randall was sure he could talk Dominic around.

"I owe Nadine fifty quid now."

Randall frowned. "Why?"

"She said you would do something like this. I told her your wedding would be traditional." He sighed. "Fifty quid!"

Randall relaxed and laughed. "Well, that's your own fault for making a bet with your wife. How is business, anyway?"

Geoff perked up. "They're doing well. May's photographs are flying off the wall faster than she can take them, and Nadine is loving the gallery job. It fits her perfectly. Going into business with Dominic's sister was one of your better ideas."

"Hey!" Randall said. "My ideas aren't that bad."

"What ideas?" Dominic said, poking his head around the corner. Randall waved his question off. "Do you want to have a game? I'm beating Owen and Evan at the moment." He grinned.

Randall raised his eyebrows at Geoff, who nodded. "Sure. We'll be there in a minute."

Dominic winked at him and disappeared. All their friends had got along well from the moment they'd been introduced, which made joint night outs so much easier to handle. But tonight was something special, and no one in their house knew about it. He wasn't sure how much longer he could keep the secret, but it needed to be, at least until they got to their destination in two hours.

They played a few games of darts before Randall said they needed to get their skates on. As far as everyone was concerned, they were going to an open-air cinema showing of *Armageddon*. They weren't, though. The five of them squashed into Owen's car, which was the biggest car any of them owned, and they headed for their destination.

When they pulled up, Owen parked the car, and everyone filed out. The entrance had a white rose archway for them to go through, which took them to a short fabric tunnel leading to where the "cinema" was happening.

Randall pulled Dominic to a stop, letting Owen, Evan and Geoff continue through the tunnel. They were no longer his problem. Portia had agreed to take care of them when they went through. But Dominic was his concern.

"You know how we were always so worried about the reporters and everyone trying to get in on our wedding?" he said to his fiancé.

"Yeah. It's a shame, but we can deal with it." Dominic squeezed his biceps. "I don't care how it happens as long as we become husbands."

"I'm glad you said that." Dominic scratched his chin, and Randall hooked his arm through Dominic's and led him through the tunnel. Dominic pulled them to a stop when they exited. "Welcome to our wedding."

Dominic looked around, glanced at Randall, and looked around again. Randall tried to see things through his eyes. Fairy lights were strung up around trees, hedges and posts. Dozens of chairs made a semi-circle around an arbour of white roses. Andrew stood beneath that arbour, waiting to marry them. But it all hinged on Dominic being okay with it.

"It's okay if you don't want to," Randall said.

Dominic peered at him, and a tremulous smile stretched across his face. "I want to. I didn't want to wait another year. I would've, but I didn't want to. Yes, hell, yes, fuck, yes. Yes. Now. Let's do it."

Randall grinned and nodded to Portia, who set the music playing. Arm in arm, they walked down the aisle towards the person who was going to make them husbands. When they stopped in front of Andrew, the music quietened.

"It is with great honour that I was asked to marry these two amazing people tonight," Andrew started. "They have both given so much of their time, energy and passion into making our lives that much better and easier. It's only fair that the same thing is given back to them on this wondrous night. The ceremony may be short, but it's binding and heartfelt."

He turned to them. "Please offer your rings to each other." Randall pulled their rings from his pocket and handed one to Dominic. "Randall, Dominic, please repeat after me in unison. I voluntarily stand before you to give you my love, my heart, my everything. I promise to cherish, support and communicate on every step of our journey. I call to these people present to witness my vows to you. With everything I am, I vow to be yours." They repeated the words and slid the rings onto their fingers. "With your vows spoken and witnessed, I pronounce you husbands. You may kiss."

They joined their lips to a muted cheer from their guests, and Dominic tightened his hold as if he didn't want to let go.

Randall hadn't wanted a long-winded ceremony, and when he'd spoken to it with Dominic, his fiancé had said, *'If all I do is say I do, that is enough for me.'* Randall had taken that to heart with this event, and he hoped Dominic was not disappointed.

"I love you," Dominic murmured against his lips.

"And I love you."

Owen's heart had been broken too many times by Evan. How can he protect his heart when it has never belonged to him anyway? Read on for information about Protecting his Heart.

Would you like a bonus story about Randall and Dominic? Well, check out Training Day, where Randall agrees to a couples massage, but what has he really got himself into? https://bookhip.com/NBRDTLF

For a taste of the free short story you get if you sign up to my newsletter...

Triplicity

Oliver and Griffin have been married for years. They've agreed to an open relationship to get what they both need as long as it's within the walls of Club Royal and there's nothing more than play. When Oliver watches Griffin play with Xan, he realises his husband has fallen in love with the sub. What can Oliver do to keep Griffin by his side?

This is an MMM romance with BDSM scenes and a happily ever after.

Get this book FREE here: https://elouiseeast.com/newsletter

Protecting his Heart

His heart has been broken too many times - by the same person.

Owen had never wanted a fancy job, he just wanted to be able to take care of his family. Losing his heart to his best friend was something he'd never expected but was inevitable, nonetheless. Despite the ups and downs of their childhood romance, when Evan moved to Italy, Owen was shell shocked. He focused on protecting the royal family and keeping his feelings to himself. It was the only way he could take another breath...and another.

One thousand miles wasn't far enough to run from his heart, but Evan couldn't bring himself to go any further. Or stay away for more than a few years. His family and friends lure him back, but it's one person alone he needs and cannot stay away from any longer. With a lot to answer for and many apologies to make, he needs to secure Owen's heart once and for all.

How can he protect his heart when it never belonged to him anyway?

Protecting his Heart is a kinky, second chance romance with a grieving bodyguard and a childhood best friend who knows him better than anyone else.

Grab it here:

https://books2read.com/protectinghisheart-guarding

Books by Elouise East

Guarding Royalty
Protecting his Past
Protecting his Heart
Protecting his Secrets

Club Royal
Royal Firsts
Rogue Royal
Secretive Royal
Grieving Royal
Disowned Royal
Trained Royal
Awakened Royal
Commanding Royal

Illuminate Matchmaking
Ignite
Blaze
Kindle

ELOUISE EAST

Scorch

Boys, Daddies, Snuggles & More
Need Him
Trust Him

Daddy
Love Me, Daddy
Soothe Me, Daddy
Spoil Me, Daddy
The Complete Daddy Series

Love in Flames
Out of the Frying Pan
Smokescreen
Breathing Fire
Love in Flames Collection

Crush
Love Conquers
Instant Desire
Primary Seduction
Deep Down
A Crush for Christmas
Life Support
Covert Strength
Love Scene
Lawful Attraction
Crush Collection Volume 1
Crush Collection Volume 2
Crush Collection Volume 3

Just A Little Crush

First Kiss
He's Behind You
A Special Love

Standalone
Treehouse Whispers
Star-Crossed
Protecting the Thief
Sizzling Chauffeur
A Home for Barney

Elouise R East (taboo)
Dark & Divergent
Forbidden Temptation
Too Many Secrets: A Life of Secrets
Too Many Secrets: The Lake House

Collide
When Fantasies Collide
When Dreams Collide
When Pleasures Collide
When Cravings Collide
When Hungers Collide

About Elouise East

Elouise East writes sweet and steamy connections in gay romance. She also touches on taboo stories under the name Elouise R East.

Books that tell the stories where friendship and family are the focal point - be it blood family or chosen - are very important to her. That's why she includes a variety of personalities, talents, ages, situations and abilities as she believes a story or character needs. She wants her characters to be real, to be relatable, to be free to have whatever views they tell her they have. And trust her, most of the time, she does not have *any* say in the matter!

Her characters come to life on the page for her as well as her readers. Their stories unfold in front of her as she writes, and she has very little input into how they want to be shown. Just like real life, the lives of her characters change with every choice, every interaction and every conversation. And she wouldn't have it any other way.

She writes books that are emotionally realistic, even if liberties are taken with other aspects of the stories. She doesn't know any other way to write. It comes from deep inside.

Who is she? A single parent to two children living in the UK. An avid reader who still tries to devour every book she can get her hands on. A student of learning about any subject that takes her fancy. An author of books she would read herself. And a romantic at heart who loves anything cheesy.

Who's joining her on her journey?

Stalk her here... ;-)
Website : https://elouiseeast.com
Newsletter : https://elouiseeast.com/newsletter
All links : https://elouiseeast.com/links

The QUEST for EAST AFRICA

Greg Lane

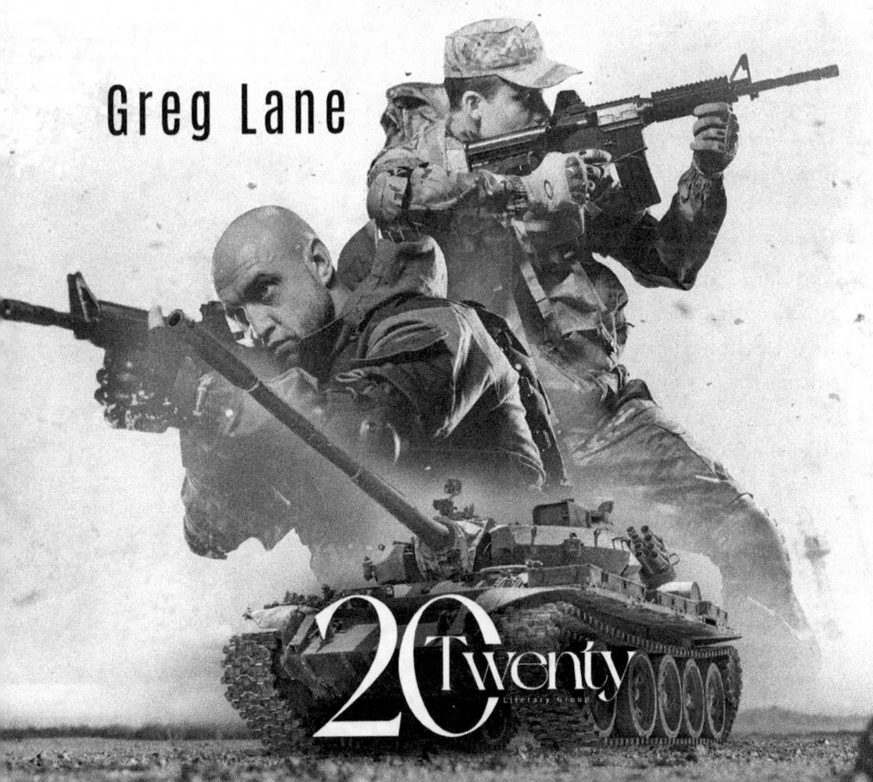

The Quest for East Africa
Copyright © 2023 by Greg Lane

ISBN
978-1-961250-06-2 (Paperback)
978-1-961250-07-9 (eBook)
978-1-961250-05-5 (Hardcover)